FRIGHT NIGHTS BIG CITY

A CANADIAN WEREWOLF NOVEL

MARK LESLIE

Stark Publishing

PUBLISHING

Stark Publishing
Waterloo, ON
www.markleslie.ca

Publisher's Note: This is a work of fiction. Names, characters, places, and incidents are a product of the author's imagination. Real locales and public and celebrity names are sometimes used for atmospheric purposes. Any resemblance to actual people, living or dead, or to businesses, companies, events, institutions, or locales is either coincidental or used in a fictional manner.

Fright Nights Big City / Mark Leslie. — 1st ed.
Hardcover ISBN: 978-1-989351-51-2
Trade Paperback ISBN: 978-1-989351-50-5
eBook ISBN: 978-1-989351-52-9
Audiobook ISBN: 978-1-989351-53-6

First paper printing December 2021.

For Laura

Table of Contents

Tuesday, July 4, 2017

Prologue: Wolves on a Plane

I was used to waking up naked in strange places with foggy memories of what I'd done the night before when romping around as a canine.

It's amazing how accustomed one can become to the strangest things. But those odd moments, the things we never thought we'd get used to, can, over time, evolve into habits, rituals. They might even become comforting in a bizarre way.

This time I woke in a sitting position. The feel of clothes on my body informed me of something important: it must not be that time of the month for me. When the moon is at 80% or more, my body undergoes a metamorphosis from a six foot-two two-hundred-pound male Homo sapiens into a six-foot long Canis lupus.

As consciousness returned to me, and I took in the sounds and smells around me—the base low rumbling of engines I could both hear and feel vibrating through my bones, the recycled air, the sweat, perfume, halitosis, heartbeats of more than a hundred other humans in a tightly closed environment—I remembered I was on a plane. It was a flight from Los Angeles, where I'd spent the past several weeks. I was returning home to New York.

The scent and distinct heartbeat of the traveling

companion sleeping beside me brought an immediate wave of warmth and passion. It was Alexandria. Lex. She was, of course, more than my traveling companion. She was my partner, my lover, my confidante. Meeting and getting to know her just a few weeks earlier had been a significant turning point in my life. She'd come along at just the right time for me, as I had been rejected, again, by the only woman I had ever truly loved up to that point in my life.

Prior to my trip to Los Angeles, my dear friend and former girlfriend, Gail, had made it clear that, despite how we both felt about one another, there wouldn't be a return to our earlier relationship. That part was over.

Getting away from New York, and from the serial rejection of Gail, seemed to be just what I'd needed. And exactly what my literary agent, Mack, had intended when he forced me on that work trip as a script consultant for a movie based on one of my novels.

Damn, I hate when that gruff, crude, cigar-chomping loud-mouth was right. He wasn't a pleasant man to be around—he came about his nickname of Mack "the knife" Halpin quite honestly—but he had never steered me wrong in all these years.

Mack surprising me with the trip to LA had come at exactly the right time; and I'm not just talking about my emotional life. The trip had been scheduled, without my knowing it, almost exactly between the lunar phase cycle that would have me turning into a grey wolf.

It meant I could be human and not worry about the lycanthropic change the entire time I was hanging out in

Hollywood.

And during that time, I had met and almost immediately fallen in love with Lex.

We shared a roller coaster of adventure, fearful encounters with a few nasty characters, and in-depth explorations of one another, both physically and emotionally.

I couldn't have even imagined meeting and loving someone like Lex on my flight out to LA, but here she was, such an integral part of my life that she was leaving everything she knew behind to be with me in New York.

No, it wasn't as simple as that.

We were distancing ourselves from a disturbing group of people she had gotten mixed up with. Terrible people. Evil people. A racist hate-group cult that also possessed oddly supernatural powers.

I might have the heightened senses, strength, and agility of a wolf, even when in human form, because of this inexplicable curse running through my veins; and I might have been able to take out a few bad guys over the years—petty thieves, bullies, attempted rapists, even a handful of mobsters. This was a side-effect of my boy-scout tendencies, likely derived from reading too many Spider-Man comic books in my youth. But I was not prepared, equipped, or trained to take on such a group.

I realized, after a few encounters with this group where I'd been over-powered, and where my meddling led to the death of an innocent bystander, someone I considered a friend, that I was in well over my head.

I needed to leave dealing with this hate group, the neo-Nazi Proud Fighters for America, to the professionals, the police, the FBI, the special task force assigned to tracking and stopping them.

And I needed to focus on having a life again; building a new life with Lex, this amazing woman who had given me a new outlook on life.

When Gail and I had been together, I'd kept my werewolf nature from her; and that deception had led to the dissolution of our romantic relationship. She'd been previously lied to, deceived, cheated on, one too many times in her life. My unwillingness to share my secret other life wasn't something she could get past.

But with Lex, despite a bit of a rocky start, I revealed the deception about my true nature before it could tear us apart. Because we both had been hiding supernatural secrets.

Not only had Lex loved me despite my awkwardness, faults, and emotional scars, but her presence came with a most welcome side-effect. When I was with her, my heightened wolf senses and powers faded.

Which meant that I fell in love with her in the depths of normalcy. I didn't have insights into her emotions through her scent or heartbeat or any of those obvious tells. I had to navigate my feelings for her, and her feelings for me, like an everyday human.

It felt amazing to feel so normal, and yet so extraordinarily blessed by being with Lex.

We had figured out, by accident, that Lex possessed a strange ability that caused bad luck to harmful actions directed towards her, as well as a side-effect of nullifying my special senses and powers. It only seemed to work when I was near her. The effect faded when she was asleep, like she was now.

But it meant that when I was with her, I could be a normal human. I could live a normal life.

Well, apart from the fact that, for about ten days every month, I morphed into a wolf.

Lex was the first person with whom I had willingly shared the details of my affliction. Technically, she was the second. But the first person I told was in a situation when I had no other option—because the change was coming at me like a freight train—and I had no choice but to explain what she was about to witness.

But with Lex, it was voluntary, and built off the mutual trust and late-night in-depth conversations and sharing.

She had confided the details of the violations of her own morals by joining the PFA in order to try to save her best friend from their clutches. And how, despite leaving, they had still maintained a hold on her, and power over her.

We relayed the curses we had both been living with alone and became stronger for the sharing of those experiences. Because we no longer had to bear those curses on our own. We had one another. And we were on our way to building a new life together.

Among the sounds of murmuring voices of the other passengers, I heard the pilot speaking. It wasn't on the intercom, though. My super-enhanced hearing was picking up his voice talking to the co-pilot. He was talking about the heat wave in New Jersey and how the thinner air would make it more dangerous to land. Flight take-offs and landings had been delayed, and they needed to circle over the greater New York area waiting for the sun to set and the air to cool down enough before they'd likely get the go-ahead that it was safe to land.

This wasn't good. Because timing wise, tonight the moon was expected to be at 82% in New York City. Lex and I had devised a plan on how she would help me get to a safe location to change into wolf form shortly after we landed.

But this new delay, staying in the air until after the sun set, that would not go over well.

I don't think that this airline was prepared to deal with any sort of *wolves on a plane* scenario.

I opened my eyes, just as the pilot was coming on the PA system to announce this update to the passengers.

Lex woke as the pilot made his announcement.

"What do I do now?" I asked Lex, when he finished sharing the delay that would mean landing after nightfall. "Lock myself in the restroom?"

"I don't know," she said.

"Oh," I said, feeling the tingling and ringing sensation in my head, the aura that I knew meant the change was about to happen, coming over me. "It's happening now. It's happening early."

"The altitude must be causing an altered reaction," she whispered.

I looked down at my hand, the one Lex was clasping, and watched incredulously as tufts of fur grew out of the back of it. Simultaneously, I felt the tautness of my arm muscles stiffen and jerk.

I had never been conscious of the change into wolf form before; I had always blacked out and never experienced it happening.

This was different.

Lex and I stared at my hands as my fingers retracted and the bones of my hands compressed.

It was excruciating, and I let out a squeal of pain.

What the hell was happening? Why was I experiencing the change consciously? With the pain I was feeling this early in the process, was it even possible for me to maintain sanity while it was happening?

There's no way a person could remain of sound mind experiencing this intensity of anguish.

I looked into Lex's eyes, tried to tell her I loved her, but my lips no longer worked. My face was distorting as my jaw started to elongate.

She didn't look horrified about the creature I was turning into; she appeared empathetic; and the scent rolling off her was of love, compassion, and concern for my well-being.

"It's okay, Kal. I'm here. I've got you. We've got this."

Her words were soothing, and I focused on them as the pain in my body and my entire head intensified. She started calling me Kal that first night at the bar where we'd met. Her full name was Alexandria, but she preferred to go by Lex. So instead of calling me Michael, she nicknamed me Kal. It was short for Michael as well as for Kal-El, the name Superman had been given at birth. It was our little inside joke of Kal and Lex being partners.

I closed my eyes, prayed that Lex would be okay in dealing with the bizarre repercussions of her travel companion morphing into a wolf in the middle of a flight. And all without the help of Samuel L. Jackson.

Suddenly, the pain retreated.

The aura, the tingling, the crushing pain in my bones, all faded away. I looked back down at my one hand that had been morphing into a paw and saw it was reforming back to its normal size and shape. The tufts of fur had returned to regular dark human hair on the back of my hand.

I moved my jaw as I tried to speak.

"It's... not happening," I said. "I'm not changing."

"Thank God," she said.

"No," I said, realizing what was happening. "Thank you, Lex."

"What do you mean?"

I thought back to the odd things I'd witnessed her doing that led us to believe she had a bad luck curse. How, when she was conscious, my paranormal senses didn't work around her.

She didn't just possess a good luck charm aura that protected her from harm. She also could completely neutralize magic and the supernatural.

Lex herself was the charm to the curse I had been living with for years.

When I was with her, I could be one hundred percent human and normal.

All the time.

No more nocturnal escapades in canine form.

Talk about an amazing new chapter in my life.

"It's you, your charm," I said. "It isn't just reducing the side effects of my enhanced wolf powers as a human. It's working to allow me to maintain my full humanity.

"It's you, Lex. You're giving me a new lease on life."

I paused and grinned at her as the horrible pun came to me.

"Or maybe I should say a new *Lex* on life."

She groaned.

"Why don't you just stick to writing mystery thrillers and leave the comedy to the professionals?"

"Lex my love," I said. "I'm going to do more than that. I'm going to leave the comedy, and the heroics, to the professionals."

She squeezed my hand and I lost myself in her beautiful eyes as the Rush song I'd been thinking about on my flight to LA just a few weeks earlier came back to me.

Fly by Night.

"Change my life again, indeed." I whispered.

"Change our lives again," she replied, and kissed me.

The plane remained in the air, circling the city I had fallen in love with years ago, for another hour and a half. Lex and I held hands as we looked out the plane window together.

Her face beamed so magnificently as she marvelled

at the view of The Statue of Liberty from the air.

"Oh Kal," she said. "It's spectacular."

"It sure is," I said, realizing how much I missed seeing that beautiful sculpture, not that I'd seen it from the air very often. I realized that being with Lex was going to give me a whole new perspective.

Lady Liberty, like Lex, was a glowing beacon of light in the midst of the dark water. The flood lights lit her from below, and her torch gave off its own light. But there was an additional light hitting her from above.

The moon.

I tilted my head to look up and see the almost full orb in the sky and realized how long it had been since I'd been able to look at a full or mostly full moon; well, at least in this human form, with a consciousness I could remember.

Lex squeezed my hand.

"You haven't seen that in a while, have you?"

"No," I said. "I haven't seen a full moon in years. I've *never* seen a full moon over New York City. And there's nobody I'd rather share that experience with than you."

I turned to see her looking not at the moon, but at me. Her face was beaming, so filled with unadulterated joy at watching my reaction to seeing the moon. I had no special heightened sensory input on what she was feeling; no scent, no heartbeat indicators.

But I didn't need any of that.

I could see it in her eyes. I could feel it in the way she squeezed my hand.

"This is one of so many amazing things you bring to my life. I love you, Lex."

"I love you, Kal."

That heightened mutual passion continued to grow as we sat there silently, holding one other's hands and staring out the window.

It remained as the plane landed and we disembarked along with the other passengers, keeping our hands clasped tightly almost the entire time.

Now that I'd found her, I didn't want to let go.

We made our way, in that same fashion, through the terminal within the flow of the crowd, a part of them, and yet uniquely alone together, on our way to the baggage claim area.

The pounding of passion in my chest for Lex seemed to grow exponentially with each new beat of my heart. Here we were, starting a new life together, in my city. She knew who I was, what I was, and she not only loved me, but her proximity allowed me to live a normal life.

Just when I thought my burning and throbbing heart might burn a hole through my chest, I was hit with what felt like a jolt of cold water.

As we were standing in a tight crowd of people gathered around the luggage carousel, I looked up and recognized a stunning brunette woman hustling in our direction from across the room. From over thirty feet away, I could make out the mixture of tension, concern, and confusion in her beautiful green eyes.

And I knew exactly what she'd been worried about.

She not only knew I was a werewolf, but she was familiar with the cycles that affected me. And it was more than an hour after sundown on the night of a near-full moon.

What the heck was Gail doing here?

Chapter One: An Awkward Terminal Encounter

"Gail!" I said as she got within a few feet of us, my voice cracking as it came out much louder than I had intended. "What are you doing here?"

Gail tapped the back of her left wrist, the universal gesture for indicating the time, while rolling her eyes up as if looking at the night sky.

"More like: *What the heck are YOU doing here, Andrews?* I would have expected to see your, er, companion at this late hour."

"Well," I said. "It's a…it's a long story."

She shook her head. "I…don't understand. But it's so good to see you." She stepped forward, her arms open, coming in for an enormous hug.

I started to move in response to the incoming hug, and Lex squeezed my hand, a subtle reminder to me that she was here.

Coming out of her shock and confusion, Gail seemed to notice Lex for the first time—in particular, the fact we were holding hands—and slowed in her forward hug approach, her face twisting into a deeper mode of confusion.

I let go of Lex's hand and gave Gail a quick cursory hug—the way one might try to gently embrace a porcupine, more of an 'air hug' than anything—then stepped back and placed one hand on Lex's left shoulder and the other on the middle of her arm.

"Gail, this is Lex. Lex, this is my friend Gail."

I worried if I had placed too much emphasis on the word *friend* in that statement. But of course, Lex knew exactly who and what Gail was to me. I had explained the details of our past relationship and longer-term friendship to her.

"Gail," Lex said, stepping closer to Gail and embracing her in a quick hug—this one a genuine and warm embrace, unlike the pathetic excuse of a hug I'd given—before stepping back again and reaching down to take my hand once more. "Kal has told me so much about you."

"Kal?"

"Sorry," Lex laughed nervously. "It's my pet name for Michael."

Gail was quiet as she looked down at our clasped hands. A moment later, she responded.

"It's nice to meet you, Lex. I assume Lex is short for...?"

"Alexandria. But you can make plenty of different names from those five syllables. I've gone by many different names spun off of my full name."

The three of us stood in silence for a moment.

"So," Gail said. "I, uh, rented a car to come pick you up. I had expected you might need to...er...get out of here rather quickly because of...what day it is."

"Lex knows about what you're referring to," I said.

"Oh."

There was another long pause.

"I see our bags," Lex said. "I'll go grab them. It'll give you two a chance to catch up." She shoved her way through the crowd toward the luggage carousel.

"I told her about my...er...affliction. She knows."

"I see." She was quiet for a few seconds. "But I don't understand why you're not currently in your alternate form. It's well after sundown. I was expecting to see a bit more fur, you know?

"What's going on, Michael?"

"Long story. But, ultimately, meeting Lex has been good for me. Really good for me. On many fronts. One of them is this unexpected effect she has on my canine nature." I paused to glance at the people around us. I couldn't pick up on scents or heartbeats or any of those indicators I'd normally have that would show if anyone was attending to our conversation. But there were too many ears close by for me to properly explain the details.

"So, you told *her* about it?"

"Yeah."

"After just meeting her?"

Gail knew I was a werewolf. But I hadn't actually told her. She had figured it out on her own after putting several things together, including me constantly having some excuse to be unavailable after dark during the cycle of the full moon. It made sense. I met her several years ago when I was doing research for a novel involving black magic. She owns an occult shop in the East

Village and is an expert on understanding paranormal phenomena. So, if anyone could put together the pieces of why I was behaving so strangely during a particular cycle of the month, and a few other side effects I might have let show, it would have been Gail.

"Yeah," I said. "She also has experience with people with…uh…special talents. Including one of her own. Her affliction is very compatible with what I have. Somehow, she neutralizes my abilities. Her presence prevents my alternate self from appearing. I don't know how, but I'm rather pleased with it."

While I wasn't great at reading people without my heightened senses, I could tell Gail was intrigued and wanted to learn more. As far as I knew, I was the only paranormal person Gail had encountered. Well, apart from that other werewolf we had both met a few years back, that shock-rock bad boy, Knell.

"Lex and I will explain it to you once we get to the car and away from this crowd."

"Okay," Gail said, just as Lex was making her way back with our bags.

"Thanks, Love," I said, leaning down to kiss Lex as Lex stepped up beside me, taking my bag.

"The car is this way," Gail said, turning on one heel and briskly walking away as she spoke.

I moved to follow her, but Lex pulled down on my arm, holding me back.

"Why'd you do that?" Lex whispered.

"Do what?"

"Call me *Love* and kiss me."

"Because I love you, and you're hot?"

She rolled her eyes. "Yeah, I know. But why in front of Gail? She's still into you. That was a cruel thing to do."

I had to suppress a laugh.

"No, she's not. There's nothing between Gail and me. I told you, she made that very clear before I left for LA."

Lex shook her head, sighing. She muttered something under her breath. It might have been *"Men!"* but without my supernaturally enhanced hearing, I couldn't pick it up.

"Oh no, there is something between you. And that's very clear to me. Like the way she was glaring daggers at me when she saw we were holding hands. How can you not see that? Are you sure she dumped *you* and it wasn't the other way around?"

"Yeah. One hundred percent. I was moping around Los Angeles, drowning my sorrows by eating ice cream out of the tub, playing Phil Collins and Alicia Witt records, and getting drunk with strangers and sexy blonde women in bars, remember?"

"Oh, I *do* remember that," she laughed. "And the fact you said you were 'mostly single.'"

"I explained that. It was my awkwardness in the moment. After years of pining after Gail, and knowing that, despite her telling me it would never happen, my senses were telling me she was still in love with me. So I'd still been feeling like I was committed, connected. I'm not good at navigating these things."

"No shit, Sherlock," she giggled. "And I may not

have the enhanced wolf senses you had, but it's very obvious that woman is head over heels in love with you. It's screaming from her every pore."

Gail was still motoring her way, well ahead of us, through the crowd.

"We're losing her," I said. "C'mon. Let's pick up the pace." Following someone through a crowd by scent wouldn't have been an issue for me in the past. But with my senses muted in Lex's presence, we had to rely on keeping Gail within visual range. "We'll discuss this later, okay?"

"Oh yeah, we most certainly will."

Chapter Two: Taking for Granted You're Always There, You Just Don't Care

The ride from Newark back into Manhattan was one of the most uncomfortable forty minutes of my life.

Gail had rented a four-door Kia Forte to surprise me at the airport. She'd known what day I had been planning on returning. And likely through my agent, Mack, or his assistant Anne, must have learned that my return flight had been delayed by a day. Anne had made those arrangements when I'd asked if she could find a seat beside me for Lex to return to New York.

So why hadn't Anne told Gail I'd be accompanied by a girlfriend I'd made while in LA?

Before I left New York, Anne had counselled me about the need for Gail and me to be apart. She'd offered advice in line with the *if you love something, set it free* school of thought. I knew Anne was in my corner and wanted to see Gail and me back together.

But she hadn't mentioned Lex to Gail. Obviously.

And Gail, knowing my lycanthropic nature, realized what day it was, and the cycle of the moon. When she saw the flight delays on my return flight, she must have panicked, realizing what time the delayed flight was expected to arrive.

Which led her to the last-minute renting of a car to surprise me at the airport and whisk me out of there so I would be away from prying eyes when I turned into a wolf.

Gail had been with me for the transformation to a wolf and back to human several times over the years. And even within a closed space. My wolf form apparently recognized our special kinship and knew her, despite me having no human consciousness and all save for the briefest few snippets of memory as a wolf.

Meeting me at the airport in this way was something a dear friend would do without thinking about it.

But Lex said Gail was still into me, and that it was obvious.

Apparently, a woman's intuition is on par with a wolf's enhanced senses or something, because I didn't see that at all.

I sat in the back seat and listened to Lex explain a ten-thousand-foot view version of meeting and befriending me and how we discovered, quite accidentally, that she had this nullifying effect on my wolf-enhanced powers and my lycanthropic curse. She left out any of the romantic or falling-in-love aspects of the story. Lex also shared some of the background about the alt-right white supremist hate-group the Proud Fighters for America. She shared how her best friend had gotten involved in the group without revealing just how deeply she ended up inserting herself into their ranks in an attempt to get her friend out. It was enough to let Gail know they had expelled her from the group because they found out she was half-black and that the ritual they'd performed to give her enhanced abilities seemed to have failed. Only, of course, Lex and I learned, it was just that her abilities weren't easily evi-dent; or perhaps they developed more slowly, and over time.

Despite the awkward tension since Gail had met us at the terminal, it was an interesting and odd experience to sit back and listen to the two women talking in the front seat. Their voices seemed polite and courteous. They seemed to get along smashingly.

I thought about that.

Less than a month ago, all I had wanted was a way for Gail and me to be together again, like we had been, in that short-term relationship when we'd first met. Though it had only lasted for a couple of months, it had been the highlight relationship of my life. We had been good friends for years, much longer than our limited time together as a couple. But I'd never stopped yearning for Gail.

Not until my agent had forced me to go on this work trip to Hollywood, and I'd met Lex at that bar.

Lex seemed to have come around at exactly the right time for me. And apparently, I'd been there at the right time for her.

So there I was, sitting in the back seat listening to the only two women I'd ever loved, and two of only three people in the world who knew about the cursed blood running through my veins, chatting comfortably with one another.

I still had feelings for Gail, of course. Although I turned into a beast during a full moon, I wasn't a monster. And I'd likely always have feelings for her, always care about her. I had already become used to pushing back on any feelings other than the platonic relationship we had cultivated over the past several years.

My heart, and my passion, were with Lex. We had connected in the most intimate way with one another, and she brought new things to my life that I never thought I would have.

That part of my own feelings was clear to me.

But Lex said she could clearly see Gail was still obviously in love with me?

I thought back to the number of times Gail had called and texted me when I was in Los Angeles. She'd texted and called more often in this last month than in the past several years, come to think of it. And I'd been busy pursuing Lex, so ignored half of her texts and only sent back token and polite responses.

I pulled my phone out of my back pocket, wanting to review those texts. That's when I realized I'd left my phone in airplane mode. I toggled it back to regular mode, and a handful of notifications of voice mail and texts popped up.

I brought up the text icon.

There were four unread messages. All from Gail.

Based on the time showing, the first one had been sent just as we'd been boarding the plane and I had switched the phone over to airplane mode. Being a model airline passenger, I was in the habit of switching my phone to airplane mode the moment I boarded. Don't laugh at me. It helps ease my flight anxiety by knowing there was one less mobile device potentially interfering with whatever function of the airplane it might unintentionally mess with—or whatever reason they made us shut them off.

Hey, Andrews. I see they pushed your flight back to today. I got us tickets for the opening of Spider-Man in a few days. See you in a few hours.

The next text had come in a few hours later.

I see they delayed your flight multiple times. It's going to be close. But don't panic. I've got your back. I'll figure something out.

The following text was about twenty minutes later.

I've rented a car to meet you at Newark. There's a nearby park I can whisk you off to for the change. We got this.

The last one had come in at 8:25 PM, just minutes before the sun was about to set.

I don't know what to do. You're still in the air. I know it's about to happen. I'm so sorry. I love you, Andrews. Please know that I never stopped loving you. And I realized I want to try again. I want to try

US again.

I put the phone down and looked up at the back of Gail's head.

Okay, then.

That was awkward.

Gail had assumed, rightfully so, that I would turn into a wolf while in the air. Who knows what sort of mayhem might have happened? A wolf on board would have led to ridiculous panic. Even if I'd locked myself in the restroom for the change, there'd be no escaping being found out. And if there had been a Federal Air Marshall on board, chances are, I'd be shot dead.

Or, if not, I'd be captured, imprisoned, locked away for private study in some Area-51 type of facility.

I chewed on what she thought would be her last words to me.

She never stopped loving me.

I knew that. Not just with my wolfish senses. But she'd admitted it to me, the week before I'd left New York for Hollywood. She'd admitted that love but said she couldn't be in a relationship with me, or potentially anyone else.

Had that changed?

How? And why?

Gail's eyes in the rear-view mirror locked onto mine. She had seen me checking my phone; had likely realized I was finally looking at those messages that came in when I was in the air.

I wasn't quite sure what the look on her face was, but

if I didn't know any better, I'd swear it was a look of hurt. I'd grown used to being able to detect emotions via scent and the sound of a person's heartbeat. This time I didn't have that.

But there was a moistness in her eyes I recognized, despite only having seen it a few select times. Gail rarely cried. In all the years I'd known her, and despite living through incredible struggles or when sharing painful personal memories, I could count how many times I'd seen her tear up on one hand and still have a few uncounted digits left.

So, to see her eyes mist up like that was a dagger to my heart.

I was the cause of this pain.

And I hated myself for it.

In particular, I hated how I was causing this pain just by being the happiest I had been in years; thanks to what I'd found with Lex.

In the front seat, Gail and Lex continued their pleasant exchange of small talk. It sounded like a normal exchange between two people who had just met and shared a common friend. But even I recognized the small talk as being filled with a layer of discomfort, unease, and tension.

Lex, of course, confirmed that for me after Gail had dropped us off.

Gail let us both off in front of the Algonquin Hotel in mid-town, where I lived. It was a quick exchange of *thank-you* and *goodnight* as we collected our bags from the trunk and moved inside.

Paul, the doorman who had been working here for a long time, greeted us, offering to help take the bags off our hands.

"Good evening, Mister Andrews. How was your stay in LA?"

"Hey, Paul. Good to see you. And thanks for asking. It was pretty good."

He smiled, taking a quick glance over at Lex, and then slipped me a surreptitious wink. "Looks like it was."

"Paul, I'd like you to meet Lex, my, ah..." okay, so we hadn't defined what we were calling one another.

"Girlfriend," Lex said, stepping forward and putting out her hand. "Pleased to meet you, Paul."

"Likewise, Ms...?" Paul said.

"Jones. Alexandria Jones. But I'm not into formalities. Please call me Lex."

I laughed. "I've been trying to get Paul to call me Michael for the better part of ten years. And nothing I've tried works."

"Force of habit, I'm afraid," Paul grinned. "I come from a stubborn lot. I like to stick to familiar patterns."

"You certainly do, Paul. But speaking of patterns, you normally work the morning shift. Why are you here in the evening?"

"Bruce had a death in the family. I'm covering for him while he's out of town." He glanced at his watch. "I'm off in about fifteen minutes or so when Ryan gets here at 10. But I'll be back at 7."

"Sorry to hear about Bruce."

"It was an aunt. They weren't close. More of a family obligation thing for him. He'll be back on Thursday."

"And you'll be back here in the early morning. Not much of a break."

"It keeps me on my toes," Paul smiled. "Speaking of which, I'll see you then too, won't I?"

"What do you mean?"

"Well," Paul pointed up to the sky at the more than three-quarters full moon. "It's the right phase of a full moon for you, isn't it?"

Lex looked at me, her eyes wide and her mouth forming a large "O." *He knows?* she mouthed.

It was exactly what I'd been thinking too.

How could Paul know about my affliction?

Chapter Three: Separation Anxiety

"I'm familiar with your monthly ritual," Paul said.

It felt like my heart had gotten caught in my lower throat.

"Sorry, Paul, what do you mean by *my ritual*?"

"Your early morning writing strolls, where you go for a long walk with one of your characters. It has become obvious to me, over the years, that you only take these strolls during a specific phase of the moon."

I stared at him silently, relief pouring over me.

"There's something to the way the moon's gravitational pull affects the human brain," he continued. "I figured, based on your consistent pattern of early morning walks over the years, that you either write best, or perhaps have those long walks with characters during the full moon."

"Interesting," I said. "I didn't realize you'd noticed."

"Oh, I notice a lot of things working the front of this hotel. Mr. Andrews," Paul smiled.

"So you do, Paul. So you do.

"Of course, considering how exhausted we are from this travel—we sat on the plane on the tarmac in LA for almost longer than the flight was—I might just be sitting tomorrow morning's early constitutional out."

"Well then, there's a first for everything. Are you sure I can't help you with your luggage?"

"No, Paul, we're fine. But thanks, my friend."

We went inside, and I had the pleasure of seeing Lex's reaction to this classic hotel associated with literary history. Matilda the cat wasn't around, but I was looking forward to introducing Lex to her.

"I'm famished," I said to Lex as we walked past the Lobby Lounge where groups of people were having drinks and enjoying appetizers. "But let's enjoy this amazing lounge when we're less exhausted."

"How about I order us some classic New York pizza? It's not exotic like the salmon pizza we had in Venice Beach, but it's a unique experience, unlike any other."

"I'm game," Lex grinned as we walked towards the elevators. "But first things first. I really have to pee. I should have gone when we landed. But I don't think I can hold it until we get upstairs."

She handed me her bag and hustled over to the lobby restrooms.

I stood there, holding our bags and thinking about how different it had been the last time I'd been hanging out in this lobby.

It was on the evening of the last night of my previous werewolf cycle. I hadn't turned into a wolf, despite the moon being at 84% that evening. It was rare, but it did occasionally happen. Who really knows how this body chemistry is supposed to work, anyway? It's not like I could check in with my doctor about it.

But, I had expected to be turning into a wolf that night, which was the night before I'd headed off to Los Angeles for my nearly month-long trip.

Only it never happened. I ended up spending much of the evening in this lobby with my laptop and riffing off observing the couples at the other tables around me for an exercise in free writing; inspired by the stories I imagined coming from them.

When I got to LA, my enhanced senses continued with their odd coming and going. It had partially been the effect of the volume of alcohol I'd had. But later, I'd realized it was a side effect of being close to Lex.

Little did I know, the last time I'd spent time in this lobby, that I wouldn't be returning back to wolf form. That curse was finally behind me. So long as I was with Lex.

As I stood on that spot reflecting on the events of the past many weeks, I wondered what was taking Lex so long. It had been going on five minutes since she'd slipped into the bathroom.

And that's when something odd happened.

I was picking up snippets of the conversation from several of the couples well across the lobby. The scents of the room, and the people inside were coming to me. I could even detect the scent path of the last time Matilda had walked past this area. Her unique odor had passed right through here less than an hour ago, according to what my senses were telling me.

Then a strong tingling and ringing sensation started buzzing in my head, followed by an intense ache that shot through my bones.

Oh no.

It was happening.

I was turning into a wolf.

I dropped the bags and shuffled over in the direction of the restrooms. Lex's scent was a magnet pulling me forward. Hearing her heartbeat and the sound of water from the taps running from inside the ladies' room, I moved closer, needing proximity to Lex to prevent this lycanthropic change from coming over me. I opened my mouth to call out to her but found myself unable to do more than grunt. My vocal cords were already starting to morph in my throat.

As I got to the restroom door, my legs seized up, as if the bone structure was shifting, and it was difficult to move my legs the way I wanted them too. I hobbled forward, and the pain screamed through my back as I hunched forward.

In that position, I could see the fur on the back of my hands start to grow; excruciating pain fired through my fingers as they twisted like I was overcome with terrible arthritis.

I collapsed to my right against the women's room door and fell inside as it opened, spilling onto the floor in the doorway.

"Kal!" Lex called, followed shortly after by the feel of her hands on the backs of my shoulders.

The pulses of pain echoed through my entire body as she whispered gently to me. "I'm here, I'm here, I'm here. It's okay. I've got you."

The rhythmic pain lingered, not getting worse, not getting any better.

She continued whispering assurances to me, and

slowly the throbbing pain in my bones and the ringing in my head lessened.

"Is he okay?" I heard a man say. I didn't recognize his voice or scent.

"Yeah," Lex said. "He's okay. He'll be fine."

I turned my head, able to move again, like a normal human, and saw a waiter from the Lobby Lounge standing in the hallway.

"Does he need an ambulance?"

"No, it's just low blood sugar. I'll get him back up to our room and he'll be fine."

Lex helped me get back to my feet. My heightened senses receded, but I was still feeling rather dizzy.

"Thank you," I said to the waiter. "I'm fine. But that's the last time I try sticking to that damned Keto diet. Too many unexpected side-effects."

Assured I was okay, the waiter went back into the lounge area.

I was returning to full normal human again, and we moved back toward the elevator and our bags. Lex hit the button to call the elevator, and we stood together in silence waiting for the door to open.

After we stepped into the elevator and I hit the button for my floor number, the doors closed.

"Well, that was certainly scary," I said.

"No kidding."

"I suppose we'll just have to stay as close as possible."

"I think that can be arranged."

"Then I'm in," I said, dropping my bag and sliding

closer to Lex, placing my hand on the small of her back.

"Speaking of in," she said, sliding up against me. "It's been almost twelve hours since I've had you inside of me."

"I think *that* can be arranged," I grinned.

We wrapped ourselves in one another's arms in the manner that had become so natural to us recently and we kissed passionately, staying in that tight embrace until we reached our floor.

With one arm still wrapped around one another, and the other holding our bags, we moved down the hall until we got to my room. I had to temporarily let go of her while retrieving the key from my pocket and opening the door.

But once we were inside, and the door was closed we dropped our bags and were back in that tight embrace.

We desperately tore off one another's clothes and made love standing just inside the closed door of my room.

Wednesday, July 5, 2017

Interlude—Wolf Night—One

The wolf woke with a start, at once aware it was in a closed area and covered with an inorganic material.

The smell of the enclosed space was familiar. The wolf knew this room, both by the scent of it, and the sounds of the traffic outside muffled by the walls.

There was a human inches away. A female human. She had a somewhat familiar scent, but different from the two other female humans the wolf knew and trusted.

She was sleeping—that was easy enough to tell by the rhythmic and gentle sound of her breathing and movement of her chest. Her eyes were closed.

It passed its snout close along her body and took in more of her scent. Instinctively, it felt this female could also be trusted. And, though this female human was new and unknown, there was something unique in her smell. A subtle undertone, perhaps, not unlike the undertone of the female the wolf had encountered repeatedly, and many times in this same setting.

A painful throb starting in the wolf's head and cascading through its bones caused it to shudder. It stood and shook the light sheet off its back, then leapt off the structure it had been laying on with the female human and paced about the room.

The act of moving about reminded it of the burning desire inside to run, to race, to hunt in an unencumbered open landscape.

It needed that. Desperately.

It could, at times, remain restrained in this environment. But the wolf knew that part of the throbbing sensation in its head and entire being was related to being prevented from that freedom.

The female human could navigate the structures of this prison with its upper appendages.

She could help it get free of this limiting enclosure.

It leapt back onto the bed and gently licked the side of the woman's face. She tasted familiar, though the wolf had no memory of having previously licked this woman. Her breathing changed as she was coming back to consciousness. The wolf then nuzzled up against her, pushing against her to further wake her up.

She awoke and gave off an immediate bolt of shock and fear.

The wolf whined at her, eager to show it would not harm her.

"Kal?" the woman said, and her fearful scent dissolved into warmth, love, and compassion. "Oh my god. Kal. You're magnificent. Beautiful."

The noises the human female was making were unrecognizable but the feelings that came with them were familiar. This human female loved the wolf. Just like that other one who the wolf had encountered in this same space on numerous occasions.

Could that be the familiarity of part of her odor? No, it wasn't the emotion, it was something deeper, not about a feeling, something underlying that it couldn't figure out.

But the important thing was, this human female was a trusted and safe companion, like the other one had been. It would want to help the wolf.

The wolf jumped off the bed and walked toward the part of the wall that it knew the woman could open.

The woman just stared at it.

She wasn't getting it.

The wolf repeated the movement of moving back toward the bed, then turning again to the enclosed part of the wall, turning its head to glance back toward her.

"Oh," she said. "You want to go out."

The words had no meaning, but the wolf could tell she now understood what it wanted.

"No," she said.

The wolf knew that particular human sound well, having heard it repeatedly from that other female human.

"No," she repeated. "We can't go out. It's not safe."

She then patted the bed in front of her.

"C'mon, Kal. Hop back up here. Now that I'm awake, you'll likely change back." She patted the bed again. "C'mon."

The wolf recognized that gesture and that other vocal sound.

It whined again, feeling a deeper throbbing in its head and bones, then leapt onto the bed.

The woman wrapped its arms around the wolf and buried her face in the fur on the back of its neck. That was one of the *most vulnerable parts, but the wolf fully trusted this human female, knowing she would not bite it there.*

The throbbing in its head grew, and a burning like it had never experienced before shot through its body.

It let out a low howl of pain, then another whine, this time not one of disappointment, but of extreme pain.

The woman pulled it closer into its embrace, stroking it and uttering a stream of words in a repeated rhythm that accompanied the wolf as it fell in a swirling mass of intense throbs of pain toward the blackness.

Like before, the wolf couldn't understand the vocal noises coming from the human female, but it understood the soothing intent that came with them.

Chapter Four: While You Were Sleeping

"How did you sleep?"

I opened my eyes to see Lex sitting in the armchair near the foot of the bed resting a cup of coffee on the top knee of her crossed legs. The morning sunlight was streaming in from her left, casting the perfect angelic glow across her beautiful face.

Lex was wearing one of my t-shirts and nothing else. I could feel myself stirring with excitement just looking at her. Wow, you'd think I was a horny seventeen-year-old boy who hadn't ever been laid. When we had arrived at the apartment, we'd made love right in the entranceway the moment we got in. Then we'd moved around the corner to the bedroom, leaving our clothes and bags there on the floor, where we'd made frantic love again before falling asleep, exhausted, in one another's arms.

I realized, only now, that we hadn't ordered the New York pizza I had been looking forward to introducing her to. Which was a reminder of all the amazing things I had still to share with this woman whose very presence made my heart yearn for with increasing passion. As I looked at this gorgeous woman and thought about all the things I could show her about this city I adored, I marveled at how lucky I was to have found this amazing person.

And, on top of that heartwarming feeling, despite the glorious love-making sessions we'd engaged in last night, as famished as I was for food, looking at this magnificent woman right now, I was feeling turned on again. I wanted nothing more than to pull her back into the bed with me. Perhaps it's true that you can't get enough of a good thing.

"Like a baby," I said. "What are you doing up so early?"

She tightened her lips and paused before replying.

"Well, I wasn't able to sleep so well."

"What's wrong?"

"For one, I woke up at 2 AM to find a large grey wolf sleeping beside me."

"Oh my God! I morphed in the middle of the night? Did I try to harm you in any way?"

"No, you were nuzzling me gently, trying to wake me. Then you bounded off the bed, and headed for the door, then back on the bed again, as if you'd wanted me to take you outside. I'm guessing you wanted to run free somewhere.

"I patted the bed, and, like a compliant dog, you jumped back up and nuzzled me again. Then you let out a yelp of pain, and that's when I held you and whispered comforting words to you while you morphed back into human form. I was horrified at the look on your face and the howls and wails, both human, and canine, that were coming from you.

"It sounded, at times, like you were dying. Oh, Kal, it

was horrifying to watch. No wonder you have no memory of those transitions. It looks excruciating. Do you remember any of it?"

"No, none of it."

I've long believed that having no memory of the change, nor even of my consciousness as a wolf, was a factor in me maintaining my sanity. My memory typically blacked out several minutes before, and after, a transition between human and wolf form. And my memory of the time as a wolf were tiny fleeting glimpses of sights, sounds, smells, and feelings at best. Nothing coherent. Like miniscule memories of a vague dream on the best days. Most days, I had nothing.

"It happened because I fell asleep," Lex said. "I can't be apart from you at night during the cycle of a full moon. I also can't fall asleep; or else the effect I have on nulling your wolf blood retracts."

"I'm perfectly fine with not being apart from you. Especially not when you look like that." I let out a playful purr-growl sound that made her smile. "But it's not fair for you to be missing out on sleep."

"It's not that bad. I can catch some sleep when the sun's back up. And besides, your moon cycle lasts, what, ten days?"

I grinned at her. "Lex, you're amazing. I love you so much."

"Right back atcha, Kal."

"Do you need to sleep now?"

"Naw," she grinned. "I am tired. But this is my second cup of coffee. Maybe I'll have an afternoon nap."

"Well then," I said, pulling the sheets off to reveal the effect seeing her in only my t-shirt was having on me. "Can I interest you in a different bed-related activity?"

She put the coffee mug down on the floor and slid into the bed beside me. We then made slow, careful, and passionate love with each other.

"I still can't get over how you couldn't see it at all," Lex said from across the table at The Brooklyn Diner.

I picked up my coffee to take a sip. This was the third time we'd been over it, but Lex wanted to keep returning. Fair enough; I had walked her right into an odd and uncomfortable situation, and yet she had handled it with ease and complete calm. It would have been understandable had she been catty to Gail, refused to accept the ride from the airport, and decided to not come home with me.

"Well, when I had my wolf senses, I could tell that Gail still had feelings for me. But like I said, she made it quite clear that despite those feelings she wasn't interested in or prepared for anything more than a friendship."

"It was obvious to me that simply wasn't the case. Something must have changed. She's so into you it reeks."

"Maybe I stopped seeing it after a while. Of course, as you have experienced yourself, I'm not all that good at this relationship stuff. I'm awkward at best. Prior to the enhanced canine senses, I wasn't very good at reading people. And I'm obviously not all that good at it with those senses removed."

"Well, it's clear to me how much she loves you."

"I don't love her anymore. Lex, I love you."

I thought about what I'd just said. Of course I still loved Gail; I likely always would. That's not something a person can turn off, no matter how hard they try. And I had tried—numerous times over the years. I don't think I'd ever not love Gail. But I had, at least, given up on the idea of romantic love with her. Gail was an important person in my life, and I cared for her deeply. Heck, we'd been friends a lot longer than we'd ever been lovers.

Lex was giving me a look that suggested she didn't believe what I had just said.

"I know you love me, Kal. I knew how you felt long before you told me. But you can't tell me you don't have feelings for Gail."

"Okay," I said, throwing up my hands. "I still care for her. Like a friend. Like a sister."

"A sister you slept with."

She started laughing and kicked me in the shin under the table.

"It's hilarious, when you think about it. I meet this guy, in a bar, of all places—although, when you think about it, I'm in a lot of bars, so that shouldn't be surprising. But we hit it off. He's a nice guy, an ex-pat Canadian. A bit of a pushover, actually. But he's sweet, a boy scout by nature. He's awkward, but obviously into me. I fall for him, later learn he's not just an eager-to-please beta human, but also an alpha wolf. We end up fighting side-by-side against a neo-Nazi hate group, then I uproot my life to move across the country to start a new life with him in New York—only to be met at the airport by his ex-girlfriend, the woman he was trying to get over when he went to LA.

"It makes for one hell of a paranormal romantic comedy, don't you think?"

"I prefer silly comedies. Classic Monty Python. Or adventure comedies. Those *Vacation* movies with Chevy Chase."

"Wow," Lex laughed. "What are you, one hundred years old or something?" She descended into a fit of giggles.

It wasn't that funny, but I suspect the lack of sleep was a factor, making her a bit punchy. Seeing her laughing made me grin from ear to ear.

"I'm surprised," she snorted, "that you mentioned movies filmed in color."

"Hey," I said with a tone of mocking indignation. "I'm still trying to get used to this newfound triumph of the talkies in the film industry. I stand alongside Charlie Chaplin. Physical humor comedy becomes 'lost' with dialogue."

That set her off even more. Lex was laughing so hard her eyes were watering. I started laughing along with her. With an audience of over-tired people like this, I could start a new career as a stand-up comedian.

Lex was laughing so hard she snorted again just as our waitress arrived with our breakfast order. The surprised look on the waitresses' face set Lex off even more.

"Thanks," I said to the waitress as she was setting down our plates. "And sorry about this. My girlfriend is mocking my taste in *older* comedy films. And she's a little punchy from lack of sleep."

"Well, I'm sorry, ma'am," the waitress said, adopting a similar mock indignation to the one I'd just used. "But I'm going to have to ask you to stop. You're sitting in a snort-free section of the diner."

That launched both Lex and I into a fresh round of giggles. Lex snorted again, then started laughing harder. The waitress laughed along with us.

"Glad you two lovebirds are having so much fun," the waitress said. "If you need anything more, just give me a holler. Or a snort, if you prefer."

More laughter from Lex.

"Actually," I said. "Do you mind taking this sugar? I'm thinking she's had enough, don't you?"

"Oh," Lex beamed. "And when you get a chance, can you top up his glass of prune juice?"

The waitress shook her head. "You two are adorable," she said, moving on to greet newly arrived customers at an adjacent table.

"She was pretty cool," Lex said.

"Yeah. People in New York can be awesome. I can't wait to share more of this city with you."

"Me too."

We looked at the New Yorker Special breakfast plates in front of us. Three eggs with a side of crispy corn polenta, sausage, and toast.

"This smells delicious!" Lex said. "But I've got to visit the ladies' room before I dig in." She leaned in and whispered. "I was laughing so hard I think I might have pee'd a little."

She got up from the table, taking the time to lean in and kiss me before heading to the restroom. "Don't wait for me. Dig in."

Watching her walk away I again marveled at this incredible woman. I then looked down at my plate. I was indeed hungry, but I wasn't as ravenous as I normally felt on mornings after I'd spent the entire night tearing around Central Park on four legs. On those mornings, I would have ordered a double helping of the eggs and all the meat options and still been hungry afterwards. It was likely my body needing to replenish from the metamorphosis and the calories burned while running in wolf form.

I poured a hearty helping of ketchup onto my plate, then sunk my fork into the scrambled eggs and lifted it to my mouth. It was, as always, as delicious as it smelled. And once the food touched my lips, I realized just how hungry I was.

It didn't take long for more than half of the food on my plate to disappear. I had to consciously try to slow myself down. Okay, so apparently the near change in the lobby of the Algonquin and the temporary change to wolf up in my room had burned a significant number of calories.

I kept shoveling the food into my mouth, barely taking a breath and planning on ordering another plate.

Towards the end of finishing the food, I realized my sense of taste was growing. As it returned, so too, did my appetite. But it wasn't just my taste returning. I smelled more than just the food at our table. I could smell the food from other plates, from the kitchen, the perfume and body odor and breath of others in the diner. The conversations from the surrounding tables were crisp and clear.

Lex had been gone long enough for my enhanced senses to have returned. It was a curious thing, having my senses go in and out like that.

I was considering the logistics of how to navigate this new coming-and-going of my senses based on her proximity when I picked up a sound that made my blood run cold.

"No!"

It was Lex's voice, coming to me all the way from the bathroom hallway, startled and terrified. It came with a whiff of shock and instantaneous fear.

Chapter Five: Do You Think it's a Sign?

I was on my feet without thinking about it, and already halfway to the restrooms when I realized I still had the fork in my hand.

It was the fearful scent of a woman from one table who'd seen me rushing past determinedly and assuming I was on the attack that tipped me off. "He's got a weapon," I heard her utter to whoever was at the table with her.

Her assumption made sense. I was over six feet tall and must have had a wild look in my eyes—my panic and concern for Lex—as I suddenly bolted from the table, the fork I'd been eating with clutched tightly in my fist.

I dropped the fork on the table of one booth I passed as I continued to rush toward the pair of men's and ladies' rooms at the back. They were single use restrooms, and I could tell by scent and sound that Lex was the only one inside.

Lex's heartbeat was elevated, and I could hear her breathing heavily. There was a terrible anxiety coming from her as she sobbed under her breath.

"Lex," I called out, "Are you okay?" The door was, of course, locked. But that didn't stop me. My enhanced superhuman strength allowed me to force the door open easily, the deadbolt cracking through the door jamb. I stepped inside. "What happened?"

"Kal?" Lex said, in the middle of splashing water onto her face from the sink. She was startled to see me burst into the ladies' room.

"Are you okay?"

"Oh, you heard that? Your senses are back? I suppose I was gone long enough for that to happen."

"What frightened you? Your reaction was pretty intense."

She took me by the hand, pulled me all the way into the small single person restroom, and let the door close behind me.

"I didn't see it because I was browsing Instagram on my phone when I first sat down. It wasn't until I finished washing my hands and was about to leave that I saw it."

She pointed to the top left-hand corner of the door, just above the top hinge.

It was small, maybe only half an inch high, and scratched lightly enough that you had to catch it at the right angle to see it. But once you did, there it was, clear as day.

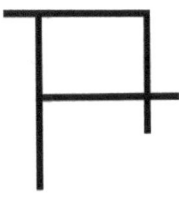

The PFA symbol of the Proud Fighters for America.

We had seen it enough times in Los Angeles to know it all too well. This white-supremacist hate-group cult typically left this symbol spray-painted in red, on the sides of buildings of businesses they had attacked, or near where they'd attacked visible minorities from cultural or LGBTQ groups.

It was a symbol that was usually large and blatant and proudly claiming responsibility for the assaults, attacks, and destruction of property.

But this one was subtle and difficult to find. Almost as if it might be a member of the group letting other members know they had been here.

"Kal, they're here in New York too."

I turned to look at Lex and saw the fear clearly on her face. Her heart was still pounding, and the odor of her fear was still coming off fresh and strong. I couldn't blame her. She had been deeply involved with this cult in her attempt to rescue her best friend Sacha from their clutches. Their experiments with some odd combination of cultist rituals and chemical injections to create a race of super-powered beings ended up killing Sacha.

Because their injection didn't seem to have any effect on Lex—not to mention they'd discovered her Black heritage—they had removed her from the group. But they'd continued to use her for intel and access to files based on the tech work she did.

After several encounters with the group where we just couldn't get the upper hand, we ended up being spotted by Marco, the leader Lex had been involved with, who recognized her.

Realizing how powerless we were, and that my attempts to fight them, even with my enhanced wolfish powers, led to the death of a good person I'd befriended, Lex and I decided to leave the crime-fighting to the police and a special domestic terrorist attack force.

We had also decided it would be best for her to leave Los Angeles, where this group was operating, and come back with me to New York, where we could build our new lives together. Normal lives. Free from having to deal with my werewolf curse. Lex finally free from having to bend to the wishes of the PFA.

But this symbol suggested this malicious group had members in New York.

In *my* city.

I reflectively let out a low growl that startled Lex.

It happened rarely, but the wolf blood flowing through my veins occasionally affected more than just my enhanced senses. During rare moments, it affected the core of my emotions too.

They had invaded my territory.

"What the hell was that?"

"It's a territorial thing. Part of the instinctual nature of the wolf blood running through my veins."

As the brief overwhelming wolf emotion receded, so, too could I feel my enhanced senses begin to slowly fade.

But they were still strong enough to pick up, faintly, the voice of the woman I'd passed and frightened in the diner.

"He went in the women's room, officer. And he's

armed with a steak knife."

I mused at the way we could interpret things in the heat of the moment; we often see and hear the things we expect rather than what's actually there. This woman saw a large man with wild eyes storming across the diner with a utensil in his hand. Of course she saw it as a knife. Perhaps that's one reason eyewitness accounts could be so suspect.

My slowly fading senses picked up the shuffling of feet and an authoritative male voice, likely one of the officers, ushering people out of the restaurant.

"Oh oh," I said, pushing my hand against the door to hold it closed. "The police are here."

"What?"

There was a loud knock on the door that visibly shook it.

"This is the police," a gruff male voice called out. "Come out now with your hands up."

"A woman in the diner saw me rushing through the diner with my fork in my hand, then breaking into the ladies' restroom. She must have thought I was some sort of crazy or drugged-out maniac."

The second knock—more of a pounding which I'm surprised didn't crack the door—came with a louder and more forceful order. "Come out, *now*! With your hands up!"

"Okay," I shouted through the door. "We're coming. We're not armed."

Lex grabbed my shoulder and pulled me back.

"Let me go first." She then turned back toward the

door and called out. "We're fine, officer. Everything's fine. Everyone's okay. This was a misunderstanding. We're coming out."

She turned her head back to me with a smirk on her face and said, "Something tells me my breakfast will be cold before I get to it," before opening the door.

Lex took a single step out, with her hands raised above her head. I stood behind her, my hands also up, with my left elbow holding the door open.

A female police officer who was the spitting image of a young Halle Berry stood in the aisle straight ahead of us, legs parted, and knees partially bent, her gun in both clasped hands pointing in our direction. Several feet behind her, another officer was still clearing the last few people out of the restaurant.

I picked up the sound of the breathing and masculine scent of another officer from the right of the door; that was likely the one who'd been pounding on it. Most assuredly, his weapon was also drawn.

"Step this way ma'am," the black female officer said. "Come stand behind me."

Lex complied and stepped forward. In a much quieter voice, one a normal person standing where I was wouldn't have been able to hear, the officer asked her if she was okay. "Yes, officer. I'm fine. We're together. It was a misunderstanding."

The tall thin male officer who'd been clearing the restaurant rushed back from the front entrance to meet Lex. This guy reminded me a bit of Ben Stiller, but he wasn't being funny in any way. He was all business as he produced a pair of handcuffs and looked her up and down, studying her. "No signs of defensive wounds," he whispered to the other officer. Then he asked her to lower her hands and cuffed her hands in front of her.

"Step forward, out of the restroom!" the female officer called to me. "Keep your hands up."

I complied, stepping out, and glancing to my right. The older white male officer with the gruff voice who'd pounded on the door with his ham fists looked exactly like I'd pictured. He was standing in a similar pose as the female officer directly in front of me. He was much older than her—old enough to be her father—and reminded me of William Shatner in that 80s television show *T.J. Hooker*.

"Keep moving forward, slowly," officer Berry said to me.

I did what she said. My senses were now muted close to normal human range. I wasn't able to pick up on emotive scents, heartbeat, any of the things that usually helped me navigate challenging interactions.

Officer Shatner moved in behind me.

He quickly patted me down, likely checking for weapons. He pulled my wallet and cell phone out of my back pocket and tossed them onto a booth table.

"Listen, officer—" I started.

"Hands behind your back!" he ordered.

As I lowered my hands and brought them behind me, I felt the cold steel of the handcuffs snap around my wrists.

Shatner then man-handled me into the booth where

he'd dropped my wallet and pushed me to the back. He slid in beside me.

Officer Berry took Lex by the shoulders and moved her into the booth opposite me before sitting down beside her.

The look on Lex's face as she was being shoved into the booth was clear panic. I didn't have to have enhanced senses to tell what worried her. We needed to explain this and ensure I didn't somehow get locked into a cell overnight. That wouldn't be a pleasant scene.

"Officer," I said. "We can explain."

"Yeah, you will," Shatner replied. "But first, what are your names?"

"Michael Andrews," I said.

Shatner had my wallet open and was confirming what I had just told him by looking at my ID.

"And you are?" he asked Lex.

"Alexandria Jones." she said.

"Do you have any ID?"

"It's in my purse at our table. Around the corner. Second last table on the right. Brown suede bag."

Officer Stiller nodded and moved off to go get it.

"What is your relationship with one another?" Shatner asked.

"Boyfriend and girlfriend," I said.

"Is this true?" The question was directed at Lex.

"Yes."

"For how long?"

"A few weeks."

"Where do you live?"

"Los Angeles. But I just moved here."

"And you?" he asked me.

"Manhattan. A few blocks from here. The Algonquin."

Shatner paused and looked me up and down. "That's a hotel. Where do you live?"

"I live at the Algonquin. In one of their residence suites."

"What are you, some kind of big shot?"

"Oh, I know," Officer Berry said. "Andrews. Michael Andrews. I thought that name sounded familiar. You're a mystery writer."

"Yeah. That's me."

"I've read all your books," she grinned. "*Print of the Predator* was much better than the movie. I hear that JP Heartschwinger is filming *Tome of Terror* right now."

I smiled back at her. "He is. I just got back from the set in LA yesterday. That's where Lex and I met."

The female cop beamed a huge smile and was about to ask something else, but Shatner threw a glare at her that stopped her.

I couldn't tell if they were playing "good cop, bad cop" or if she was a genuinely personable police officer and her much older partner was just a crotchety curmudgeon.

The tall skinny officer returned with Lex's handbag. Shatner grabbed it from him, reached into it and pulled out her wallet and flipped through it. "Her name checks out.

"So," he said, returning his gaze to Lex. "What was

going on? Why did this guy storm through the restaurant and break into the restroom? Were you having a disagreement?"

"No," she said. "We were laughing, having fun. I just went to the washroom to freshen up. Then I saw something that startled me. I called out."

"And I heard her, and went running."

"You heard her from behind a door and well across a packed restaurant?"

"I have exceptionally strong hearing."

Shatner glared at me silently. It was obvious he didn't believe me, but I'm pretty sure the furthest thing from his mind was that I might have wolf blood coursing through my veins that gave me superhuman abilities.

"So I rushed to see what—"

"What about the knife?" Shatner interrupted.

"What?"

"The eyewitness who called this in said you were rushing at the restroom door with a steak knife raised like you were going to attack with it."

"She must have been mistaken," I said, internally cringing at the realization he hadn't revealed the sex of the person who'd called this in. He didn't seem to notice, so I continued. "In my panic to get to Alexandria when I heard her call out to see what the matter was, I realized I was still holding my fork. I tossed it onto one of the tables before I got to the door."

"So, let's pretend that you could actually hear her call out amidst all the noise in a full diner. Why would you jump out of your seat, with your fork still in your hand, and race to get to the washroom? What, is she deathly afraid of bugs?" He swung his gaze to Lex. "What'd you see? A giant cockroach?"

"No," she said. "Something much worse."

"Which is?"

"The PFA symbol carved into the back of the door."

"PFA?"

"The Proud Fighters for America," the female officer said. "They're a suspected domestic terrorist group operating in the greater LA area. They've been extremely active lately…"

Shatner glared at her as if to tell her to stop talking.

"Why don't you go with Officer Johnson here and show her this symbol."

Johnson slipped out of the booth and helped Lex out and to her feet. They headed to the washroom.

"That's a bit of an over-reaction to a bit of graffiti, isn't it?" Shatner asked me after they left.

"Well," I said. "We had a number of pretty nasty run-ins with the PFA in Los Angeles. They completely trashed Alexandria's apartment. They spray-painted their swastika-like calling-card in two-foot-high letters all over her walls, too. That's one reason she came back to New York with me. We figured we'd be safe from them all the way across the country.

"You can check with Detective Hank Reynolds, of the LAPD. He is one of the lead investigators in the Office of Special Operations that has been following this group. He knows us and can attest to all of this."

He stared at me silently. A few seconds passed.

"Reynolds, eh? How do you know him?"

"He's the brother-in-law of a friend I'd been working with when in Hollywood. That's how I know him. We witnessed them attacking racial minorities on multiple occasions. They shot a man in front of me. Detective Reynolds can corroborate all of what I'm saying."

The older cop sat quietly staring at me. It made me uncomfortable. I'd purposely used the terms *attest* and *corroborate* because it was terminology often used by law enforcement according to the research I had done for my mystery novels. And I knew that the silence was a technique often used in interviews or interrogations. If an authority figure remains silent, or only responds with minimal words, like Shatner had been doing, the interviewee would often, out of nervousness, keep talking, to fill the uncomfortable silence. I realized I had been doing just that.

I told myself to shut up—and I actually listened to myself too, though I did have to consciously clamp my lips together because I often spoke more when I was anxious—and looked back at him, trying desperately not to look nervous.

"I'll be sure to check that out," Shatner finally said.

Lex and Johnson returned. The female officer slid her phone in front of her partner without saying a word. The screen was at enough of an angle for me to see it was a picture of the PFA symbol from the ladies' room door.

Shatner looked at it silently saying nothing. He

handed the phone back to her.

"Okay," he said.

Officer Johnson and Simmons, we later learned was his name of the elder partner—though I still thought of him as Officer Shatner—spoke with us for a few more minutes, taking down our contact information. The conversation was a lot less confrontational at that point.

Johnson left the booth and walked several feet away down the aisle to call something in on her radio, before returning and asking if we would be willing to stay to talk to a local detective.

They uncuffed us and asked us to go back over the details of this morning. They also asked about everything we'd done since we left Los Angeles. We shared the details, without mentioning the total panic over me turning into a wolf on the plane, nor the near-wolf incident in the Algonquin Hotel lobby or the waking wolf in the hotel room.

We made sure, if you will, not to cry wolf.

Fifteen minutes later a tall middle-aged white man in a brown sport coat and black tie, with grey hair and large bulbous eyes that overshadowed his thin face arrived. He introduced himself as Detective Wagner.

Detective Wagner took Officer Simmons' spot beside me and asked us to share the specifics of what had happened in Los Angeles. Lex and I took turns relaying the same details we had shared with Detective Reynolds about our encounters with the PFA. He gave us a card and asked us to contact him if we remembered anything else, or if we saw or spotted any other activity that might be related to the PFA.

He also mentioned something that struck me as interesting when he lowered his voice so that the police officers nearby couldn't hear him and asked us to report anything regarding the PFA. His wording was peculiar. He said: "If you see anything that might not be explainable by natural occurring phenomena; something that gives you the heebie-jeebies or makes you feel like you've walked into The Twilight Zone, call me."

It suggested he was familiar with the experimentation and bizarro science-meets-occult rituals of the PFA.

That entire process took another half an hour.

By the time we were finally free to leave, just happy to get out of that restaurant, neither one of us said anything while still in earshot of the police. I think that, Lex, like me, was just relieved that we weren't in any trouble, and also took comfort in the knowledge the local police force was familiar with this hate group and were prepared for them.

After we walked past the tall thin officer I had nicknamed Stiller, Lex turned to me with a serious look on her face.

"Before we talk about what just happened and what this might mean," she said, "can we grab something to eat? I'm famished."

Chapter Six: Mack Attack

On the way back to our place we stopped in at a deli and picked up three breakfast sandwiches. Lex hadn't had a single bite from her plate earlier, but she was only having one of them. The other two were for me. Even though I had finished most of my own generously portioned plate at The Brooklyn Diner, I was still feeling hungry.

I normally was ravenous after a night of tearing around on all fours during my monthly cycle. I had always thought it must have been because my midnight canine romp resulted in the burning of a shit-ton of calories.

But I realized it might not be that—or at least all that. I had been on the brink of conversion twice last night. Once on the plane, and then again in the Algonquin Hotel lobby. And then, up in our room, after Lex had fallen asleep, I'd gone through a full conversion into wolf form, and then back again.

The conversion, and potentially even the near conversions themselves must consume a considerable number of calories. My body undergoes a vigorous transformation; one that plays a role in significantly speeding up my body's ability to heal from injuries and even viral or bacterial infections.

"So," Lex said when we were back on the street, un-wrapping the sausage and egg sandwich—these sandwiches were definitely not going to make it back to the hotel with us. "The PFA is here too."

I had unwrapped one of my own sandwiches but hadn't yet taken my first bite. "They must have some sort of offshoot branch. I suppose it's inevitable in any movement; including a hate movement."

"Do you think they followed us here?" she asked around a mouthful.

I had half the sandwich from a giant bite already crammed into my mouth, so I responded by shaking my head and holding my left hand up to indicate a verbal response was coming.

"I don't think so. The scratching in that bathroom wasn't fresh. It looked like it had been there a while."

"Have you ever seen that symbol around the city before?"

"No. Not that I can remember, at least. I mean, now that I know what it is, it stands out, you know? But I could have seen what appears to be an innocuous tag from a random graffiti artist or gang a dozen times and never registered it."

"I wonder how big the group is locally. And do they have special powers too?"

I thought back to the fact that the only supernatural foe I'd encountered prior to my recent trip to Los Angeles was here in New York. It was a few years ago, when the shock-rock star who called himself Knell turned out to be a werewolf. But he was a musician who'd spent most of his life on the road; there's no way he could have been part of some local sect of the group.

"No. The only person with special powers that I ever met here in the city wasn't even from here. Remember I'd told you about Knell?"

"Yeah. He was the only one?"

"The only. Funny, I wandered around for close to a decade thinking that I was the only one with these odd supernatural abilities. I mean, sure, the wolf who infected me must also be a werewolf. But that was in upstate New York. Far from the city.

"In all those years since I met up with only a single other super-powered person. But these past few weeks, you couldn't even throw a Timbit in my vicinity without hitting someone else with extraordinary powers."

"Throw a what?"

"Sorry?"

"Did you say '*Timbit*?' What the heck is a Timbit?"

"Oh," I laughed. "I must have been speaking Canadian without realizing it. Tim Hortons is a Canadian donut and coffee shop franchise. A Timbit is round mini donut. What are often called donut holes. They're the size of the dough that would conceptually be cut from the center of a normal donut.

"You know that old expression *you can't swing a cat* when trying to express how close someone is? Like in Hollywood you can't swing a cat without hitting a celebrity? My dad used to use the expression *you can't throw a Timbit* or *you can't pitch a Timbit* to express the same thing.

"He really liked cats, and I suppose the thought of swinging one around was bothersome to him."

Lex grabbed my arm and snuggled up against me.

"I adore your cute little Canadianisms," she said.

"Get oot of here," I jokingly replied, purposely altering the word *out* so it sounded like the long 'o' sound in *boot*. Then, for good measure, I added, "Eh?"

Lex laughed and I thought about how it was a sound I just couldn't get enough of.

"I can't believe how much I love your laugh, Lex."

She grinned and her eyes became playful. She adopted a Marilyn Monroe voice. "Mr. Andrews, are you trying to seduce me?"

"Maybe."

Lex continued in her Marilyn Monroe impersonation. "Because it's definitely working. I certainly hope you don't try to tickle me when we get back to your hotel room."

"Oh, I'll be tickling you all over."

"Tell me more," she purred.

I suspected we might not be getting out that much today, and the idea of spending the entire day in bed with Lex suited me just fine.

The phone in my back pocket vibrated and I pulled it out. The call display told me it was Mack Halpin's office. It was likely Anne, Mack's assistant, welcoming me back to New York.

"I should take this," I said to Lex. "It's my agent."

I then hit the accept button for the call. "This is Michael."

"Hi Michael," it was, as I expected, Anne Lee, Mack's assistant. "How was your flight?"

"Good," I said. "I mean, there were a few delays in getting back, but it just meant a bit more waiting around than usual."

"That's good. And…" her voice shifted into a much softer tone on that last word, and she paused for a few seconds. I could almost hear her blushing when she continued. "How is Alexandria?"

Anne was one of the sweetest, kindest, and most thoughtful people I'd ever known. And despite being a decade younger than me, she was kind and motherly to me. Before I had left New York for LA, she'd given me some advice about Gail. I'd been mooning over Gail despite her repeatedly stating we could only ever be friends and that she wasn't ready for any sort of romantic relationship.

Anne's advice to me had been to go to Los Angeles, to be away from Gail for a while, and that would offer me a fresh perspective. She'd suggested I should allow myself to be open to the possibilities of the world. Her talk, followed, a few days later by a particular song performed live by Alicia Witt at an intimate live music venue I visited when I first arrived in LA, allowed me to open up to those possibilities; and I met Lex shortly after that.

"She's good." I said, looking over at the beautiful woman walking beside me. I suppose I should send Anne a giant bouquet of flowers for how she helped me.

"That's great. Oh, Michael, you know I do like Gail,

but I'm so glad you and Alexandria found one another. I'm looking forward to meeting her. Are you bringing her with you to your appointment this morning?"

"My appointment?"

"With Mack. It's at eleven. In half an hour. I was calling to remind you in case you forgot."

Oh, crap. That meeting was today. I'd remembered it being set up for two days after I arrived back in New York. Of course, I'd had to re-arrange my flight by one day to accommodate a seat for Lex beside me. Which meant the meeting *was* today.

"Half an hour?"

"You forgot, didn't you?"

"Yeah," I said. "I thought it was tomorrow.

"No," she said. "It's in half an hour. Well, technically, twenty-eight minutes and thirty-seconds. Glad I called to remind you. You'd best be on your way quickly. You know how Mack is about tardiness."

Oh, I knew that very well. Mack waited for no one. Ever. He was impatient and preferred being an hour early over even being one second late. I could imagine his gruff voice booming from his mother's womb when her doctor told her the expected delivery date that he'd be coming out the second he felt his gestation was completed, and not a bloody second later.

"We're on our way," I said. "See you soon, Anne."

I thumbed the hang-up button and pocketed my phone as I raised my arm to hail a cab.

Mack's office was perhaps a dozen blocks from where we were. We could have walked there in roughly the same time, hoofing it at full pedestrian speed; but I preferred explaining it to Lex while we sat comfortably in the back of the taxi.

I'd already told Lex about my agent, cautioned her about his crude bedside manner, and reminded her it would be a good idea to not kick him in the nuts, which had been Gail's instinctive reaction the first time she'd met him.

I also apologized for the quick change of plans but assured her she was going to love Anne, and that Anne had been looking forward to meeting her.

As I suspected, Anne and Lex hit it off marvellously. When we got in, Anne gave me a big hug and embraced Lex as if they were long-lost friends.

"Thank you for coming into Michael's life," Anne said to Lex as they hugged, "I haven't seen him this happy in years."

I apologized to Anne that we'd left in such a hurry I didn't have time to bring her the coffee beans I'd picked up for her from a San Diego coffee chain that had been growing significantly throughout the state. "I'll come back later today to bring them."

"Oh, don't make a special trip on my account."

"It's no bother, Anne. I know you'll love their coffee."

"I'm sure I will." She turned to look at Lex again. "He likely hasn't had time to take you to any of the best coffee shops in Manhattan."

"No," Lex replied. "Not yet."

"Excellent." Anne moved back to behind her desk. "Perhaps you and I can meet up at one of my favorites. Just us girls. It'll give us a chance to get to know one another."

"That sounds fun," Lex said.

I grinned. Anne had done the same thing when I had first started dating Gail all those years ago. She was such a protective motherly figure to me—despite being about ten years younger than me—and was looking for an excuse to spend time with any girl I'd fallen in love with so she could really check her out.

"Andrews!" A gruff male voice called from the right. It was Mack.

I turned to see him standing in the now open doorway of his office.

"Look at you. You're five minutes early. How unlike you. You usually arrive with barely a second to spare. Seems like that time in California has been good to you. Looks like you got a little sun—a dramatic improvement over your normally pasty white complexion."

"And look at this absolutely gorgeous doll!" Mack let out a whistle as he looked Lex up and down. "When I sent your miserable whiney bitch-ass to LA, I figured you might get your rocks off somewhere, but had no idea you'd net such a foxy Hollywood babe."

I looked at Lex and could tell how hard she was suppressing her instinctive reaction to Mack's degrading words. She gave me a quick look that told me she'd be good at keeping it under control.

"Hey, Mack. This is my girlfriend, Lex."

Mack whistled again. "Good to meet you, Sexy Lexy." He stepped forward and reached out his hand. Lex raised her hand to shake, biting her bottom lip so hard she wasn't able to verbalize a greeting back. Mack lifted her hand up to his thick-mustached lips and kissed the back of it.

"It's a pleasure to meet you," he said. It was a moment of old fashioned and gentlemanly respect, and I felt a wave of relief that he'd come back out of the gutter where he'd started off. That sense of relief didn't last more than a split second, because of the next words out of his mouth.

"And thank you for boning my client. If you hadn't come along, I'd likely have had to pony up some dough for a string of prostitutes just to get this guy's head out of his own ass."

"Mack," Anne interrupted. "I see there's a call from Penguin Random House coming in on line one. It's likely Ed. Should I take a message?"

"No," Mack dropped her hand. "I'll take it. I need to talk to him now. Andrews won't mind.

"Of course," I said. "All good."

Mack moved back toward his office.

"Nice to meet you, Sexy Lexy," he was saying, his back to us. He was still talking as he closed the door. "Seriously, Andrews. How the hell does a plain guy like you get to bang such a hot dame?"

Anne, Lex, and I stood there looking at one another.

"He's quite the...charmer," Lex said. "When you said

he would be crude, I never expected that."

"Mack talks tough," Anne said. "But he has a heart of gold. He likes to tease Michael, but it's just his idea of tough love."

"He's a little rough around the edges, but he's the best agent in the business," I said. "If it wasn't for Mack, I never would have gone to Los Angeles and never would have met you."

Lex sighed. "Okay, I'll give him that. But I'll be fine if I never have to interact with him again. Seriously, I'm surprised he grabbed my hand and didn't grab me by my—"

"Why don't the two of us go downstairs to the lower-level concourse in this building?" Anne interrupted. I'm due for a break, and I know a fantastic little donut shop there that I think you'd love. Their coffee is not as good as some of my favorite places, but it's pretty solid.

"You and I can head down there and we can get to know one another a bit now. Mack will probably be on this call for a few minutes, then he and Michael will meet. That should give us some decent girls' time."

"Sure," Lex said. "Because I'm not sure I could handle seeing that lech again so soon."

Anne got up from behind her desk and took Lex by the hand.

Lex leaned over and gave me a quick kiss.

"Wow," she whispered. "I'm surprised at you, Kal. You let him walk all over you. All over me. I've never seen you be such a pushover."

As they headed out the office door, I took a seat in

one of the leather chairs across from the reception desk and glanced at the spread of magazines on the coffee table there.

I picked up what looked like the latest copy of Publishers Weekly. It was a stark white cover with the round green logo of the featured publisher on it. Berrett-Koehler were celebrating twenty-five years in business.

Flipping through it, skipping to the deals section to see if any of the writers I had met over the years were there, nothing caught my interest. But that's mostly because I wasn't really reading it; my eyes were barely just scanning the words without taking them in.

I was thinking about Lex's reaction to Mack as well her assertion of how I let him walk all over me.

Lex was right, I was a complete pushover in front of Mack. He didn't just walk over me; he led a full-fledged state university marching band over top of me. But it had always been that way. I mean, it's not like I'd ever been a forceful and domineering person to begin with. I was easy going, a people-pleaser, and rarely incited aggressive situations.

My default response to almost any incident was to immediately apologize and then ask questions later.

I suppose the one area where I was a little more confident and forceful, would be whenever I used my heightened senses and strength to help others. But, even when that led to a fight with some thug or bad guy, it was usually out of a position of protecting or helping their victim rather than an aggressive attack.

No, while I might have become an alpha wolf a little

more than a decade ago, I'd been a beta human my entire life.

Mack had long been the dominant alpha in our relationship. Heck, the terms *alpha* and *dominate* are far too subtle to express his default manner of exertion. Mack's bold demeanor makes the old *bull in a china shop* expression a quaint little happenstance event practically unnoteworthy by comparison. He's more of a *remove a splinter using a flamethrower* kind of guy in terms of his subtlety.

But as frustrating as all that could be, I was thrilled to have him as my agent. Because most of the time he was aggressively pushing for me. He'd been the one responsible for landing me a rock-solid contract with Staadt Publishing, had sold film and television rights to my Maxwell Bronte novels, booked me onto the Late Night with David Letterman Show, and even got me a job as a script consultant on the latest film being made from one of my books.

I was still flipping through the magazine without really reading it when the buzzer from Mack's office sounded on Anne's desk. I knew it well, since he rarely would get up and come to the door. He preferred the power statement of buzzing from behind his closed office door.

Since Anne was downstairs with Lex, and I knew that he'd been signalling to let Anne know he was done with his call and I could now enter his office, I got up and stepped inside, closing the door behind me.

Mack was seated behind his large mahogany desk

with an unlit cigar peeking out from under his thick and narrow toothbrush moustache.

He struck a match and lit the cigar as I took a seat in the chair in front of his desk.

"Your babe didn't want to come in with you, Andrews?" he asked after he got the cigar lit. "She's pretty damn pleasing on the eye; I wouldn't mind another gander at her."

"No. Anne took her downstairs to get coffee."

Mack nodded and sat there staring at me.

With Lex having been gone for several minutes, my enhanced senses began to return. It was oddly disconcerting to have my senses go through this multiple times in a day. It might be akin to the subtle—or perhaps not-so-subtle—difference when your ear has been clogged with water, but then clears. You could still hear, but it was slightly muffled. Or when your sinuses are congested, and you can still smell things, just not as well.

Mack was giving off the scent that he was impatiently waiting for something as he stared at me. And the longer he waited, the angrier he got.

"Well?"

I had no idea what he was waiting for.

"*Well* what?"

"Aren't you going to thank me?"

Mack had used this tactic before when he was about to announce something he'd arranged for me. I shook my head in response, indicating I did not know what was coming.

He just shook his own head back, wordless. And

wordless was not a term many people would ever use when describing Mack. So the whole thing made me rather uncomfortable.

"I'll bite. What? What do you have for me?"

Finally, he broke the silence, pulling the cigar out of his mouth and gesturing with it as he spoke.

"What do I have for you? For fuck's sake, boy, I sent you on a luxury trip to LA to hang out on the set of a Hollywood film with JP Heartschwinger, one of the most renowned directors in the business. And while you're there, you land a delicious piece of ass that actually comes back to New York with you.

"You hadn't been fucked in a coon's age and you were moping around here like a pathetic loser. I sent you to LA, and you get your pole polished by that sexy creature.

"And you're asking me what to thank me for?

"Okay," I said. "I get it. Thank you, Mack. Meeting Lex has been really good for me."

"You're damned right it was." He stuck the cigar back in his mouth, took a long pull on it, then let out a large puff of smoke. "You know what else worked out brilliantly? The fucking PFA."

"The PFA?"

"Yeah. The fact you ran into them and they stomped all over your pansy ass was one of the best things that could have happened for you and for this film.

"Nielsen BookScan numbers show a dramatic lift in sales of *Tome of Terror* ever since you were attacked by the PFA. Sales on a backlist title usually never see that type of significant jump in sales until the release of a movie tie-in. But this was off the charts.

"Heartschwinger, that brilliant and always-thinking director—God, I love that guy's moxie—played it up in the press as an attack against Hollywood Jews and will use that again close to the film's release for garnering further publicity for the film.

"But we need to leverage that as well, not just for sales of *Tome* and your other novels but so I can use that to get your next Bronte novel into a bidding war."

I had one more book to write in the contract of the last seven-figure advance Mack had negotiated for me with my publisher. I was about halfway through the first draft of it, and it was due to them in the fall for a late summer 2018 release.

"But Staadt has been a great publisher to work with."

"And they'll be even better if they're willing to pay what you're now going to be worth.

"The additional movie would mean enough of a boost in sales; but this PFA business is controversy. I just got off the phone with Penguin Random House. They're interested in you. If I can get PRH and Hachette and Staadt all horny to sign you for the next three book deal, we can play those suckers for a high seven-figure deal this time around."

The scent of Mack's excitement at the thought of the money was as thick in the air as the stench of the cigar smoke. He really did like negotiating and scheming.

"We need to play up anything related to you being a minority. You being from Canada and being whiter than the underside of a fish doesn't play nearly as well as if you'd been from Mexico. So we can't go with that.

"What background are your parents? Is there anything there we can use? Your mother was Polish, wasn't she? Was she, or were her parents in Auschwitz? Is there something there?"

He didn't wait for me to answer.

"We'll get to that; we'll figure that out later. But right now, I've got you lined up for a feature cover-story article with *The Inquiring Entertainer*. It'll be a first-person account of the nightmare of being attacked by the PFA and then witnessing their attack and murder of that black limo driver."

"You really want to exploit the actions of a white-supremacist neo-Nazi hate group?"

Mack stared at me for a minute.

"Yes, I want to *exploit the actions of a white-supremacist neo-Nazi hate group!*" He repeated those words of mine in a high-pitched mocking sing-song voice. "Fuck's sake, Andrews. Yes, we do."

"Isn't that just going to give the PFA even more press? Isn't more press what they want?"

He again repeated my words back to me with a mocking tone. "*Isn't more press what they want?*

"Who gives a fuck what they want? They're deranged cockwomble deplorables. They deserve to be strung up by their balls, the whole lot of them. But if we can leverage their attack on you to our advantage, you're goddamn right we're going to do just that."

I often had a tough time getting a bead on Mack's

emotions. His gruff and aggressive manner was usually so dominant that it overshadowed the other inputs. But it was extremely clear to me just how emotionally and personally vested he was in his hatred for the PFA. It was extremely powerful—the most intense emotion I had ever scented from Mack.

It lasted just a few seconds, then was gone again; but the raw strength of that hate; and perhaps a little bit of fear mingled in there, had captured my curiosity. This was extremely personal for him. I wondered where that came from. Mack was Irish, at least by descent, since he'd been born in the United States—third generation, if I remembered correctly. I knew little about his past, but knew that his father had been a New York City police officer.

"Andrews, are you paying attention?"

I realized he'd been talking, and I hadn't been attending to that at all. I nodded.

"Good. As I was saying, I need, by the end of the week, a three-thousand-word article outlining your experiences with the PFA in Hollywood.

"Once this article is published, I'll be able to line-up a few radio and maybe even a few television news spots. We have to prime you into the media as much as possible. This'll help me play the publishers off one another and drive the bidding on the advance for your next several books through the roof."

I considered the article deadline. Three-thousand words wasn't all that much. Even though I hadn't written a single word since leaving New York in the middle of last month.

That realization caught me by surprise.

It had been the longest I'd gone without writing.

I didn't travel all that much, except when on limited book tours, but I usually enjoyed writing in hotel rooms. Heck, I *lived* in a hotel room, so I often felt right at home in one, no matter where I was.

But I hadn't written since I left for Los Angeles.

Of course, I had Lex to distract me for these past several weeks. When I hadn't been on the movie set of *Tome of Terror* Lex and I had been together. Putting my hands on a keyboard was the last thing from my mind when she was around.

That differed from the way it had been when I'd first met Gail. I mean, of course I'd been into her in a major way, in the way that new love often comes with a significant degree of infatuation and a layer of obsession.

But when Gail and I had been first dating, I'd been on a tight deadline with a manuscript and had to keep writing in order to meet it. Even if I wasn't on a deadline, writing was in my blood, much more so than turning into a wolf during the full moon cycle was in my blood, since I'd been writing, and wanted to be a writer since I was in my early teens.

With Lex, the desire to sit in front of a keyboard and compose words barely registered.

Because we were too busy composing sweet love together.

Mack whistled, breaking me out of my revery.

"Yoo hoo. Andrews. Stay with me."

"What's that?"

"I was asking if there were any pictures of you bruised up from the attack.

"Dammit, man, you're sitting there with a glazed and moony look on your face. What the hell kind of monster have I created here? I thought you were pathetic when you were lusting after Sommers for years after she dumped you; but I think you're even worse now that you're getting so much fuck action with this hot new Jones chick.

"Your head's not in the game at all, son." He paused for a moment, stroking his chin. "Not that I can blame you—that's one fine piece of ass you brought home with you. I just hope that you can tear yourself away from that sexy hot mama long enough to write. I know, just looking at those huge tits can turn practically any man into a motorboating maniac—"

"Shut your fucking mouth!" The words were out of my mouth, and I was on my feet before I even realized what I was doing.

An intense rage beyond any I'd ever felt filled my body. I'd heard Mack use derogatory terms to describe women before, but it had only made me uncomfortable and want to wither away. I'd never confronted him about it before.

Again, before I even realized I was doing it, my right arm shot out with lightning-like speed across his desk, grabbing him by the collar of his jacket.

"That's the woman I love you're talking about," I said, pulling him forward and leaning in close, snarling into his face. The fear and utter shock that beamed off of Mack only made me want to attack harder, make him cower before me.

"She's MY woman! And I don't appreciate you disrespecting her!"

I realized, just in the nick of time that I had raised my left fist and was preparing to strike Mack with everything I had in me. Given the time of month for me, which was the height of my super-enhanced strength, a single punch at full strength would have shattered his nose, likely killing him as a shard of his broken nose lodged into his brain.

I hadn't ever punched anyone with full strength; nor could I recall ever feeling such pure and unabashed anger flowing through me.

Letting go of Mack's collar, I sank back down into my chair. As I moved from attack to neutral position, the scent he was giving off morphed from a mixture of shock and terror to bewilderment and indignation.

"Jesus Christ, Andrews! What are you, a caveman? *My woman! Me Tarzan, her Jane.* You can relax. Put your damn pecker back in your pants. I'm not after your woman. She's not my...type." He laughed at his own joke.

I shook my head, not getting it.

"Lex may be stunning and beautiful, but I'm not interested. She doesn't have the right parts."

The right parts? I realized something I had never attended to or even noticed before. Mack was gay? He rarely spoke about his personal life—it was something he kept rather private—and had never mentioned any sort of partner, male or female.

The hatred and fear of the PFA I'd smelled on him now made sense.

"Sorry, Mack. I don't know what got into me. I wasn't worried about you wanting Lex. I was just frustrated that you were using such derogatory terms when talking about her. Enough is enough."

"Derogatory is my schtick. Perhaps you've picked up on that over the years. It's part of my brand, Andrews."

"Well, you don't have to use it around me."

"It's a long-term carefully curated persona and disposition. I use it to keep people on the defensive. It works brilliantly in business negotiations. It's not something I can easily turn off."

This might have been the most frank and authentic few seconds of discussion Mack and I had ever had. I mean, he was always brutally frank and forthright, at least when it came to being aggressive. But he'd never opened up even a crack of his kimono.

"From the look on your face, Andrews, I'd say you had no idea I was gay."

I shook my head. "No. No clue."

He laughed. "You are adorable, Andrews. But I suppose that, apart from my impeccable dress and style, there really isn't anything stereotypical to suggest that, is there?"

"No. Not really. So why haven't you come out?"

"Because my personal life is nobody else's goddamn business, that's why.

"But speaking of business, I've never seen you so ballsy. It looks like this chi—er, this new woman in your life is having a solid and important effect on you.

"Let's see you take some of those balls and aggression onto the campaign we have to embark on in order for me to get a huge bidding war going for your next books. Does that sound like a plan you can work on?"

I heard the women returning from their coffee trip.

"It does. Thanks, Mack."

"Good. Now piss off. I've got work to do. Real man's work, while you likely spend the rest of your day traipsing around the city like a tourist with your new babe. I bet Anne has already told her a half dozen places she needs to see.

"Close the door behind you, Andrews."

I left Mack's office, closing the door as he'd ordered, to find Lex and Anne engaged in small talk about an Italian restaurant Anne had been recommending. The scent coming off both woman was mutual admiration and respect.

It was great to see how well they'd hit it off.

Not that I could scent it before, but I'd imagined when Lex left the office, she'd likely been giving off an odor of hatred and anger toward Mack. But there were no remnants of that on her now.

We bid our adieu to Anne, the girls promising to connect so they could continue to get caught up, and we left.

"Anne is a pretty amazing person!" Lex said. "I just love her."

"She is, indeed. I'm sorry about Mack, though. He's something else."

"It's okay," she said. "I get it."

Lex told me about the discussion she'd had with Anne, and how Anne explained to her that Mack was really a sweetheart beneath his gruff exterior.

"Yeah, she'd been telling me that for ages, but I'd never really seen the man behind that gruff and aggressive demeanor. Until just a few minutes ago, that is."

"Anne saw how upset I'd been, and she knows a little bit about what I'd been through. She's such a nurturing and caring person. I admire how much she wants to protect Mack, but also how much she cares about you, and, because I'm an important part of your life, of me."

"She has always treated me in such a caring and motherly way. They don't make 'em like Anne anymore, that's for sure."

"Did you know Mack is gay?"

"Well, no. Not until a few minutes ago. He shared it with me after I called him out for the way he spoke in such a misogynistic way about you." I thought about how I'd leapt to my feet, prepared to attack him but didn't mention that. I was still trying to process where that had come from.

"You stood up to him?"

"Yeah, for the first time ever, apparently. He came as close to an apology as I've ever seen him do. So that was pretty startling. But him being gay doesn't excuse him for the way he was speaking about you, or women in general, for that matter."

"No, it doesn't. But there's a lot more to him I know you don't know."

"Wow, you and Anne were only together for maybe

twenty minutes. You certainly shared a lot."

"We did. Mack's rough surface hides some pretty rich flowing waters that run quite deep."

"So, I'm learning."

"You likely weren't aware of the number of refuge foster children he has taken in over the years; or the community-based organizations he privately funds, including women's shelters, orphanages, kid help-line clinics."

"No. None of that. Why hasn't Anne told me any of this?"

"He's very private, she told me. He wants to keep the philanthropy and his personal life under wraps. She didn't get into any detail, but she shared that something in his own childhood was quite traumatic, and he wants to make a positive difference. She's one of the only people who knows all this about him. Anne explained how he purposely puts on this overtly domineering personality to keep people he is negotiating with on the defensive."

"Yeah, he sort of explained that part of it to me just now. I never knew."

"I suppose it makes sense," Lex said. "If anyone caught wind of how much of a softy he was, of the compassion he had, they would be able to call plenty of his business negotiation bluffs."

"And he wouldn't be the Mack that we love, and love to hate," I laughed.

"So, big guy, tell me about how you stood up to Mack in my defence," Lex said in a teasing yet seductive voice while taking my arm and batting her eyes at me. "Just thinking about that is turning me on."

Chapter Seven: We Built This City on Rock and Rolling Like Thunder Under the Covers

We mostly kept our hands off one another until after we got behind the door of our hotel room at the Algonquin, but that's only because we had to share the elevator with another couple.

But once we were back, we got right to the carnal activities we'd been planning before Anne had called to remind me of my appointment with Mack.

It was a mini marathon of exploratory passion as we made love, held one another while we talked, then took part in Act Two. I was amazed at how, despite how many times we'd already expressed our love to one another in such physical ways, we applied ourselves with the same commitment and dedication of the first time we'd made love.

"It keeps getting better with you, Lex," I said as we lay entwined in one another's limbs. "Every time we make love it's even better than the last."

"Well," she giggled, nuzzling her face into my neck. "We've had plenty of practice. But we have *so much* more practice to do."

"Yeah?"

"Of course. I mean, we want to get to that ten thousand hours Malcolm Gladwell wrote about, don't we?"

"Sounds like a plan I can live with," I said, kissing her forehead. "I love you, Lex."

"I love you," she said, yawning on the last word.

I held her as she slowly fell asleep, marveling at how comfortable she was in trusting me. We had started off our relationship with mixed messages and a few layers of deception. Technically, I'm deceptive with pretty much everyone I interact with, as I always hold back the lycanthropic curse. But we cut through that layer of mis-truths, confiding our deepest secrets to one another early in our growing relationship.

If you told me that I woman I'd just met would believe and accept the condition I was afflicted with and move across the country to live with me prior to me leaving for Los Angeles, I would have asked you if your delusion came with its own tin foil hat. But it was amazing just how good it felt to be in a relationship where there was such mutual trust.

Gail and I had the same sense of passion, and a prominent element of trust; but I'd kept my wolf nature from her which created a gap between us that was too much for us to bridge. Prior to my trip to LA I would have vehemently declared that I needed Gail. But the difference is, I did need Lex. Not just her love, but her proximity. She made me normal again. And she'd told me, prior to meeting me, that she didn't know if she could ever again feel normal or even a good person herself; because the only other people she'd known with supernatural abilities were truly bad people. With me, she realized, there were good people with extraordinary superhuman powers.

Lex started snoring softly. She was so exhausted, the poor dear. Losing an entire night of sleep to keep me from turning into my wolf form was just further evidence of how much she cared for me.

I held her quietly, unable to sleep myself. I continued to bask in the moment, appreciating what Lex and I had.

After some time, I carefully extracted myself from the delightful entanglement with my beautiful lover and left her to continue sleeping peacefully. I figured I should get up and start working on the article Mack wanted from me.

I pulled my briefs on and went into the living room to the work desk. Realizing I hadn't even unpacked my laptop reminded me I didn't do any writing while in LA. It had been nearly a month since I'd written anything.

I opened up my word processing program and started writing. I didn't even give the document a title. I just created a bullet-form list of the things that had happened to me related to the PFA.

When I made the list, I stared at it:

- Interrupted an attack of three masked individuals beating on a black man in a parking lot on Highland Avenue and Sunset Boulevard in the early morning hours on June 16.

- Was beaten up in place of the original victim, who, fortunately, escaped.
- Was rescued by a passerby who happened to know me.
- Witnessed another group of masked PFA thugs harassing an East Indian woman and her white female companion in the neighborhood outside Skull Crusher Brewery on June 17.
- My girlfriend and I overheard gunshots in early morning hours of June 29. A black woman and her son had been shot. Called 911 then encountered the PFA thugs who'd done it to them. Witnessed them shooting another black man.
- Sharing the details of that attack with the local police and a domestic terrorist unit of the LAPD.
- June 30th. My girlfriend's apartment was trashed by PFA as a warning about us talking to the police. Graffiti including the PFA symbol was left there.
- She decided to return with me to NY.

I kept plenty of details out of that summary, as I intended to in the article.

Such as the fact that Buddy J. Samuels, a long-time traveling salesman friend, was the passerby on June 16th who showed up with a gun and saved me. I still had to figure out why Buddy had this knack for seeming to appear at the most opportune times. There was something he was hiding from me; I just couldn't figure out what.

Also, I left out that Lex had been intimately involved with the PFA and they ransacked her apartment not as a threat about us talking to the police for the shooting we'd witnessed, but as a warning to her not to share the details about the group that she knew.

I figured that, before I started writing, I would see if there were any news reports about the PFA I could draw upon.

I toggled over to an internet browser and typed "Proud Fighters for America" into Google.

A list of results came back immediately. Several pages worth. But near the top was a story from one of the local news sites.

I clicked onto it.

SOMETHING ROTTEN IN NEW YORK'S CORE

Hate is alive in this fine city yet again.

Fear, hate, and prejudice reign supreme. Mid-year statistics indicate that New York and Los Angeles are among the cities expected to see numbers that approach a 30% year over year increase in hate crimes.

According to a release from the FBI, who have been collecting statistics that include reports from regional police departments and a victimization survey since the 1920s and a report from the *Center for the Study of Hate & Extremism* from California State University, San Bernardino, hate crimes are up about 20 percent in the nation's largest cities and are expected to hit as high as 30% by the end of the year.

The FBI defines a hate crime as a "criminal offense

against a person or property motivated in whole or in part by an offender's bias against a race, religion, disability, sexual orientation, ethnicity, gender or gender identity."

Most of the agencies reporting on last year's statistics showed a dramatic increase during election time in November 2016. Here in New York, the two-week period around the election saw a five-fold increase over the same period in 2015.

According to Mark Potok, a senior fellow at the SPLC (Southern Poverty Law Center), Donald Trump's racist and xenophobic remarks on the campaign trail resulted in buoying the white supremacist movement and electrifying the radical right. Anti-Black, anti-Semitic, anti-gay and anti-Latino remain the most common type of hate crimes.

The NYPD, which has the largest and second oldest hate crime unit in the nation, is no stranger to dealing with crimes against property and individuals. But according to a source within the department the 2016 election not only exposed a deep divide in America related to race, ethnicity and sexual orientation, it emboldened vicious attacks on individuals.

"The most violent attacks," an un-named source from the NYPD Hate Crimes Task Force says, "seem to be associated with a West-Coast group called the *Proud Fighters for America*." Founded in, and most active in the greater Los Angeles area, the group is known for stealth and violent attacks on both people and property, leaving a red marking that appears to be an overlap of the capital letters, P, F, and A. "We have tracked half a dozen local attacks in the past three months to the PFA, and we believe the group is looking to grow its presence in our city.

According to this same source, residents should be on

the lookout for the PFA symbol in spots where graffiti typically appears. In addition to the PFA symbol being displayed prominently in areas immediately after these stealth attacks have taken place, members often begin their recruiting by leaving less easily spottable tags of the logo to communicate to other members of locations where meetings can take place to plan out attacks.

Police are asking citizens to report *any* sightings of this logo to authorities, or to contact the NYPD Hate Crime Task Force at 1-888-440-HATE.

The article included an image of the PFA symbol spray-painted in red on the side of a Synagogue in Forest Hills below the words "Dye Jews."

One problem when you were living in a world with so many uneducated morons was, I couldn't be sure if "dye" was mis-spelled, or if it was perhaps a reference to a request that Jewish people be dyed and marked, like the Nazi era Germany badge used to stigmatize, humiliate, and segregate anyone of Jewish heritage.

Or maybe I was guilty of the act of assigning own's own intelligence and knowledge to another. When humans do that with an inanimate object it's considered a form of either personification or anthropomorphism.

I typed both words into Google and hit search.

As I was scrolling, I realized what I was doing here— it was something I was often guilty of doing when writing. I would start doing research, then that research would lead to a series of rabbit holes where reading one thing would lead to another, then another. Then, the next thing I knew, an hour had passed, and I was still not a single word further ahead in the writing I'd left to go do that research.

Long ago, I had learned that, whenever I caught myself doing that, it meant I wasn't in the right headspace for writing. And I needed to do something else.

I'd gotten a start on a skeleton list of things that happened so I could write about my experiences with the PFA. But my brain had had enough.

When writing fiction, and something like that happened, I would take a walk with one of my characters and listen to what they might have to say about a particular topic, or just pay attention to what they observe on that walk.

Why couldn't that work now?

I was feeling hungry after the back-to-back lovemaking sessions with Lex. And I'm sure that she would also be famished when she woke up.

A walk down to Sarge's Delicatessen for a couple of Reuben sandwiches would take me about twenty minutes each way. I could pick up a couple of their Reuben's or maybe a Reuben and The Monster, a 12-inch pastrami, corned beef, roast beef, and turkey on three thick slices of rye bread and hailed as New York's largest sandwich. Heck maybe two of those. I was feeling particularly peckish today.

That mini quest would get me on a decent enough walk and away for a good hour. Plenty of time for Lex to get her rest and for me to listen to how my series character Maxwell Bronte might describe the encounters

I'd had with the PFA.

I quietly got dressed, grabbed my phone and then jotted a brief note for Lex to let her know where I was in case she woke up while I was gone. Then I slipped into the bedroom and kissed her softly on the cheek.

But not before admiring just how beautiful and peaceful she looked in her slumber.

It took everything in me as I stood there watching her to not disrobe, slip under the sheets with her, snuggle into her and slowly wake her so we could make gentle and deliberate love with one another.

Something to look forward to when I returned.

Little did I know that this excursion would lead me on the trail of something a lot less desirable, downright unpleasant, and quite disturbing.

Chapter Eight: Elementarily Rambling, My Dear Andrews

My wolfish senses were back to full strength well before I was out the front door of the Algonquin and on West 44th Street.

It was strange getting used to my senses coming and going like that. The entire process was a little disconcerting. Being with Lex was significantly life-changing when it came to walking around with these enhanced powers.

Having her in my life *is* life changing in and of itself, of course. Dramatically. I love her so much, and the time spent with her is the kind of bliss I never thought I'd experience again. But when it comes to living a normal life, being a normal human again, I'm coming to realize I can only be normal when I'm with her. Whenever we're separated for more than a few minutes, the wolfish strength and senses come back.

Not to mention the odd experience of them also returning when she falls asleep. I suppose having her stay up all night for the ten days during the monthly full-moon cycle to prevent me from morphing into a wolf is a pattern we'll have to get used to. It certainly beats my previous attempt at having a relationship and having to stay completely away from Gail and deceiving her about my wolfish nature.

It only took a couple of blocks before Maxwell Bronte's voice materialized in my head. I headed east and turned right onto 5th Avenue. Bronte's voice came to me just as I was crossing West 42nd with the New York Public Library on my right.

"Did I ever tell you," Bronte whispered, "that my mother took me here several times when I was a kid?"

"You talked about going to the library with your mom every Saturday morning," I replied. Then I picked up a sharp and harsh judgemental *he's off his meds* vibe from a woman in a business suit walking parallel to me about a foot away.

I decided it was best to reply to Bronte in my head.

You shared that in the first book. I replied to him in my mind. *You went to a branch of the Queens Public Library. That revelation came about one third of the way into* **Print of the Predator**. *It came out in a conversation with Trudy, one of your long-time regular customers at the bookstore.*

"I suppose I did."

You grew up without much. Books were the only entertainment you had, and since your family couldn't afford them, that weekly library trip was deeply meaningful to you.

"It was, indeed. Every Saturday we'd go to one of the smaller branches of the library where we lived. But every once in a while, maybe it was every two or three months, my Mom would take me into Manhattan, into the big city, to visit this branch of the New York Public Library."

"I don't believe I ever explained the nature of the intense journey, the epic adventure it was for us to get here from where we lived in Queens.

"It maybe only took about an hour—it was a walk to the Rego Park transit stop where we'd take a train to Jackson Heights to transfer to another subway that would take us into the city—but, to me, it was a grand voyage.

"We weren't just heading into the downtown core with the deep caverns from the enormous towers that cut off views of the sky in places, but we were on a pilgrimage to a building that was like a mecca to me. A single structure filled with so many books, resources and access to knowledge that could be the portals to a multitude of universes and possibilities."

That is fascinating, I replied. *But can you get to the point? I was hoping I could get your perspective on some of the things that happened to me in Los Angeles.*

Bronte offered a tsk, tsk noise while fingering the long thin pointy goatee on his chin. "You, my friend, need to have some patience. What I'm telling you is directly related to your trip to the city of angels. You're always wanting to skip to the end of a good mystery and see how it ends before you even sit down to read a good book."

I do not.

"You do. I've seen you. I pay close attention to the habits of readers. It's my livelihood. You even peek ahead when reading a chapter, to see how it's going to end."

I shook my head. He nailed it. Of course he did, the guy was born in and lives in my head. He has access to all of that.

"Now can I finish telling you my story, so that I can 'get to the point' as you so bluntly stated?"

Sure. Knock yourself out.

"Because we couldn't afford to take the train into the city more than every few months, I wasn't able to check out any books. The longest loan period for most books was two weeks. And so, if we checked anything out, they'd be dramatically overdue; and we couldn't afford the overdue fine fees.

"So, whenever my mother and I went into the city on this epic voyage, we would spend the entire day in the library, taking full advantage of what we had right in front of us, while we were there."

I'm not grasping what you're trying to get across.

"That's because I'm not done. Tut-tut.

"There was this one novel I adored when I was a child. It was George R. Stewart's post-apocalyptic novel from 1949 called *Earth Abides*. I started reading it when I discovered a copy on my first trip there. But it took me several trips, over the course of several years, to finish it.

"On some visits, it was checked out, and I couldn't read it then. So it could be up to six months, at times, between reads.

"But every time we arrived at the library and I found a copy available, I would read it, continuing where I'd left off the previous time."

But didn't the Queens library have a copy of it? Or

couldn't you request one be brought into your local branch if they had it?

"That's not the point, my boy. The point was the experience, the patience, the commitment to the long-term experience, rather than the short-term satisfaction and pleasure.

"Too often we want immediate gratification. Like in a story. Some of the best stories in the world's history come from literature, and yet in modern times we barely have the patience to consume them in digest format in movies.

"Consider Stephen King's *The Stand*. The 1990s TV series was told in 4 parts and had a running time of about 6 hours. And yet it didn't come close to the fullness of King's 1100-page unabridged version. Even the abridged one ran 700 pages after the publisher insisted he cut 150,000 words from it.

"Or modern classic movies compared to the books. *Gone with the Wind* the film ran just shy of 4 hours. And yet the movie was a significantly truncated version of Margaret Mitchell's thousand-page tome.

"The movies *The Godfather* and *The Godfather Part II* which ran over 5 hours combined, were still abbreviated adaptations of Puzo's 1969 novel.

"*A Tale of Two Cities* by Charles Dickens is one of the best-selling novels of all time. But even the 1980s made-for-TV adaptation, which ran about four hours doesn't incorporate all that appears in the over 400-page text.

"A book like that would take the average person between 9 and 10 hours to read. But even that is an abridged version of the experience.

"When Dickens originally wrote much of his work, most of his novels were published in monthly or weekly instalments in serialized format with cliff-hanger endings that the public had to wait for. This instalment format delivery process even allowed Dickens, as a writer, to evaluate his audience's reaction. He would sometimes change his characters or plot based on reader feedback.

"Not everyone could read back in the day, but his works were so highly anticipated that masses of the illiterate poor would pay—upwards of a halfpenny each—to have monthly episodes of his serialized novels read to them."

Boy, but this guy could blather on. We were already at East 36th Street, where we—rather, I should say I— needed to turn left. And he just kept rambling on and on, never tired of the sound of his own voice.

I had honestly never really noticed that about him in all these years, but reflecting back, Bronte did like to ramble on when revealing how he had deduced to solve the crime; likely something inspired from how Sherlock Holmes liked to slowly reveal the details that allowed him to unravel a mystery.

How my readers put up with, and yet seemed to admire Bronte, was beyond me.

Get to the bloody point! I wanted to yell at him. *I've got things to do, places to be. And you, you bookish snob, you have readers to bore to death.*

Bronte was quiet while we crossed 5th Avenue and

headed East on East 36th Street. He spoke up again once we reached the far curb.

"Today's point-and-click culture and Netflix binging society doesn't properly understand and appreciate the joy of sitting for hours enthralled in a book.

"Nor could they even comprehend the patience required for reading a thousand-page serialized novel over the course of a year, or more, in monthly installments.

"It's all about instant gratification. Patience is the rarest of virtues. The best of things in life come to those who are willing to wait."

He fell silent again.

After another minute where he said nothing, I had to ask what that was all about.

You said you were getting to the point.

"I did."

I don't understand.

"You will, young man. You will. All in good time. If you stop trying to force it."

Shaking my head, I kept walking on. Yeah, I know. Bronte is just in my head. But sometimes a character can feel like they are coming to life, which is one reason I liked to walk and talk with them.

I hadn't expected to be lectured by Bronte on this walk. And I had no idea what he was getting at. But I figured it was something my subconscious mind wanted me to better understand. Which I'm sure I would, in time.

We walked a couple of blocks, and I waited to see if

he had something more to say. It wasn't until we were almost at the intersection of East 36th and Lexington when Bronte stopped, raised his left hand, and said something.

"But soft, what scent through yonder window breaks."

"What's with the Shakesp—" I started to say, but then I smelled what he was referring to. Or rather, what my subconscious mind had picked up and was trying to tell me about.

From the passing cab that had the back window rolled down, I picked up the very distinguished scent of the male passenger in the back seat.

The scent was strong.

And it was as clear and powerful as his scent the day I first encountered him—in my human form, at least— when, in front of a large studio audience of witnesses, he'd looked me in the eye, said, "Pleasure to meet you, mate," and squeezed my fingers in a bone-crushing grip.

It was Knell.

The only other werewolf I'd ever encountered.

But that was impossible.

I'd watched him fall to his death.

Chapter Nine: You Look Like You've Seen a Ghost Werewolf

I stood unmoving in the middle of the sidewalk, completely stunned, as the cab turned right onto Lexington and disappeared around the corner.

This wasn't possible.

Knell, the shock-rock star *couldn't* be in the cab that had just passed.

But I had smelled him.

And I never forgot a person's scent. At least not someone whose presence had that kind of impact on me. It smelled like him; or at least—and I'm not sure how to describe this combination of scents I had picked up in the brief second, but the human scent of him differed from what I remember. It had a bitter tinge to it that I didn't recall, a different olfactory sweaty odor. It wasn't just that he was wearing a different cologne than the one he'd been wearing when I met him years, ago—there was something more to it. I know that a person's scent can change depending on the foods they consume. But, regardless of the difference in the body odor, the wolfish scent coming off him was unmistakable.

I'm not sure how long I stood there, likely looking like a stunned tourist who had just spotted an iconic movie-star and was frozen on the spot, tongue-tied and unsure what to say. I may even have looked down to ensure my chin wasn't resting on the sidewalk at my feet.

I was nudged out of my temporary paralysis when a pedestrian who'd been walking behind me ran into me at full walking speed. He'd likely been looking down at his phone rather than the sidewalk ahead. Of course, when moving in a flow of pedestrian traffic, one doesn't expect the person in front of them to suddenly stop.

"Out of the way, asshole," he said, the quick angered response a pathetic attempt to cover up the embarrassment I could smell oozing out of him.

"Sorry," I instinctively replied, then took a few steps to the right to get out of the way of anyone else.

I wondered if Knell had either recognized or scented me. He, after all, knew my scent well. In fact, he knew mine better than I did, because he seemed to keep his human consciousness in wolf form. While I had only vague snippets of memory of my encounters with Knell when we were both in wolf form, Gail had been there the night of our first encounter and had witnessed him turning from wolf back into human, seemingly upon his own will.

Knell was more adept at this werewolf thing, particularly since he'd mastered control over the metamorphosis.

Unlike me.

As I was standing there, trying to make sense of it all, I realized he was getting away.

I was at my absolute strongest; and maybe he hadn't

scented or noticed me. All I had picked up was his scent, but not any sort of indication from the smell coming off of him that he recognized me.

Realizing the cab had enough of a head start, I raced to the corner and turned right on Lexington in the direction the cab had gone.

Focusing in on the specific exhaust smell from the cab because the scent of Knell in the back of the cab was a much fainter presence, I realized it was almost two full blocks ahead. The lights on Lexington worked in favor of the cab, as it had cruised through the green lights on East 35th and was about to go through the one on East 34th.

I ran as fast as I could without putting any of the pedestrians I was racing past in danger and was slowly closing the gap between myself and the cab, when the light at East 34th turned yellow, then red, just as I was getting to it.

A traffic cop was positioned across the street at the intersection of East 34th and Lexington, and I slowed as I approached, waiting for her attention to be away from my direction, before dashing across between cars, and continuing south on Lexington.

I detected the surprise in her scent as she noticed me once I was halfway across, but it's not like she was going to be able to do anything about that.

I kept moving.

The cab continued to hit a string of green lights through the next ten blocks, and I kept hitting yellow lights on the way down, picking up my pace enough to avoid most of the red lights.

The scent of the cab, and the occasional smell of Knell inside the cab, wafted back to me.

At one point, I picked up Knell's scent as giving off an eau of flight; as if he recognized he was being tracked and chased. The cab sped up, increasing the distance between us.

Dodging a few pedestrians and people on bicycles slowed me down enough that when I reached the intersection at East 23rd, it was a red light for me.

I could have dashed through the intersection, but a large furniture delivery truck and a UPS truck that were stuck getting through the intersection in the two-way traffic blocked my way. That delayed me further. After the truck cleared the intersection, I slipped through the remaining traffic, waded my way through the red light at the next intersection, then saw and smelled the cab as it was turning the corner of Lexington and East 21st.

The cab was in slower moving traffic now and I realized the trailing scents of the cab and Knell had parted ways. Knell's continued south through Gramercy Park, while the cab was heading west.

I stopped at the locked gates of Gramercy Park and spotted a blond man on the other side of the black metal fence running west inside the park. The scent he'd left behind told me this was my quarry.

Running west in parallel to the fence along East 21st I tracked his scent moving further away to the south. I leapt the Gramercy Park fence by stepping onto the curb at the bottom of the black metal fence, placing one hand onto the cold steel bars, and propelling myself over.

I rushed south through the park, but then up ahead, overheard a woman shouting to someone else. "Oh my god, was that a wolf?"

He'd changed into a wolf?

I raced southwest through the park, following his scent, and picking up some confused looks and accompanying emotive scents from that same woman and the man she'd been sitting with on the bench.

I pressed on.

When I got to the corner of the park at East 20th and Gramercy Park West, I realized he'd leaped over the fence there. Because I had a good run at it, I vaulted over the six-foot-high fence in standard hurdle pose, landing on the sidewalk on the corner of those two streets.

His scent continued west down East 20th. Up ahead were a few more startled shouts of "wolf" from pedestrians and screeching brakes.

But the wolf was nowhere in sight.

He had quickly and efficiently moved on, evaded me, and there was no way for me to catch up with him now.

Realizing that a pair of men walking together across the street had seen my leap over an object that stood twice as high as a standard Olympic hurdle and were staring at me, their mouths agape, I decided it was best to move on. I hastily turned the corner and headed east.

My initial focus had been getting as far away from this other wolf and those men who had witnessed my spectacular leap. I hated calling attention to myself.

The men didn't follow me, but I did manage to pick up their mumbled conversation wondering how it was possible for a man to jump that high. They then started debating the possibility of it, when one of them, consulting his smartphone, mentioned the world record hurdle was recorded as being completed by a man named Adrian Wilson of the Arizona Cardinals who completed a five-and-a-half-foot hurdle with a three-step start.

"That dude just cleared a fence that has to be at least 6 feet tall," his partner responded. "Too bad I didn't have my phone out to record it."

Too bad for them; but fine with me.

I didn't need the attention; and besides, I had been hoping to not be living with the side-effect of these powers. Lex being with me was supposed to be allowing me to just live like a normal human.

So far, I hadn't been all that good at sticking with that plan.

Of course, with Knell back in the picture, I wasn't sure I was going to be able to return to a normal life just yet.

Because Knell knew what I was.

And he was one nasty dude.

Evil. Insane.

Reckless and dangerous.

He was back in New York, which was bad enough.

But worse than that, he was back from the dead. That made no sense. People didn't come back from dead.

Yeah, I know, I get it. People also don't turn into wolves during the light of a full moon either. People don't walk around with extraordinary supernatural powers.

But I exist.

And so does Knell.

So, if that can be true, why couldn't I wrap my head around him somehow having come back?

After I had moved another block, I couldn't pick up their conversation any longer and there was no distinguishing scent from anyone in my vicinity who had seen me sprinting and jumping in that extraordinary way.

And I realized what neighborhood I was in. I was close to the East Village, where Gail's boutique occult shop, *Enchanting Magic* was located.

If anyone knew anything about the resurrection of the dead, it would be Gail.

I kept walking in the familiar direction of her store.

Chapter Ten: Those Enchanting Magic Memories

*E*nchanting Magic was a small single step-down from street level shop on East 9th Street in the East Village. It felt like just yesterday that I had first walked to this store to pick up Gail for one of our first dates as the scents from the store came to me when I was still almost a block away.

The scented candles, oils, herbs, and incense mingled with Gail's scent in the air. She was there all right.

My heart did a bit of a backflip as it raced along memory lane. I realized that last night, when Lex and I had met up with Gail at Newark airport I hadn't been able to smell Gail the intimate way I always had before. There was no reading her emotions based on the pattern of her heartbeat.

I hadn't, in fact, fully experienced Gail with those enhanced smells and sounds since before I'd left for Los Angeles. It had almost been a full month. A matter of just a few weeks, but as significant to me and the things I'd experienced as a full year or more.

It's amazing what we can pack into such a limited amount of time.

And how much our worlds can change in those little instances.

The thought of being able to sense Gail's emotions now bothered me. If she was still quite into me, like Lex suggested, and I suppose I'd witnessed when I saw her eyes misting up in the rear-view mirror of the car last night, I didn't want to be able to fully detect that.

I paused a few doors down from the shop and looked over at the beer store to my right. I'd walked past this beer store dozens of times in half as many years, and yet never been interested in it.

But suddenly, now, seeing that beer reminded me of the wonderful night of meeting Lex at Gulp, a beer and cocktail bar in an L.A. neighborhood I had wandered into. Or a few nights later, looking for her at Skull Crusher Brewery.

Both times, I'd drank more beer than I ever had before in my life. And the alcohol had dulled my enhanced senses. Of course, I later realized my proximity to Lex had been having the most significant effect on me; but the alcohol did mute my senses as well.

I wondered if I needed that now.

Then started wondering if I needed the alcohol not just for the effect it had on my senses of smell and hearing, but if I needed it for the emotion-dulling impact.

A white man in his early twenties in a hoodie stepped out of the door to the beer shop. I shuffled forward to catch the door before it closed and watched him walking down the street, surprised that he could actually walk with his pants riding low and bunching in between his legs like he'd dropped a full load in them.

His blue boxer briefs were on display as the pants

seemed to defy gravity because they were resting below his butt cheeks. What could they possibly be held up with except a hope and a prayer? And yet, despite his nearly bare ass, he was wearing multiple layers and a thick hoodie. He was a startling contrast in fashion and sensible weather wear. Hot and sweaty and over-dressed upstairs, yet cheekily putting his underwear on display while he waddled down the street.

I shook my head and let out a laugh as I stepped into the store.

The beer store had such an overwhelming selection that I could have spent hours admiring the names of the different beers from hundreds of breweries from across the US. But I was on a mission here. I found, in one cooler, a cider and a pink lemonade sour, which I fig-ured I could drink quickly because they would be light tasting—prior to my recent visit to LA I hadn't ever been much of a drinker—but then also grabbed a 12% imperial stout.

After making my purchase I surreptitiously chugged the two lighter drinks just outside the shop. It was ille-gal to drink on a city street in New York, so I needed to be careful. However, if that young man in the hoodie wasn't busted for indecency, the bylaw enforcement was likely a bit lax.

The stout took me longer to put away. It was thick, rich, and chocolaty, and might have been a beer I would have enjoyed drinking casually. I figured Lex might en-joy it too, as she was partial to sweet and chocolate stouts. I made a note of the brand. It was *Liquid Double*

Fudge from Evil Twin Brewing. The brewery was a local one. It would be fun to visit with Lex.

I alternated between looking at the bottle and the time display on my phone, waiting for the alcohol to kick in. It had been close to ten minutes, and I wondered if I should go back into the beer store and buy something more. Despite my strengthened constitution, my lack of ability to handle alcohol should kick in relatively soon. But I realized I was stalling.

I focused on the sounds from all around me—over time I have developed the ability to not attend to the often-overwhelming streams of sensory input—and picked up Gail's voice from inside the shop. It sounded like she was on the phone with one of her suppliers. I could also smell another person's scent from inside the store. A male. His odor was hesitant and nervous. It was either his first visit to an occult shop, or perhaps he was there to shoplift.

Nope, the alcohol was not having the intended effect. Not yet at least. But maybe it would help loosen me up for seeing Gail face to face.

Raising the bottle back to my lips, I drank down the last few swallows from the stout.

I placed the two empty cans and empty bottle on the side of the steps leading down to the beer store, figuring someone would scoop them up for the return deposit, and steeled up my courage to walk over to Gail's store.

When I stood back from the crouch and took my first step, a tiny wave of vertigo hit me, and I recognized that the alcohol had kicked in at least a little, which was good. But I hoped it would help relax me to prepare for this conversation I was about to have.

Gail was just putting down the receiver of the phone and looking at the front entrance when I walked inside.

A barrage of emotive scents from her hit me in rapid succession. Surprise. Loving warmth. Inquisitiveness. Relief. Confusion. Hopefulness.

Surprise—that I showed up unexpectedly at her shop.

Loving warmth—she was genuinely pleased to see me.

Inquisitiveness—curiosity at whether I was alone. Would Lex be walking in immediately behind me?

Relief—at seeing I was, indeed, alone.

Confusion—at what I was doing there.

Hopefulness—that I was there to see her, without Lex, and would have some brilliant explanation about this mysterious woman I'd brought back to New York with me.

Like I said, we can pack a lot of things into a short time. A lifetime of change can happen in one week. But we can also pack a crap-ton of emotions into a single moment that lasts perhaps two to five seconds tops.

All those things came to me, instantly, and I was reminded of just how well I knew Gail. Those same emotive scents off someone I didn't know so well wouldn't have been interpreted as effectively. But that's the brilliance of knowing someone that intimately. At a glance you catch the tiniest change to their facial expression and know exactly what they are thinking.

While I'd never had that sort of relationship with anyone in my life, because prior to gaining my wolfish senses I wasn't all that intuitive—I was, perhaps, oblivious to those kinds of cues—I definitely had that with Gail.

And she had it with me.

It reminded me of how much my relationship with Gail might have depended upon my ability to—consciously or subconsciously—have a manipulative advantage. When you can so intuitively read and detect someone else's emotions, isn't it a form of deception? Aren't you the one with all the power in that one-on-one dynamic? Had I been taking advantage of Gail as our relationship had been blooming? Using all those additional sensory clues to work things in my favor?

Did she actually ever fall in love with me, or merely love the way I could manipulate my reactions and interactions with her in a way I knew was a pleasant experience? And, by attribution, think she loved me?

Had it ever been real, or just me pulling at all her heart strings and manipulating her?

I felt a sense of anger and disgust with myself for ever taking advantage of another person's vulnerability in such a way. It was wrong. Gail deserved better. Gail was an amazing woman. She deserved more. She deserved genuine love. And I know I loved her—would always love her. But that love I had for her came with a fundamental caring and desire to see her happy, truly happy.

How could she ever be happy with me? Having been

manipulated, controlled, dominated, lied to, and cheated on by almost every single man in her life—her beloved Uncle Albert had been the only man in her life who was a positive male influence, a caring and supportive man—she deserved a love that was born out of organic two-way genuine reciprocity. Not the deceptive way I could manipulate a relationship.

Damn. I wish I had seen that so much sooner. I would have stopped trying so hard to force an intimate relationship beyond our dear friendship. That was selfish of me. Only thinking about what I wanted, and not what Gail needed in her life.

I suppose it took stepping back from the situation in order to see it. Dammit if Mack hadn't been right about sending me away to Hollywood.

That trip led to me finding perhaps the only woman I could properly love in that natural and organic way. With my wolfish senses muted around Lex, our relationship was built upon a foundation of mutual conscious and intended sharing, rather than a deep violation of the other person's most intimate thoughts and feelings.

Lex's love for me was built out of that, not out of my ability to manipulate her based on the powerful and unfair feedback mechanism.

I'm so lucky to have found her, and to finally understand this about myself.

"Michael," Gail said as I stepped up to the cash desk where she stood. "What brings you here this afternoon?"

"Gail, I owe you such an apology," I said, feeling tears coming to my eyes immediately. Dammit, I hated the fact that I could barely express emotional things without choking up and blubbering like an idiot. "I am so sorry."

Pausing to gather my voice back, because it cracked on that last word, the scent of hope and love for me grew dramatically in Gail. I tried hard not to focus on that, steering my focus to the nervous young man browsing the herbs a few feet away. But it was hard.

"You don't have to apologize, Michael. I'm the one who pushed you away for so long. I can't blame you."

"No, Gail. I'm not apologizing for that. Though I am sorry about how that happened. I should have told you." Damn, my voice again cracked on every second word.

I flashed back to one of those movies I'd seen a dozen times, *Die Hard* and the scene where John McClane is asking Al to relay a message to his wife. Focusing on something like that allowed a reprieve to take me out of the moment. McClane says: *She's heard me say I love you a thousand times. She never heard me say I'm sorry. And I want you to tell her that. I want you to tell her that John said that he was sorry.*

Focusing on that Hollywood scene in my mind allowed me to block much of the emotion coming from Gail. Because it was damn overwhelming to hear her heart beating so fast, scent the hope and love and passion she was exuding.

"All I've done these past several years is try to get

back to that thing we found when we first met. But the truth is, Gail, something I've only recently come to realize, is how wrong I'd been, and how harmful I've been to you.

"I fell in love with you because of the spectacular and amazingly caring and passionate woman you are, Gail. But you only fell in love with me because of the way I manipulated and deceived you."

She started to say something in denial of that, but I raised my hands to let her know I wasn't finished.

"No, I might not have been doing it intentionally. But that's how it happened.

"And when you," I paused to look over at the young man who had progressed deeper into the store in his browsing. He was clearly out of ear-shot but I still lowered my voice slightly, "found out about my actual nature and that I hadn't trusted you enough to confide in you, you broke it off.

"You did the right thing, Gail. But then, when you returned into my life because you needed a friend, I saw it as what I wanted it to be. I kept forcing the issue; wanting to return to what we'd had.

"But what we had was built upon my lies, my deception, my manipulation.

"You deserve so much more than that, Gail. You deserve to fall in love with a man you can genuinely fall in love with rather than someone who can manipulate and engineer a relationship based on feedback that nobody should have access to.

"For the first time since this happened to me, I'm able

to live and love normally, because I've found the only person I'm able to do that with, to be that with.

"So, I'm sorry, Gail. I'm so sorry that I never saw the harm of what I'd been doing. I'm so sorry that for years I've pressured and pushed you into something that you never should have been involved in."

Despite my voice cracking many times during my little speech, I got through it by continuing to picture John McClane in my head, sweaty and bloody, hunkering down on a deserted floor in a tall building and talking on the radio to his cop friend. It prevented me from choking on many of my words, but it didn't prevent the tears from flowing.

That movie scene reel kept my attention as much away from Gail's emotive scents as possible, but there was still a significant amount of confusion, pain, and love for me radiating there.

This little speech was having the opposite effect of what I'd intended. Her admiration and respect and love for me grew. But it also came with an intense burst of anger at being insulted.

"I'd like to address what you just said," Gail said after taking a deep breath. "If you'd let me.

"But first, I would like to deal with that young gentleman over there. He's here looking for a love potion. I know you have already determined that about him likely based on the scents he's been giving off. But one thing you need to remember about me, Michael, and this is one thing that attracted you to me in the first place, is that I have a similar ability to understand people."

She walked over to the nervous young man and immediately engaged him in the type of interaction I'd seen her do dozens of times in her store.

He was trepidatious about asking what he'd come there for, but Gail immediately put him at ease.

Originally, he'd been feeling awkward and disgusted with himself for wanting to find something to get this girl he worked with at the restaurant where they were both wait staff, to pay attention to him. But Gail's gentle approach allowed him to relax and share it.

They spoke for about ten minutes, and I marvelled at how brilliantly Gail explained she could help him with love, but how it was important for him to not focus on that one particular girl, but on love in general.

She explained that often people think they are in love with a person, but they're actually in love with their idealization of that person. Then she pointed out a candle carved and embedded with oils that would aid in his quest for love in general, rather than love for this specific young woman. She also helped him pick out some incense that would assist with clearing his intentions. She asked if he could focus not on this girl he was fixated on, but on all the attributes he would want in the perfect love—the type of person. Then she suggested a ritual involving tea leaves and another incense to perform first so he could ensure that he was starting by loving himself, loving the good things about himself.

I marvelled at watching her in action, putting this frightened and love-yearning young man at ease, helping him see something deeper and more meaningful than the infatuation he was obviously feeling.

As Gail was ringing in his items, I heard her tell him that if this lovely young waitress he was working with was the one, these rituals would help create the right space for it. But if she wasn't the one, his internal and emotive life would be openly prepared to accept the love that might come his way.

The intense appreciation and relief the young man felt was thick in the air as he thanked her profusely and left the shop.

I was in awe at how he came looking for some magic love potion to have his way but ended up leaving with a mini therapy session in loving himself and being open to the infinite possibilities of the universe.

"Wow," I said, re-approaching the cash desk. "You're damn good at that."

"I know," Gail said. "Like I said, I can read people. I can sense what they're looking for, what they need, even when they can't see it themselves.

"You might think that you've been manipulating our relationship, but I'm no powerless pawn in all this. And I'm furious that you would dare even think that. You know me too well for that. I might not have supernatural abilities, but I can read people too, Andrews.

"I was able to read you and play off the tells you were giving just as much as you were with me.

"So don't you dare take responsibility for something that we are both responsible for. Don't you dare put this all on yourself."

The indignation and anger in her clearly struck with those words, and I stood nodding, unable to say anything. She stared at me, and I could feel her probing the depths of who I was.

"Fair enough," I finally said.

"And I don't think I need to tell you how those assumptions you just shared makes me feel. I'm sure you're getting that strong and clear."

"I am. Gail, listen—"

"Now," she said, cutting me off. "There was a particular look on your face when you first walked in that leads me to believe you didn't come here planning on apologizing to me. There's something you were worried about; something pretty damn important. Important enough to overcome the awkward discomfort you wore last night when I picked you and your new girl up at the airport. You couldn't get out of that car fast enough, Andrews. And yet, despite not wanting to see or face me, you came here because you needed my help.

"So, it must be really important."

Damn she was good. I forgot just how good.

"Yeah," I said. "It is. You're right. That's true."

"Out with it, then."

"What can you tell me about resurrection?"

"Resurrection?"

"Yeah."

"Why?"

"Remember Knell?"

Just hearing his name brought immediate underlying flashes of tension, fear, and anxiety from Gail. She'd been a direct part of the melee attack on him. In fact, she'd been the one to strike the first effective blow on the sick creep. A good one too. Why the heck was I always underestimating her kick-ass nature?

"He's back," I said. "I just saw him; just chased him down Lexington. First in a cab, then on foot. At least until he morphed back into a wolf and could out-pace me."

"Knell? But we watched him fall to his death. Could he have survived that fall?"

"There's no way. We both heard the bone-crunching impact of what was left of him on the ground. I could hear that he wasn't breathing, that his heart had stopped. He is dead, Gail. Or he *was* dead. I need to understand how he could have been brought back to life."

"Are you *sure* it was Knell?"

"I'm sure."

"Did you see him?"

"No, not full on, but I didn't need to see him. I can tell a person by their scent; sometimes even the distinct pattern of their heartbeat if I know someone well enough.

"And, besides, when he was running away from me, he morphed into a wolf. Who else do we know that can do that?"

Gail bit her bottom lip; her heart was racing and the odor she gave off was panic mixed with a sense of deep contemplation.

"And this man-wolf you saw smelled like Knell?"

"Yeah." I thought about it further, remembering my initial confusion. "Well, he definitely smelled like Knell, but there was another odor to him. He smelled a bit off."

"Off? How?"

"He smelled like Knell, mostly, but there was another smell about him, and it was more than just the cologne he was wearing. There was something different about his body odor, his breath. It was like he was Knell, but also different.

"I mean, I'll never forget his scent. And it was there, but either muted by these additional bodily odors, or changed somehow."

With the perky air of an *aha* moment Gail walked across the aisle and looked at the spines of the books on the shelves there.

"That makes me wonder," Gail said. "Let's say he died. I mean, we saw his dead body splattered on that alley floor. But two things that *could* change his scent, I'm thinking, might be a blood transfusion and the effect of decomposition on his flesh.

"If he was revived, brought back from the dead, maybe the revival didn't happen right away. It could have been hours, days, maybe, before he was brought back to life. I'll need to do some research."

She pulled a few books off the shelves. I caught the covers of a couple of them. One was titled *Raising Hell*, by someone named Masello and the other, which didn't have an author was named *The Complete Book of Black Magic and Witchcraft*.

"This'll be a good start," she said, walking over to the cash desk. She dropped the books on the counter and perched on the stool behind it, cracking the pages of the one on top.

A minute later she looked up from the book.

"Are you going to stand there all day watching me read, Andrews?"

"Uh," was all I managed to say. I can be quite the conversationalist at times.

"Why don't you head back to whatever you were doing. I'll reach out once I figure out a bit more."

"What about Knell?" I asked.

"What about him?"

"Isn't he a threat? Shouldn't we track him down somehow?"

Gail gave off the scent of exasperation. "There are eight and a half million people in this city. I know that when you're not with Lex, you can track someone down by scent.

"But let's think this out here. It has been how many years since we last saw him? Three years? And, given he has the same abilities as you, he should have been able to track either of us down in all that time, right? If Knell was a threat to you, or me, don't you think he would have already come after us?

"Perhaps, after he was resurrected, he lost part of his memory. That's one thing I need to research.

"Besides, you said that he ran *away* from you. He didn't attack. He ran. So, it's likely that *something* in him changed when he was brought back."

"Okay," I said. "You're right. I hadn't thought of that."

"Off you go, Andrews. I've got some reading to do."

Chapter Eleven: When You Swiftly Get Caught Between the Moon and New York City

While New York is a magnificent and dynamic city with so many neighborhoods and unique elements to enjoy, there's nothing like experiencing it through the eyes of someone who was seeing it for the first time.

Admittedly, it had been a long time since I've been able to experience that joy.

Earlier that afternoon when I had returned home from the excursion that resulted in chasing a werewolf, or an undead werewolf, or whatever Knell currently was, then a confrontational and in-depth conversation with Gail, I introduced Lex to the magnificence of Sarge's deli sandwiches. We then re-introduced one another to the exuberance of mutual carnal lust.

I decided not to share any of what had gone down earlier with Lex; at least not yet. I figured I would tell her in the morning. What I needed was to escape into the high emotive throes of passion and be normal.

Just for one day. Or at least, the last half of one day.

No paranormal bullshit, no heroic posturing and

chasing bad guys, no baggage of past relationships. Just Lex and me. In love, and thirsty for the thrill of being together in the moment.

She was awake and listening to music when I returned. I could smell her sweet scent complete and deep, something I only had the pleasure of knowing through fleeting glimpses when she first woke, or when we were first reunited, since my enhanced powers faded shortly after I was in her presence. It only took about five minutes for those enhanced senses to mute themselves into veritable non-existence and the two of us could be normal together.

Well, normal in terms of humanity and supernatural powers.

Because there was nothing normal about our love making.

As I stepped out of the elevator, I heard the sounds of Taylor Swift's *1989* coming from my room. Lex loved her music and told me two things about that album. One, that the song "Shake It Off" had long been her personal theme song and mantra. Two, that, the night she first met me, she'd been so intrigued and turned on by our mutual flirting that afternoon and night that she'd played the song "Wildest Dreams" over and over.

In that song, Swift sings to an ex-lover that she pleas to remember her despite their brief relationship, even if it were just in his wildest dreams.

We'd made love to that Taylor Swift album several times back in LA, and as I approached the door "Wildest Dreams" was just getting to the part where Swift describes the memory of them being tangled together all night and burning it down.

By the time I opened the door, I was so turned on by her smell, the sound of her heartbeat, and that passionate song that I was instantly erect. I put the sandwiches down and ripped my clothes off—that's not an expression, I actually tore and ruined my shirt and pants— desperate to show her the effect that smelling her had on me.

All she had on was one of my t-shirts; nothing else. It was a look I quite appreciated. We said nothing to one another as I approached her. I lifted her into my arms, and we made quick and rushed love standing in the front entranceway to the place.

Being inside her while my enhanced senses were still active and hearing her heartbeat, smelling the heights of her pleasure and the passion she had for me was exquisite.

After we finished, we ate the sandwiches, naked, then made love again, once in the living room on the floor, then moving to the bed.

After we finished in the bed we showered together, making love again under the water, then finally getting dressed.

By that time, it was evening. And I was famished again.

I took her out to John's Pizza in Times Square, which had incorporated the spectacular opulence of a previously abandoned old Gospel Tabernacle Church, including the perfectly intact original stained-glass ceiling that resembled, ironically, a giant pizza pie.

We then wandered through Times Square, where Lex marveled at how the street performers and characters dressed up as fictional characters and movie stars reminded her of parts of the Hollywood Walk of Fame.

Then we meandered, hand in hand, down Broadway to where it intersected with West 34th Street and 6th Avenue, when we headed east.

It had been years since I'd gone to the top of the Empire State Building. And I had never had that type of view of the city with someone I loved.

The first time I'd gone there I'd been alone, and relatively new to the Big Apple.

But standing with Lex with our arms wrapped around one another and looking out over the city lit by the near-full moon, I marveled for what felt like the hundredth time in the past several days, at just how lucky I was.

I hadn't ever seen a full or near-full moon over New York since I had arrived because I'd never been in human form during this cycle of the moon.

But now, here I was with Lex, enjoying the type of romantic evening that would have been impossible for me with any other woman.

"I know what you're thinking," Lex whispered to me, nuzzling the side of her head against my neck.

"What's that?"

"You're appreciating being able to see the moon."

"Yeah, that's part of it," I said. "But I was also thinking of something beyond just that."

"Which is?"

"That you're the only person in the entire world I could ever share this experience with. You're the only person I would want to share this with. I love you so damn much that it feels like my heart is going to burst out of my chest."

I turned my head to the left and down, looking her in the eyes.

"You have given me the moon, Lex. You're the only one who could ever give me the moon."

She lifted her head up to kiss me. It was a sweet, gentle, and loving kiss.

At least, it started off that way.

Because moments after our lips parted, and we stared at one another, our faces still just a couple of inches apart—the moonlight reflecting mystically from her eyes—we kissed again, this time with passion and intensity.

Lex had a way of turning me on like nothing I'd ever felt. And, regardless of how many times we had sex in the recent several weeks, or even earlier today, every time we connected, my desire for her felt uniquely new and just as impassioned as the first time we'd connected.

I felt myself growing hard, knowing she could feel it pressing against her.

Lex giggled mischievously. "I suspect that you're done with this view and would like to get out of here?"

"Yeah," I said. "There's another view I am much more interested in."

"Oh yeah, what's that?"

"You, naked."

"My God, Kal. Again? What's gotten into you? Don't get me wrong. It's amazing. But I lost count after we made love half a dozen times. You're turning into a real animal."

"I can't help the effect you have on me, Lex."

"I am flattered. And you have that effect on me, too. But I'm pretty tender. And exhausted. I haven't ever come that many times in a single day."

I rubbed up against her. "Neither have I, but I can't help myself. We still have a few hours left in the day to see if we can keep raising that bar."

She responded by letting out a low moan. I had no additional sensory input from her heartbeat or emotive scents but could tell she was turned on.

"Let's get back to you naked," I said.

"Where am I?" she whispered, pressing herself harder against me.

"Standing in front of me. Writhing under me. Moaning in pleasure on top of me."

"All that can, of course, be arranged," she kissed me again.

I started to move my hands exploratively around her body, grabbed her ass and pulled her even tighter against me, writhing up against her.

"Oh," she whispered, surprised at my aggressiveness. "Slow down, there, Tiger, we're still in public."

I reached my right hand around to the front and squeezed her breast through her jacket and shirt.

"Ow," she said. "Stop it. Not here." She gestured with her eyes at the nearby crowd of people on the observation deck.

Startled at what I'd just done—what was I, a seventeen-year-old horny teenager?—I let go. "Sorry, Lex. Sorry."

"What the heck has gotten into you? I've never seen you so aggressive."

"I don't know. I just, wow, my hormones are raging like crazy."

"It's okay," she said, then grinned. "I've always had that sort of affect on men. And it *is* a full moon, after all."

"Well, you've always had that effect on me for sure. I'm sorry, Lex. I just can't seem to control myself. I want you so badly all the time."

"I'm fine with that. I much prefer that over the alternative of you never wanting me. But not here. C'mon, let's get home and let it all out."

We headed for the elevators, and I consciously did nothing more intimate than holding Lex's hand on the ride down, despite feeling an urge to wrap my arms around her and press her against me.

Sure, she was a hot and beautiful woman who turned me on; but why was I reacting, or over-reacting with such aggressive and raw sexuality?

That wasn't like me at all.

Was there something wrong with me? Could it be related to the full moon? Was the moon having a powerful effect on me even though I wasn't shifting into wolf form? Was there some animal instinct making its presence felt because it was pent-up?

Gail would likely know the answers.

But how could I run to Gail and talk about my overly hyper sexual desire for another woman?

Damn, I needed to find a different specialist in the occult and magic.

Lex and I exited right from the Empire State Building and then turned left on 5th Avenue, the quickest way to get back to The Algonquin. We spoke little to one another in the elevator ride down. I suspect we were both processing what had come over me.

Once we reached the first block, Lex took a deep breath before speaking.

"Can we," she said, gesturing to our left down 35th Avenue, "take a longer route back home? I'd love to see Times Square again. It's such a dynamic place at night with all the lights and the people."

She then quoted a line from Taylor Swift's song "Welcome to New York" which she had sung multiple times since arriving in the city. It was the one about the lights being so bright but they never blinded her.

The burning desire in me to get her back home and rip her clothes off was powerful. I inadvertently let out a low growl under my breath.

A look of shock came over her face.

"Was that you?"

"Yeah. Sorry. It just came out. I'm good. Let's head to Times Square."

We turned down West 35th Street.

"Are you sure, Kal?"

"Yeah. Yeah, I'm sure."

"It didn't sound like you're sure."

"What do you mean?

"That noise you made in the back of your throat. It didn't sound as if you were sure."

"That happened automatically, Lex. Honest. I had no control over that. Just like, before, when we were at the Empire State Building. I have no idea what has come over me. It's like this animal instinct is increasing in intensity, trying to make its way out."

She was quiet for a moment, considering.

"Maybe we need to talk to Gail about it."

"Gail?"

"She's a specialist in supernatural things, right? You told me you'd first met her because you were researching paranormal and occult details for a book.

"If anyone you can trust might know something about your condition, it would be Gail."

"Are you sure you want me spending any time with her? You're the one, after all, who recognized, immediately, that she was still *into* me in a major way."

"I know you love me, Kal. And I know that what we have, this unique situation of our own supernatural enhancements interacting with one another is something that bonds us together in a way like no other. But it's also of an other-worldly nature. And neither one of us knows enough about that type of thing. We could use the insights."

"I suppose."

"Besides, Gail already knows about your condition, and you can still trust her. She has never given your secret away all these years. And it's obvious she loves you."

"Therein lies the rub. If she loves me, wouldn't it be best for me to keep my distance from her?"

"Normally, sure, that would make sense. But because she loves you, it means she wouldn't want any harm to come to you. True love is when you put the other person's needs ahead of your own."

I stopped walking and turned to smile at her.

"Like what you're doing right now by supporting that I talk to Gail, despite my past with Gail and the obvious way she feels about me," I said.

"Yeah, something like that."

I leaned in to kiss her. It took everything in me to force back the overwhelming desire to do more than touch our lips together gently and lovingly. The heated passion and desire I felt was overwhelming I managed to pull myself back again. "I love you so much, Lex. I can't believe just how much." I thought about the afternoon activities that I'd kept from her. "Listen, I need to tell you something that happened earlier to—"

A shrill call for help from somewhere behind me interrupted my admission.

Chapter Twelve: I Feel a Blood Rage Rising, I See Trouble on the Way

I nstinct kicked in, and I turned away from Lex to run toward the alley about thirty feet away where the shout had come from.

Okay, I suppose it hadn't been instinct. Because I definitely had not been born with the innate reaction to rush toward potential confrontation. If anything, I might have had a desire to help while hiding and cowering. No, that "just rush in" aptitude had come after I gained my wolfish superpowers. But it had become enough of a habit over the years that it felt like instinct.

Especially now.

I reached the alley to find three men scuffling together. Two of them wore masks and were holding and beating on the third mask-less fellow. The one throwing punches was wearing a green skull mask and the one who was holding the man by pinning his arms behind his back to offer clear access to his stomach sported the white grinning face from the *Jigsaw* movie franchise.

"Son of a bitch," I said, recognizing the modus operandi of the Proud Fighters for America. "You deranged dickwads couldn't give me just a single night of normalcy, could you?"

"Mind your own fucking business," the one in the green skull mask said, stopping the pummeling he was offering as he turned to face me.

That threw me off. One thing that had been part of their schtick in LA was their verbal silence while attacking. The juxtaposition was as startling as it would have been to hear a series of multi-syllabic words come out of the current president's mouth.

The other thing that was off about these guys is they were beating on a middle-aged man who was clearly white. I had only ever witnessed them picking on visible minorities.

I was gaping at them, a bit stunned at hearing them speak, when Green Skull said. "Fuck off or you'll get some of this too once we finish with this Kike."

"Death to the Jews!" Jigsaw yelled. "And to the Jew-lovers too."

Even though their modus operandi was different, this blatant racial hatred was definitely on brand with the PFA I knew.

Despite not having any of the enhanced strength and agility I'd become used to, I felt myself filling with a burning rage and lunged at Green Skull, throwing my entire weight into him.

He didn't go sprawling onto his back like I had expected, but I got him to stumble a few steps, away from his friend and their victim. He threw a right hook into the side of my head.

My ear instantly started ringing and I shook my head, thrusting my right arm into his throat. I pushed hard, trying to force him back against the brick wall behind him.

My pinning attempt failed. He was much stronger than me, and I realized I was in trouble as he punched me twice in the ribs with his left hand, then shot out another right hook that split my lip.

I staggered back, the pain and frustration roiling together in an intensity that felt hot.

"Hands off him!" I heard Lex call from behind me, followed by the sound of flesh hitting flesh. I glanced to the side and saw Lex delivering her own right hook to the side of Jigsaw's head, sending his mask flying off.

Jigsaw took a swing at Lex, but it went wild and missed her by almost six inches. She punched him in the stomach, and he doubled over.

In the split second I wasn't paying attention, Green Skull tackled me. I was off balance already and went sprawling to the alley floor.

Satisfied I was down, Green Skull got up and rushed at Lex, but she easily dodged his attack, and he ran right into the opposite alley wall.

The white guy they'd been beating elbowed Jigsaw on the back of the head and shuffled over to the other side of the alley. He was bleeding from his nose and a gash in the side of his face near his left eye. He was holding his left arm across his stomach, cradling it.

As I was getting back to my feet, Jigsaw was already up and was trying to scurry out of the alley but ended up tripping over his own feet as he passed Lex. He went down face-first in the alley.

At the same time his partner was going down, Green Skull kicked out at Lex and connected with the back of her thigh. She let out a gasp of pain and stumbled to one knee.

And that's when I saw red.

Immediately after delivering the kick, Green Skull rushed to the alley's exit, realizing the tables had turned and they no longer had the upper hand.

The fury in me was burning beyond control.

"Are you okay?" I asked Lex.

"Yeah, fine." She said. "I'm more worried about you."

"Fucking peachy," I growled, and I raced out of the alley after the fleeing thug.

Green Skull rushed across the street, dodging a honking car. I ran around behind that same car in my pursuit, still seeing mostly through a red lens as I reached the opposite side of the narrow street and continued to chase him.

He ducked left into a parking garage, and when I got to it, I saw him fleeing up the ramp on the right-hand side. I followed him up, a flash of his scent coming to me in a powerful burst.

My enhanced senses were coming back.

Because I was physically distanced from Lex.

It was after dark on the night of a full moon.

I should have been worried about the impending change. But I was so filled with anger and rage that I didn't stop to consider that. All I wanted was revenge for him hitting Lex.

All I saw was my desire to catch him and tear out his throat.

The feeling of being winded and hurt faded as a renewed strength came to my legs. I picked up the pace and raced to the top of the ramp, turning right by intuitively following his scent.

As I rounded the corner, I saw he was only about twenty feet ahead of me. But I was gaining on him now that some of my strength had returned.

Despite the passionate fury that consumed me, several sensations struck me at the same time as I closed the gap between us. From the corner of my eye, I could see the hair on the back of my hands growing in thick and fur-like. From behind me I could hear Lex, who had just entered the parking garage and was racing up the ramp. "Kal, stop!" she was yelling. She was giving off a scent of intense fear and anxiety, knowing I would morph into a wolf if she wasn't nearby.

But that didn't matter to me.

All I could smell was blood, and the fear in the quarry I was chasing.

When I got within ten feet of him, I lunged through the air, hitting with in a solid flying tackle. He landed hard on his face on the asphalt, with me on top of him.

Letting out a growl that originated from deep within, I grabbed the hair on the back of his head and smashed his face against the parking-garage floor. His green skull mask cracked and splintered as I slammed his head down again. And on the third slam I was filled with the blood-rage joy of the sound of his flesh and bone connecting with the paved surface. All the time I was doing this I was watching my hand and arms continue to sprout fur as a deep rooted and intense arthritic pain in my bones shot through my spine and limbs, a violent ringing in my ears accompanying it.

The small red-inked PFA symbol was tattooed at the base of the back of the man's skull. It hadn't been visible under his long hair, but now that I'd had a fistful of his hair it was plainly visible. That symbol served only to heighten my rage.

I was about to change into wolf form and was struggling against it, but there was no use. I kept bashing the thug's face into the pavement, letting out what I realized was a blood-curdling battle cry of a combination of anguish and fury.

"Kal!" Lex's voice came from the top of the ramp behind me. "Stop!"

I felt an odd duality in that moment.

Part of me picked up the anxiety and terror in her voice, heartbeat, and scent, recognizing that if I didn't stop what I was doing, I could kill this man; that thought came with a queasiness I don't think I'd ever felt. Yet the other part of me, the element that had taken over in a furious blood-rage, ignored her as if she were some insignificant bug, and wanted nothing more than to inflict as much pain as I could.

I was as disturbed by the part of me that thought of Lex as insignificant as much as the part of me that was relishing in the violence.

But I stopped beating his head against the ground.

Not because that concerned side of me won over; but because I physically could not keep doing it.

My ability to keep a fist-hold of the thug's hair faded as my right hand cramped up and elongated.

I collapsed onto my right side, my body twitching in a series of spasms, and I let out another howl of excruciating agony.

"Kal!" I felt Lex's hands on my shoulder and my forepaw.

The pain shot in terrible waves through me, and I convulsed and kicked—the beginning of the transformation backing off again now that she was near.

Amid the shrieking pain and fading fury, I picked up a combination of scents from Lex. Confusion, anger, worry. But stronger than any of those was fear.

She was terrified *of* me. Of seeing what I had just done.

For the record, as the pain and anger dissolved, and I laid there on the asphalt beside the man I'd been beating to death, I was just as mortified. And I burst into sobbing tears.

"I'm sorry. I'm so sorry." I kept repeating as I curled into a ball.

Thursday, July 6, 2017

Interlude—Wolf Night—Two

*T*he wolf woke in a familiar natural area.

All the scents and the sounds around it felt reassuring. The ground it lay on, the trees, the leaves, the nearby water. Sounds of small animals scurrying through the nearby brush.

The throbbing ache in its head was still there, but slowly receding.

It stood on all four paws and took in a deep breath.

Along with that breath came the scent of the woman the wolf remembered from that other familiar enclosed artificial space.

The smell came from upwind.

The wolf bolted out of the woods, off the comforting natural ground and onto the artificial rock-like surface in a path clear from the trees and bushes. It followed the female human's scent along that hard path and over a structure overtop of a body of water.

Not far after it had crossed over the water a second scent came to the wolf on the next wave of the wind.

It was the other female human the wolf had spent time with both in the enclosed space and here in this more natural environment. The original woman it knew.

The wolf stopped, confused.

It felt a strong sense of trust and love for both women.

But it was impossible for them both to be luna.

There was, after all, only one female alpha.

And the female alpha was a wolf; not a human. How could this even be?

It needed to get closer, smell both of their genitals up close, then it would know for sure which one was the real luna. But they kept their genitals covered by clothes. That made it so much harder.

Resuming its pace, the wolf followed their scents.

As it rounded another corner of the artificial smooth rock-like path, the wolf could see the two of them up ahead, in a large open clearing. They were walking together and towards an enormous structure.

The wolf suddenly stopped, several factors leading to that decision.

The first was a return of the throbbing pain. This time it was subtle and felt more like a warning buzz. But it seemed to increase in intensity the closer the wolf got to the two women.

The second reason was the clearing itself. It was a large open space, but not the open space of a grassy field. This type of open area felt instinctively dangerous to enter. It was the type of space like this within this natural area the wolf had remembered avoiding before.

Third, the wind brought the scent of at least two other humans in the vicinity. The wolf knew these two women were pack and meant the wolf no harm. But humans in general were not to be trusted.

The wolf watched the two women walk off together in the distance until they disappeared, then turned right, away from the artificial stone path, through a set of trees and onto a large open field of grass.

Once it got to the clearing, it launched full speed across the field, relishing in the grass's feel underfoot and the wind through its fur.

It needed this.

It raced across the field, turned right, then headed back across the structure crossing over the water, relishing a return to the more thickly forested area where it had spent much of its time.

Scampering about, the wolf sniffed out and tracked the scent of rabbits and squirrels, then again burst into a run through the wooded areas before discovering some other small animals' scent and tracking it along.

It continued this combination of free running and mock hunting for some time.

At another natural clearing, it was about to launch into a full out run when a startling scent came from a shift in the wind.

There was another wolf here.

But not just another wolf.

A wolf it knew.

As the familiar scent of the only other wolf it had encountered before came to it, the hairs on the back of its neck bristled and it let out a low growl.

The other it had smelled had threatened the original woman the wolf knew. It had also attacked other humans, killing one. But there was something even more startling about that wolf. It also had a human smell about it.

The wolf remembered pursuing the other wolf, and then being startled to realize that other wolf had somehow changed into human form.

Maybe that was it. Perhaps the two female humans it loved could also change into wolf. That's why they were pack.

The other's scent was coming from the left, from a rocky elevation. It took in a hearty breath of the scent.

Yes, it was the familiar wolf/human scent the wolf remembered. But there was something different about it. The wolf elements of its scent were the same; but there was something off about the underlying human odor to it. Something the wolf couldn't understand.

Regardless, its presence was a threat.

The other was encroaching on its territory.

The wolf let out a sharp bark and rushed upwind toward the other.

Instead of running, or attacking, the other wolf froze in place, whimpering and tucking its tail tight between its legs.

As the wolf got within striking range, the other rolled over onto its back, paws in the air, its belly completely exposed, and whined, not making eye contact in any way—the most submissive gestures possible.

The wolf stopped, hovered over the other, confused.

The other was not a threat to its territory in any way.

Perhaps it would become part of the pack.

The other remained on its back, whining, and then, before the wolf's eyes, transformed into a human.

The human was not the same human the wolf had encountered and chased before. It was a different one, though there was something familiar about its scent; and it still smelled like that other human.

"Please," the human said in a similar tone to the whine it had made when in wolf form. "Help me."

Chapter Thirteen: Thinking About Lying While Laying

I woke to the sensation of pine needles pressing into my back, the energetic sound of birdsong heralding in the morning, critters scurrying through nearby underbrush, and the familiar scent of the nearby Central Park Lake.

I felt at peace. Perfectly one with nature, as I laid there, completely naked in the dirt and leaves, and twigs and pine needles, feeling startlingly refreshed and relaxed.

There's nothing like letting out a little bit of your inner wolf, I suppose.

I sucked in a deep breath and enjoyed the moment. For a few seconds I could relish in that just-awake feeling. With no conscious memory of the horrifyingly painful metamorphosis, all I could feel was the regenerative effects of having shifted from human to wolf, then back to human. The bruising to my ribs and the split lip from the night before were barely present. I ran a hand over my left side feeling only the slightest ghost of pain, and the tip of my tongue touched where I'd been bleeding from Green Skull's punch to my face, but it was as healed as if several days had passed rather than a mere seven hours.

It was strange just how much comfort I took in lying there naked and relaxed, particularly given the violence and the personal trauma of the night before. But I wanted just one more moment of that tranquility before getting up and taking on the day ahead of me.

I closed my eyes and reflected on what had gone down after Lex and I had interrupted the PFA beating.

Green Skull, the man whose face I had been bashing into the asphalt, wasn't dead. But he was unconscious and likely going to have a permanently twisted broken nose and the need of much dental work.

We determined that after Lex had held me and managed to get me to stop crying. She pulled me to my feet, telling me we needed to check on the man that Green Skull and his partner had been beating on.

We shuffled back down the ramp and crossed the street to find that both the victim and Jigsaw had disappeared.

"We can't stay here," Lex said, and suggested we make ourselves scarce before the authorities showed up. Someone would find Green Skull and call an ambulance. The police would also be called, due to the violence inflicted upon him, and hopefully the visible PFA tattoo would trigger the right action from the police.

We didn't need to be in the middle of this. Not again. Not so soon after this morning's incident in the diner.

When we got back to the Algonquin, Gail was waiting for us in the lobby.

"Gail? What are you doing here?"

"I was looking into what we had been talking about earlier and—" she stopped, her face suddenly alarmed as she noticed my split lip. "What the hell happened to you, Andrews?"

"We'll explain once we get upstairs," Lex replied in a curt tone. I didn't realize, at the time, but know now, that she was extremely annoyed to see Gail there—she was even more pissed I had gone to see Gail earlier that day and said nothing about it to her. I was, of course, obliviously to her hostile reaction to Gail at the time, and all of that didn't come out until later.

But I'm getting ahead of myself.

The three of us went upstairs where, once we were behind the closed doors of my suite, we shared with Gail what had gone down that night as well as the incident in the diner.

Knowing that PFA activity was ramping up here in New York was enough to come to terms with. But what had startled us the most was my violent outburst.

"It was the oddest experience," I explained. "I hated and was disgusted by what I was doing *while* I was doing it. But another part of me was feeling great satisfaction and a massive rush the more and more I kept hurting him, even as he was lying there helpless.

"I was aware of what I was doing but was unable to stop myself. It's like something within me was taking over."

"The wolf was dominating?" Lex asked.

"No," Gail replied. "I've seen him in wolf form. He is docile. In fact, the first time I saw him in his other state, he defended me from Knell, in wolf form. And other times he easily cuddled right up to me like the friendliest of dogs."

"True," Lex replied. "Now that you mention it. When I woke last night to find he was a wolf, he was gentle, compassionate, even. He nuzzled right up against me. And I held and comforted him while he was going through the painful metamorphosis."

Gail was silent as she glared at Lex. Even in my oblivious nature, I realized there was a bit of one-upmanship going on in that exchange. Lex established she was the one who'd be cuddling with me but also with the ability to return me to human from my wolf form.

"I was that way, as well, with Bridge," I said, referring to the only other person who knew about my lycanthropic affliction; the bright young teenager I had befriended on a cross-country adventure to Vermont a couple of years earlier.

They both knew about the special bonding relationship I'd had with Bridget Wells I hoped that bringing up the fact that, in wolf form, I'd been similarly protective and nurturing with a female where the relationship was entirely platonic—Bridge and I had more of a father/daughter and mentor/mentee relationship—would ease the tension and the obsessive need for them to show who got along best with me when I was a wolf.

It didn't seem to work. They both just scowled at me.

I continued with my next thoughts on the matter that had nothing to do with me as a wolf and my female human companions.

"The wolf isn't needlessly violent, like humans. Wolves attack and kill for food or for territory. Not for sport. Not for vengeance.

"It was like the wolf strength, the wolf power was there, but it was being dominated by a separate duality within my humanity.

"As if there's a dormant counterpart to me inside me all along. But it has never surfaced before."

"Like when you attacked Mack this morning," Lex said.

"You did *what* with Mack?" Gail's eyes were wide and startled.

"I told him to shut his fucking mouth," I said.

"You didn't!"

"And I grabbed him by the collar, screaming at him and I came really close to punching him. But I kept control. It was that same wild and powerful urge to hurt, to harm, to cause him pain for talking in a derogatory way about Lex."

"You said you emphasised the words *my girlfriend* when you were yelling at Mack," Lex said. "In a very possessive and protective way. That was likely that territorial instinct kicking in."

"That's definitely something you've displayed before," Gail said. "When Knell had me backstage during the live taping of the Letterman show you were all about protecting me. And, in wolf form that one night when he was preparing to attack, you attacked him first. Protecting me.

"But that hasn't occurred when you were in human form. I mean, you've never stood up to Mack in all these years I've known you, Michael." If I wasn't mistaken, Gail emphasised the words *all these years*. It made me wonder if there was still a competitive comparison thing taking place between these two women.

"And I surprised myself when I leapt out of my seat and responded aggressively towards Mack. Only, earlier today, I was able to control it. Tonight, with that PFA guy, I was out of control."

"That's the difference," Gail said. "Daylight, moonlight. Your body needs to transform. During your natural cycle, after dark you'd be in wolf form. But you're not. There's a pent-up energy inside of you that can't come out in wolf guise, so it's coming out in human guise.

"Remember the theory we have about Knell?"

"That his insanity—his outright psychopathy—was tied to the fact he kept human consciousness when in wolf format. And he could control when and how he changed."

"Exactly. It's not the natural, normal cycle. With Knell, nature was being denied. Something has to give. And it's the same thing with you, Michael. Trying to deny being in the wolf form is causing a similar reaction in you."

The thought of that terrified, angered, hurt, and confused me. Knell was an outright sociopath. I was nothing like that. But admittedly, I was nothing like the way I had been acting today.

"Or since last night," Lex said. She then looked directly at Gail when she said the next words. "Our sex has always been hearty, passionate, and vigorous. But last night, when we got back here, it was something else. You were wilder than in the past several weeks."

Lex quietly offered a smug smile at Gail, who glared daggers back at her. No, daggers would be too small, too subtle a way to describe that look. Pitchforks? Scythes? Perhaps a pair of bastard swords might best describe that look.

I was not liking the fact I seemed to be getting slightly better at understanding those unspoken things being passed back and forth without my wolf senses. Seeing these two purposely take jabs at one another was extremely uncomfortable. There's a lot to be said about the delightful state of "blissful ignorance."

"And earlier tonight," Lex continued, turning to face me, "at the Empire State Building, you were sexually aggressive and almost animalistic. You couldn't keep your hands off me. I'd never seen you behave that way."

I was almost afraid to look back at Gail in case those bastard swords she was glaring at Lex had morphed into short-range ballistic missiles.

But instead of returning verbal fire back at Lex, she was looking at me again.

"You know what you have to do," Gail said. "You need to release the wolf. Let your wolf-self come out.

Stop trying to control the natural forces that shouldn't be messed with. That should put a stop to this inner struggle.

"If you don't, it's likely that you're going to descend further into this aggressive madness, and, like Knell, it might take you to a state of psychopathy that you won't be able to return from."

Gail was right. I needed to let the wolf in me have his time in the sun—or, in the moon, as it were—and remove the internal struggle. In human form, I could not deal with or release that wolf power and energy in any effective way.

"That makes sense," I said. "But we haven't even discussed the PFA activity in this city, or what we can do about it."

"There's not much we *can* do at this point," Gail said. We can talk more about it tomorrow.

"As of right now, we, or at least, Lex, should escort you to Central Park. Because, as I understand it, if you're not near her you'll likely change into your wolf form within a few minutes. Don't worry about packing your disposable clothes. We can meet you in the morning. The Ramble area is a good spot, heavily wooded. Let's say we meet you at sunrise near Bow Bridge."

Gail gave me a subtle wry and knowing grin as she said this. That bridge held a special meaning for us. Because it had been the spot where she had first told me she loved me.

That smile and look ran from her face as quickly as it had appeared; and I had to wonder if I had actually seen it, or just imagined it.

We decided that all three of us should head together up to Central Park. Lex wasn't familiar enough with the city and hadn't yet been to the park. And, though the park was much safer at night than it had been in years past, it wasn't a good idea for a woman to be wandering around within the park on her own, after dark.

There wasn't a lot of conversation in the cab ride to the park. We exited the taxi at the East Side Terrace Drive entrance, across from East 72nd Street. And once at the park, we discussed some of the logistics about where I'd finally part ways to head off into the thick of the forest for my conversion, when the sun would rise, and the meeting location.

Gail and I did most of the talking, and Lex remained quiet. She might have said a half dozen words on the walk through the park.

As we moved through the Bethesda Terrace, Gail shared some things she had found about resurrection in her detailed reading about various rituals. That was the reason she had been waiting for us at The Algonquin. There were specific components and ingredients needed. She rhymed off what they were. Her own shop, which focused on and carried materials related to white magic, Wiccan and other non-dark magic beliefs, only had about one third of the crystals, herbs, and talismans required for such a feat.

She called other occult shops in the area to find out if they carried such things and would continue to do that in the morning. Her thought was maybe she'd be able to determine when Knell was brought back, or even who might be responsible. It could help us locate him.

It had been a long-shot, but it was a mystery she was determined to resolve.

Gail stopped at the base of Bow Bridge while Lex and I crossed it together, telling her she'd be waiting for Lex right here so they could walk back together.

As Lex and I walked quietly together across the bridge, I reflected on that magic moment between Gail and I on this bridge, all those years ago. It was a shame there was so much tension in the air right now, because I would have wanted Lex's first visit to this bridge with me to be something special.

Finally alone since we had arrived back at The Algonquin, once we were most of the way across the bridge, I turned to Lex, who still had said nothing.

"You've been really quiet," I said.

"There's not much to say."

"You can talk to me."

"Can I?" She picked up her pace to walk ahead of me.

I walked faster to keep up.

"Lex, c'mon—"

"No. No *c'mon*! Can't you see why I'm upset?"

"Lex, I—"

"You could have talked to me earlier, Michael. You could have told me earlier. But you didn't. Instead, when you encountered Knell, you went immediately back into the arms of that woman. A woman I told you still has the hots for you. Instead of me. And you never even told me about *any* of it."

"I didn't go *into her arms*, Lex. Besides, I was in her neighborhood. And she knows about these types of things. Resurrection. The occult. She was there when Knell died."

"Sure, okay. I get that she's the occult expert. But you could have told me you'd gone to see her. Why did you keep it from me, Michael?"

"I—I don't know."

"You don't know?"

"I just wanted to have a normal afternoon, evening, and night with you. I was going to tell you in the morning."

"So, you do know. Or do you? Or are you just making up excuses?"

"Lex, I—"

"No. You had your chance to tell me. But you didn't. You kept it from me. And I have to find out when *she* is waiting for you at the hotel? Do you know how much of an idiot and fool that makes me feel like? Do you?"

"Lex, that wasn't what—"

"No. No. No Lex. No *that wasn't*. No excuses. I don't want to hear it. I uprooted myself from LA to come to New York to be with you and you can't even talk to me about something important like that? I have to hear it from *her*?"

"What the hell am I even doing here? How did I allow myself to fall in love with you, Michael?"

We were now about thirty feet past the bridge and around a turn on the path where we could no longer see it. Thick foliage was on either side. She stopped walking and looked around.

"Is this good?" she asked.

"Is what...?" I stopped, realizing what she was asking. "Oh, yeah, this is good. I can slip into the woods here." I took my sandals off and handed them to her. "But Lex, we need to—"

"No, Michael. You need to go change into a wolf. I need to go think about some things."

I knew how much I needed to change, what the lack of turning into a wolf had been doing to me. But I didn't want to leave the conversation off this way. Lex was hurt. Because of me; because of the stupid decision I'd made to try to have a normal evening with her. It was an idiotic thing for me to do, particularly because it involved Gail.

What the hell was happening here? Why were things unraveling so spectacularly? Lex and I were supposed to build a new life, together, here in New York.

My eyes welled up with tears. I reached out to take her hand.

"Lex, I love you."

She pulled her hand away from me. "I love you, too, Michael. I just don't like you very much right now."

Without another word she turned and headed down the path back toward the bridge.

I watched her leave, the tears now freely flowing down my cheeks. The further she receded, the louder the nocturnal sounds of the park and the surrounding city became. I could even trace her footsteps back across the bridge, breathe in her amazing scent in the air.

Just as I heard Gail's voice greeting her on the other side of the bridge, the tingling aura built in the back of my head. My limbs stiffened, and I felt my hands curling into elongated fists.

I pushed my way through the bushes on the side of the path and stepped into the trees. Once I was a few steps in, my walk was more of a lumbering shamble, and I pitched forward to the forest floor.

This was disconcerting. I normally had a memory block of anywhere between five to fifteen minutes before a change. I'd even had entire conversations with people that I couldn't remember because they had taken place shortly before the change.

But Lex's own supernatural impact on me changed that. I was consciously aware of more and more about the change.

Fortunately, my memory of the continuing metamorphosis ended a moment after I lay on the ground writhing in an overwhelming intense full-body arthritic style pain.

Among the various voices and footfalls of morning joggers in the park, I picked up Gail's voice, off in the distance.

She was muttering under her breath, but she knew if I were anywhere nearby, I could hear her.

"Okay, Andrews. I don't have all day. You've got to be around here somewhere. We agreed to meet near this bridge. I'm here. I have your clothes. I brought a couple of yummy dog biscuits, too."

I laughed out loud. I didn't realize how much I missed Gail's sense of humor. It was such a comforting thing to hear her voice after waking up.

Taking in a deep breath, I found her scent, determining she was perhaps a hundred yards south of me. I had woken not that far from where I'd started off.

I rolled onto my hands and knees and took in another hearty breath, listening to Gail continue to mutter under her breath.

"C'mon, Andrews. Seriously. I'm almost out of coffee and I'm really needing another cup."

The deep roast coffee she was drinking briefly came to me in a teasing whiff. As I was appreciating the mingled smell of Gail and that rich roasted coffee, I realized there was an important scent missing.

Lex.

She wasn't with Gail. She wasn't nearby.

I got to my feet and headed through the forest to where I remembered falling as I started to change. I didn't remember removing the clothes, as I normally tried to do. But based on my inability to do more than spasm uncontrollably, I doubt I'd been able to.

About forty feet through the foliage, I found my t-shirt, or at least a good portion of it, torn into a single flat fabric. My pants and underwear where nowhere near.

"Is that you?" Gail muttered from where I could now see her through a break in the leaves. She was leaning on the rail on the Bow Bridge. "Thought I caught a flash of pale flesh through the trees. Damn, Andrews, you just got back from LA. You'd think you might have gotten a bit more sun."

She started walking toward me.

There was nobody else nearby, just the two of us, so, as she got closer, I stepped a little further out from the brush.

She smiled and I picked up the scent of relief and love radiating from her. "Yep, that's you," she said, picking up her pace. Her heartbeat picked up too.

I waved sheepishly from the side of the trail.

Gail raised the canvas tote bag that was slung over her shoulder. "Got your clothes right here," she said.

Her emotive scent revealed she was appreciating seeing me naked. I shuffled to my left in order to be further covered by the leaves of a small brush.

"Oh, stop being so bashful. It's nothing I haven't seen before. And yeah, I know you can smell that Andrews. Don't flatter yourself. You know I've always appreciated a well-toned male body. I was just enjoying the view."

As she came around the corner of the path, her emotions changed to shock with an underlying layer of lust.

"Oh, Andrews," she said in a breathy voice that came with an odor of sarcastic humor. "Are you excited to see me, or is that just the remnants of a morning erection?"

Chapter Fourteen: And Now You've Got My Attention for Something Completely Different

S tartled, I looked down.

I had woken up, as I often do, with a full mast erection—something that always felt, to me, like the hermit in the Monty Python film *Life of Brian.* In the film, after eighteen years of a vow of silence, when he finally speaks, he jumps and pops as high out of his hole as he can, shouting "I'm alive! Hello birds! Hello trees!"

When I had first woken my little 'hermit' seemed to be doing just that. He usually settled down after a few minutes. It was one of those things, like breathing, that you just don't really pay attention to.

So, I hadn't even thought about it.

There were, of course, other things on my mind.

But since Gail had pointed it out, I realized I was still partially saluting. Maybe a three-quarter salute. Like a drunken soldier attempting a full-on salute but slapping himself in the cheekbone rather than strategically positioning his hand at the side of the brow.

"I've got to be honest with you, Andrews," Gail laughed. "Since I know you can read my emotions anyway. But I missed the sight of those tight abs, and the way your little Terry Jones pops up to shout good morning to the world."

She sighed and let out a breath. "And I do miss helping you put it to good use."

Her 'Terry Jones' quip was a reference to the Monty Python actor I had just been thinking about. It was peculiar just how much she could still tell what I had been thinking. While Lex and I had shared many things in the three weeks we'd been together, Gail still had years of insights and sharing.

Hearing Gail reference what morning sex with her had been like, all those years ago, conjured up some vivid intense memories that had an immediate visual effect on me, or, in keeping with the theme, on the hermit who was now being quite the exact opposite of reclusive.

What the hell was wrong with me?

I used both hands to try, vainly, to push my erection down and hide it at the same time.

Gail grinned and then burst out laughing.

"I'm sorry," she said. "I can't help it. But this is a ridiculous situation. If this exact situation had happened a month ago, a year ago, you would have jumped at the chance. I'd be naked already, and we'd be rolling in those bushes. But of course, just as I'm finally realizing a way to stop denying my feelings for you, you, a man who we all figured would be single for life, find yourself a love interest.

"And I want to hate her—part of me does—but I can see how much she loves you, and how happy you are since you got back. It's been years since I've seen you this happy. But dammit, Andrews, that doesn't make this easy.

"What the hell is wrong with the two of us?" She burst into a fresh round of laughter. "I mean, look at us. Just freakin' look at us. What the hell is this, anyway?"

I started laughing too. The air was filled with the sound, and smell of mirth and the type of nervous laughter that is often the thing that breaks the palpable tension hanging between two people.

"But those *were* good times, weren't they?" Gail said, pitching me a pair of underwear from the bag slung over her shoulder.

I slowly nodded.

"We really should talk, Andrews. I know the timing isn't right, but when will it ever be? I realize—"

"Where's Lex?" I interrupted, remembering how angry she had been with me the night before. "Why isn't Lex here with you?"

I pulled my underwear on as quickly as I could, realizing I still looked a little ridiculous with a tent pole pushing them out. But at least I was now partially covered.

"She," Gail's scent contained a mixture of sorrow with a bit of satisfaction. "She needed some time to process your behavior yesterday. With you coming to see me at the shop. And why you lied about it."

"I didn't lie about it. I just didn't—"

The scent of anger from Gail stopped me. Me lying to Gail had been the key factor in her breaking up with me all those years ago. She had been cheated on, lied to, and treated like chattel by every man she'd ever dated. We only became friends after she had no choice but return to my life to leverage my wolfish powers. To help her fiancé out of a tough situation. Only, he turned out to be an even bigger douchebag that anyone suspected. So, despite her powerful feelings for me, our relationship had been a platonic friendship. And I had stuck around, waiting, trying to see if she could ever come around, for years. Almost three full years, actually.

Gail could tell I had smelled her anger. "You deceived her. Plain and simple," she said. "You're such an ass, Andrews. I'm sure that me hanging out with her all night didn't help."

She tossed me a pair of jeans that I pulled on.

"You two hung out last night after dropping me off here?"

"Yeah, we went back to your place. We talked for a long time.

"I know how much she loves you, Andrews." She threw a t-shirt at me. "And I know how she feels about being lied to."

I pulled the shirt over my head and then she produced a pair of my sandals from her bag that I slid on.

"You talked about that?" I asked as we started walking on the path towards Bow Bridge.

"Initially, yes. We shared how we each came to know you. How it ended with you and I. The fact you kept your lycanthropy from me. And that it was a deception I couldn't get over."

"I actually defended you, Andrews. I reminded her

you might be an idiot who doesn't always know the right thing to do or to say, but that you're a loyal companion who would always be there for your friends and loved ones. And I could see how head over heals in love with her you are.

"I reminded her that while you goofed up and didn't tell her about coming to see me, that you likely did it in some stupid chivalrous desire to protect her, for a little while, from the darkness. And that while you didn't tell me about your wolf nature, you openly shared that with her."

"You and Lex sat around swapping stories about me like a couple of old friends? Some sort of pajama party?"

"Well no. We're definitely not friends. But we do share something in common that connects us. We both love you, Andrews. God help me, but we're both in love with you."

I was silent. I'd known, for years, how Gail actually felt about me deep inside. I could scent the emotions on her. But she never properly admitted it; not in those words. Her words, and actions, were always to acknowledge that just because she felt something didn't mean she wanted to act upon it.

And I honored that. She might have loved me, but I know that when a woman says "no" she means "no" and I respected that. It's not something I would ever violate.

I shook my head, thinking about the years I'd mooned over Gail, wanted nothing more than to be together with her in that deeply intimate way we had once been.

"I-I don't know what to say," I finally stammered. "Gail, I'm so sorry. I don't know what to—"

"Don't. There's nothing you can do. You're happy, and, as much as it hurts that it's with her and not me, I'm happy for you.

"Besides," she said, as we passed the Bethesda Fountain and headed toward the pathway through the terrace, "you and Lex and I have something a lot more urgent to deal with.

"I wasn't the only one sharing. Lex told me about how you met, about her background.

"We talked about the Proud Fighters for America. She explained her...deeper involvement with the group and what happened to her best friend. We talked about potential rituals that could have brought Knell back from the dead. About ways we might be able to track him—apart from the various news reports of a wolf running through the city."

"What did those reports say about Knell? About the wolf? Were there any murders?"

"No. No murders related to the wolf. But we discovered something worse."

"What?"

"We started sifting through news reports from the last several weeks and noticed a definite uprise in hate-related crimes. Personal assaults and vandalism. Only a handful of the articles mentioned the PFA, because of the logo that was found spray-painted at some of the scenes. But there were a few common themes among all the crimes."

"Such as."

"The victims of the personal assaults were all visible minorities. Race and culture—Black, Asian, Sikhs. And people from the LGBTQ community."

I thought about Mack's recent admission to me. "A person's sexual orientation isn't necessarily something that's visibly obvious."

"The reports we read about were attacks at or just outside gay bars. They attacked three different clubs on the same night. Another attack was a male couple who had been holding hands walking down the street and were beaten nearly to death."

"In pretty much every documented case where there was a personal assault," Gail continued, "there was always more than one attacker—it was never solo; they were always in packs of at least two or three. They wore masks. And they never said a word."

I thought about the first PFA thugs I'd encountered in LA and how disturbing it had been to see them beating on a helpless man while being so eerily silent. They hadn't even reacted to the teasing and ribbing that normally puts people off their game. But the thugs last night were vocal in their anti-Semitism. That threw me for a bit of a loop.

"The guys Lex and I encountered last night weren't silent. They were talking."

"Lex and I discussed that as well, so we went back to look at the reports of the cases that included verbal threats but involved two or more attackers and Halloween masks. There were at least half a dozen of those."

"So, what is this? A different modus operandi for the New York chapter of the PFA?"

Gail pressed her lips together and shook her head before responding. The emotive scent coming off her was powerful with a mixture of dread and frustration. "No. We suspect it's something much worse. Copy-cat groups or PFA wannabees."

"Copy-cats?"

"Yes. Thrill-seekers jumping on a trend. Not to mention those who may have been encouraged by the rise in open displays of hate and prejudice. Remember how Trump's rhetoric on the campaign trail normalized and legitimized, at least in the eyes of certain groups, racism? Hate crimes grew by over twenty percent last year, and, the day after election day they saw a spike.

"Those with racist views and beliefs, and even those who might not be racist in the classic sense but had a deep-rooted fear of *the other* felt seen and heard, and acted out on those feelings, incited and fueled by anti-immigrant sentiment.

"The same thing might be happening here. With the growing incidence of PFA attacks, like-minded people are encouraged to also act out on their own fear, their own passions."

"You mean to say that we're seeing a rise in violence not just from PFA, but from average citizens?"

"Yes."

I felt my own sense of anxious dread rise to match what I was smelling off Gail.

It was tough enough to fight a group of organized hate-crime thugs that were both elusive and endowed with bizarre super-powers. But how on earth could we fight the underlying plague of contempt, prejudice, and animosity that was growing?

"Just so I understand this correctly," I asked, "you and Lex spent most of last night researching the growth of violent hate crimes in the city."

"Yes. We talked and researched until about three in the morning. I stayed at your place."

The idea of these two women who should hate one another, who most likely must struggle just to be in the same room and maintain a non-hostile disposition, spending hours talking and researching like old friends was not what I expected to wake up to learn about.

"So, you stayed over?"

"Yes. She slept in the bed. I stayed on your pull-out couch. She was still sleeping when I left to get you. She was exhausted.

"You know," Gail said, taking my arm. "You can't have her staying awake during the full cycle of the moon just so you don't turn.

"I hope you recognize the absolute danger of suppressing your alter ego. You have to let the wolf happen, Michael. Look at the way you behaved when you tried to suppress it."

Gail became extremely emotional with a combination of abject terror and concern for me. Her eyes started to well up with tears. That was twice now in the past several days I'd seen her do that. That bothered me more than I can express. And it was as awkward as thinking about the overnight research and gab-fest Gail and Lex had been having while I'd been roaming about Central Park on all fours.

"I know," I said. "I get it. I don't want to turn into the same type of psychopath as Knell."

A car drove past in front of us on Terrace Drive with the window rolled down. I got both a good look and a potent scent of the white guy in the front seat with the bristly blond brush cut.

I'd know that scent anywhere, though I'd only seen his face once. During the two encounters I'd had with him, he'd worn a hockey mask over his face, like the bad guy in those *Friday the Thirteen* movies. The guy I'd nicknamed Jason.

A PFA thug from Los Angeles.

This meant the activities in New York weren't just some offshoot branch of the PFA. It meant the PFA had come East.

Had Marco and his group of paranormal miscreants followed us?

"What's wrong?" Gail said, recognizing the tension in my face as I'd stopped dead in my tracks.

"We need to get to Lex now!" I said. "The Los Angeles PFA are here. Call my place. Warn her."

Gail pulled out her phone and placed the call. I heard the phone from my apartment ringing through her speaker.

It kept ringing.

There was no answer.

Chapter Fifteen: Gone Girl

"She's not here!" I shouted, hearing the panic in my voice, as I lunged out of the cab before it had come to a full stop in front of The Algonquin.

We didn't have to go inside for me to know Lex wasn't there.

Her fresh scent was clear on the sidewalk outside the hotel.

I started tracking her scent East down E 44th Street.

Gail, who had been paying the driver, caught up to me about half a block away.

"Tell me." Her voice was calm. It helped ground my panic. "What did you pick up?"

"She left. It couldn't have been that long ago. Her scent was fresh. Maybe in the past fifteen or twenty minutes."

"Could you tell if she was alone, or if she was with anyone? Being taken against her will?"

"No," I said, "I can't tell."

I then stopped. We still hadn't made it to 5th Avenue, but her scent just disappeared.

I thought back to the first time I'd encountered hockey mask Jason in Los Angeles and how he had simply disappeared after racing around the corner of an alley. He vanished, and his scent itself stopped dead too.

It hadn't been until more than a week later that I learned how he had pulled off his disappearing trick. Jason's supernatural power had been sending concentrated blasts of energy from his clasped hands. It was Marco, the square jawed, blue-eyed blonde man who could appear and disappear using some sort of oval light bubble.

The only time I'd seen his cold steely blue eyes had been when he'd stepped out of such a portal that opened up, startling Lex and I, who had been fighting with Jason.

When Marco spotted Lex he'd yelled "You!" with as much rancor as that one syllable word could ever hold, then grabbed Jason, stepped back through the portal and disappeared.

Marco was not only the leader of the PFA, but he was also Lex's former lover.

I suspected his desire for revenge might just bring him across the country. There's no under-estimating the lengths an asshole ex-boyfriend Nazi might take in his thirst for vengeance.

"What is it?"

"Her scent stopped," I said. "It just stopped." I then explained my theory that it might be Marco, and the place-jumping portal power I'd witnessed.

"Yeah," Gail grimaced. "Lex told me about Marco and what she had to do to try to save her best friend from the clutches of the PFA cult.

"She is a strong woman, Michael. She survived a lot. If Marco did take her, she'll be okay. Besides, she's got her magic nullifying ability to protect her, doesn't she?"

I nodded. "Yes. She does. It usually takes several minutes to kick-in for me. I wonder if it's the same with Marco."

"Did you detect Marco's scent at all along this sidewalk?"

"No. I don't know what he smells like. My powers were muted during my only encounter with him. I only know what he looks like."

"Let's head back to your place. Maybe you can pick up his scent in your suite."

"Good idea."

We turned and walked back to the Algonquin.

"She was alone," I said, standing in the living room area in my place.

There was nobody else's scent here. Just the scent of Lex, most recently, Lex and Gail, from last night, and the smell of Lex and I mingled together.

As we walked around, I noticed that one of Lex's duffel bags and half the clothes she had brought with her from LA were gone. She wasn't just gone for the afternoon. This was something more permanent.

"She packed her stuff and left," I said, then turned to look at Gail. Her face and her overall scent exuded confusion, but she said nothing.

It was a peculiar feeling standing in my apartment beside Gail while smelling the still relatively heavy odor of the sex Lex and I had numerous times only yesterday afternoon.

I couldn't help but reflect on the times, all those years ago, that Gail and I had made love here.

For months after we'd broken up, I often caught myself sitting alone in here and anxiously taking in the subtle lingering scent of her.

And kicking myself repeatedly for screwing it up.

For the first time in my life, with Gail, I'd found someone truly special. Someone who seemed to complete me. But I'd been unable to hold on to that for more than a few months.

I'd ruined that special thing Gail and I had because I hadn't been able to share with her the curse that ran through my veins.

And, years later, after having found what I thought was impossible—the unique bond Lex and I had discovered, here I was realizing I'd made the same mistake again.

I'd kept something from Lex—the fact I'd gone to see Gail—and ruined this, too.

"She was alone," I repeated. "She left alone. With a packed bag. She's gone."

Like a moment earlier, the look in her eyes told me just as much as her scent did that she knew exactly what I'd just been thinking.

But her external reaction was a valiant attempt of trying to mask that feeling and the many other emotive scents that emanated from her.

Gail shook her head.

"No, Michael. She's not gone. This isn't over." The complex flood of emotions flowing from Gail was staggering. With Lex out of the picture, Gail and I might be able to rebuild what we'd had—I could sense that's what she truly wanted for herself. But the conflicting part of her knew how I felt about Lex and wanted me to be happy. Both those emotions filled the air as she continued to speak. "Lex really does love you. Deeply. I can see that. I can feel that. You know how strong my bullshit detector is, Michael. And, as much as I would love to, I never once got a negative vibe off her. Not a single miniscule tingle in my trusty old *Spidey sense*."

She laughed. Gail knew how much of a fan of Spider-Man I was. And that I'd called her overwhelmingly powerful intuition her Spidey sense.

I laughed too.

But her utter compassion and selfless love for me, wanting me to be okay, wanting Lex to be okay, was too much to bear.

Thinking about how I'd screwed things up irreparably with Gail, and now, more recently, with Lex, was too much.

The tears had already blurred my vision, and I lost my ability to speak effectively. I tried to say "She's gone. It's over." But all I unleashed was a string of incomprehensible syllables.

Sobbing, I opened my arms and stepped toward Gail.

She immediately closed the remaining few inches between us, taking me into her warm embrace. She uttered soft comforting words, gently stroking the back of my head and my back while I wept into the crook of her neck and her shoulder.

We stood like that for several minutes. Gail's words, her physical gestures, and the emotive scent coming from her intermingled into a powerfully soothing balm.

Of course, by the time I could finally get hold of myself, I realized I'd left my own less than pleasant balm-like substance on her blouse and the side of her neck.

When I finally lifted my head, three thick sinews of snotty strings continued to attach my face to her trapezius area.

"Uh, sorry," I said, snapping the strings with a quick brush of my left hand, then wiping it on the side of my leg. "I think your blouse is now ruined."

"No, it's snot," she grinned.

The play on words made us both laugh.

"I'll spare sending you my dry-cleaning bill," she said, "if you'd be so kind as to lend me a shirt."

"You know where everything is," I said, heading to the bathroom so I could blow my nose.

On my way to the bathroom, I grabbed my cell phone. And once I was inside with the door closed, I texted Lex.

Where did you go? I typed. *Can we talk?*

I put the phone down and wiped at the tears and snot with a wad of toilet paper, then ran the faucet and splashed some cold water onto my face.

When I looked over at my phone on the counter, I could see that she'd read my message but there'd been no response.

As I stared down at my phone, fresh tears welled-up in my eyes again.

I picked it up and texted another message.

Please. I love you, Alexandria.

I stared at the phone and waited a few more beats. Again, no response.

I tried one more time.

I need to know you're safe.

This time I could see the little dots appearing that told me she was typing a message back. Those simple little dots that, as you watched them, seemed to tease out the anticipated message forever.

Her text finally appeared on the screen.

I'm safe. I just need some time to get my thoughts together. Give me some time, Kal.

I nodded at the phone. Then I sent a one-word response. *Okay.*

I grabbed another piece of toilet paper and dabbed at the fresh tears on the side of my face before heading back out to see Gail.

Chapter Sixteen: Welcome to Fear City

Gail left shortly after I'd come out of the washroom; she needed to head back home so she could get changed and then go open her store.

Before heading out she advised me that the best thing to do was to give Lex a little space and to distract myself with whatever writing deadline Mack had likely recently put onto my plate.

"Thank you," I said to her as she stood in the doorway to the apartment.

She grinned and the warmth and compassion she felt for me radiated from her unabashedly. "Any time," she nodded, closing the door.

I stood looking at the closed door and following her scent as it receded down the hallway and into the elevator.

I must have stood like that for several minutes before giving my head a shake and then deciding to order some breakfast from Uber Eats then sit down at my laptop and work on the article about my experiences in Los Angeles.

By the time my food had arrived—a two-for-one omelet special—I'd written a good twelve hundred words: almost half of the required length for the article. And I was feeling pretty good about the process.

It felt good to be writing again.

While wolfing down my breakfast I read the *New York Times* that had been delivered to my place earlier that morning.

The front cover was taken with a single article and spread of accompanying images. Above the fold were the headline, the first paragraph of the article, and the images, which included a large, hooded death's head with a yellow background surrounded by an array of photos that included smashed windows, damaged and fire-torched buildings spray painted with messages of hate and one recognizable symbol—the PFA logo—burned cars, and the bruised and beaten faces of two different young men.

I unfolded the paper to read the entire article.

DEVIL'S NIGHT IS EVERY NIGHT AS NEW YORK RETURNS TO ITS 'WELCOME TO FEAR CITY' DAYS

Mischief Night has long been originally associated with October 30th, the night before Halloween, and usually involved a series of mind-mannered pranks such as toilet papering homes, knocking on doors and running away, or throwing raw eggs at houses.

In Detroit of the 1970s and 1980s, a dramatic economic downturn, rising unemployment, and the foreclosure of many homes resulted in a growing spree of vandalism and arson of many abandoned buildings. The term Devil's Night has long been associated with this decades-long trend in Motor City that saw anywhere from five hundred to eight hundred fires in any given year. That trend started to decline in the 1990s thanks to regional and government initiatives that included curfews, increased police action, and community watch groups.

But, as this paper has reported numerous times in the past several weeks, Devil's Night style vandalism combined with increased hate-crime attacks, have been spreading in communities throughout New York City.

While overall anger, unrest, and blatant race-related crime has increased during the daylight hours, when the sun goes down, those hostilities take on a much darker hue.

The past two nights have seen the highest incidence of arson in the city, a 72% increase over typical rates. Motor vehicle fires, abandoned building fires and heinous attacks on businesses, community centers, synagogues and mosques are among the reported incidents according to reports from the New York City Fire Department.

Devil's Night has become every night, and some city counsellors are calling for curfews to help keep citizens safe but also to make it easier to spot the ne'er-do-wells who are stalking the city in the night.

Bud Richards and Hailey Rosenberg, two of the counselors representing Midtown, have rallied against the call for curfews.

"Local businesses in this city rely on the evening draw of the theatre crowds." Richards said. "We can't shut these operations down. They're sustaining a vital part of our company and many local businesses. Not just the theatres, but so many of the local restaurants and shops."

"What we need," Rosenberg added. "Is increased police presence; not forcing our citizens to hide in fear as thugs attempt to bring our fine city back to the crime spike and fear felt in the 1970s and 1980s. We can't return to a *Welcome to Fear City* environment."

Council Member Rosenberg was referring to the scaremongering pamphlets that were handed out to tourists arriving in NYC in the mid-70s, causing them to be horrified and baffled.

These pamphlets contained warnings of heightened crime activities that seemed to be lifted from the scripts of popular movies at the time such as *Death Wish*, *The French Connection*, or *Marathon Man*. (See reprint of the 'Welcome to Fear City' pamphlet on Page 12).

Rosenberg and Richards are not exaggerating about the impact a forced curfew would have on the many entertainment and restaurant businesses. But the reality is that it's just not safe to be out after dark in the city lately. This is especially true for persons of color and LGBTQ communities, who have become consistent targets in increased violence. Hate crimes have increased by 91.9% year to date over last year.

According to early reports from officials in the mayor's office 2017 was on track to have perhaps the lowest crime rate since 1951. But that has changed in the past few weeks alone. Besides the increased incidents of hate crimes, felony assaults, vandalism and property damage are also showing a sharp increase.

Many of the buildings and vehicles that have been damaged and torched also have been tagged with a symbol that has become more common in the city recently: the PFA logo.

The icon (as seen in the images accompanying this article) is associated with the *Proud Fighters for America*, a neo-Nazi hate group originating in Los Angeles. Local and federal authorities, who have the PFA on their watch-lists, have been tracking the spread of their membership from the West Coast eastward.

Members of the PFA most often attack while wearing Halloween-style masks and disguises, similar to the ones worn in *The Purge* trilogy of films.

Representatives from the NYPD Hate Crimes Task Force are asking citizens to report any sightings of the PFA symbol in the city, regardless of whether they appear in conjunction of vandalism. Call 1-888-440-HATE, text "Hate" to 81336 or email: hctf@nypd.org.

"PFA members use the symbol to communicate with one another," Detective Wagner of the task force says, "

"And if you see what looks like a PFA related crime in progress," Detective Wagner warns residents. "Do not approach them. Do not confront them. They are dangerous and malicious and unpredictable. Remove yourself as quickly and safely as possible and call 9-1-1."

With the incidence of violent crime on the rise and roaming thugs terrorizing the streets after dark, making the city seem more and more reminiscent of scenes from John Carpenter's dystopian film *Escape from New York*, one wonders, if there is, in fact, any escape from the terrors that come out every single night.

When I finished the article, I flipped to page 12 and looked at the images reprinting the entire mid-1970s "Welcome to Fear City" pamphlet.

WELCOME TO FEAR CITY
A Survival Guide to the City of New York

The incidence of crime and violence in New York City is shockingly high, and is getting worse every day. During the four-month period ended Apr. 30, 1975, robberies were up 21%; aggravated assaults was up 15%; larceny was up 22%; and burglary was up 19%.

Now, to "solve" his budget problems, Mayor Beame is going to discharge substantial numbers of firefighters and law enforcement officers of all kinds. By the time you read this, the number of public safety personnel available to protect residents and visitors may already have been still further reduced. Under those circumstances, the best advice we can give you is this: Until things change, stay away from New York City if you possibly can.

Nevertheless, some New Yorkers do manage to survive and even to keep their property intact. The following guidelines have been prepared by a council of firefighters and law officers to help you enjoy your visit to the City of New York in comfort and safety.

Good luck.

1. **Stay off the streets after 6 P.M.** Even in midtown Manhattan, muggings and occasional murders are on the increase during the early evening hours. Do not be misled by the late sunsets during the summer season. If you walk in midtown at about 7:30 P.M., you will observe that the streets are nearly deserted.

2. **Do not walk.** If you must leave your hotel after 6 P.M., try not to go out alone. Summon a radio taxi by telephone, or ask the hotel doorman to call a taxi while you remain in the hotel lobby. Follow the same procedure when leaving the restaurant, theatre, or other location of your evening activity.

3. **Avoid public transportation.** Subway crime is so high that the City recently had to close off the rear half of each train in the evening so that the passengers could huddle together

and be better protected. It has been proved that increasing the number of Transit police officers will cause a reduction in subway crime, but the announced decrease in Transit patrol will have the opposite effect. Accordingly, you should never ride the subway for any reason whatsoever. In midtown Manhattan, you may, at only slight risk, ride the buses during the daylight hours only.

4. **Remain in Manhattan.** Police and fire protection in other areas of the city is grossly inadequate and will become more inadequate. In the South Bronx, which is know to police officers as "Fort Apache," arson has become an uncontrollable problem. If you remain in midtown areas and restrict your travel to daylight hours, emergency service personnel are best able to provide adequate supervision and protection.

5. **Protect your property.** Theft has become so great a problem that the City is urging everyone to engrave identifying numbers on all property, and the Police Department has purchased special engraving pens which are made available to the public. If you walk on Madison Avenue or in the other major midtown locations during business hours, you will observe that many merchants keep their doors locked and will admit customers only after careful inspection. After hours, they protect their premises with special heavy safety

gates. Accordingly, you should observe the following precautions.

6. **Safeguard your handbag**. If you carry a handbag or similar luggage, try to hold it firmly with both hands whenever you are in public, Never let it out of your hands; above all, never let it out of your sight. Places that seem most secure, such as restaurants or cocktail lounges, are often the most dangerous. Even a moment's inattention can result in a serious loss.

7. **Conceal property in automobile**. If a package is visible on the seat or floor of your automobile, even though the vehicle is locked, there is an excellent chance that your property should be locked in the trunk or the glove compartment. Do not park your car and then transfer property into the trunk; you will probably be observed. All property should be secured before you arrive at your parking place. Remember also to keep all doors locked and all windows closed when you are in the vehicle. Remember too that auto thefts have increased this year.

8. **Do not leave valuables in your hotel room, and do not deposit them in the hotel vault**. Hotel robberies have become virtually uncontrollable, and there have been some spectacular recent cases in which thieves have broken into hotel vaults. At present, bank vaults appear to be the only

depositories that offer an acceptable degree of security for personal property.

9. **Be aware of fire hazards**. The Fire Department is severely under-manned at present and further reductions are in prospect. Accordingly, you may have to evacuate quarters without assistance if fire should occur from either natural or malicious causes. Try to avoid buildings that are not completely fireproof and familiarize yourself with exists and escape routes wherever you are. In hotels, try to obtain a room that is close by the fire stairs.

These guidelines have been prepared and distributed as a public service by the Council for Public Safety, Room 516, 299 Broadway, New York, N.Y. 10007.

When I finished reading the reprint of the fear-mongering pamphlet, I put the newspaper down and released that, mid-way through reading the main article and this piece, I had put my fork down as well.

Half of my breakfast remained completely untouched.

This was far worse than I'd thought and seemed to be ramping up exponentially.

I must have been sitting like that for a few minutes before I heard a text coming in.

It was from Lex.

I'm ready to talk. Can I call?

I picked up my phone and immediately texted her back. *Of course. Any time. But can we do this in person?*

It's best if we don't.

I shook my head. Was she really going to dump me via a phone call? Well, at least it wasn't a text message. *I miss you, Lex. And I'm sorry. I'd like to apologize in person. I need to see you. Please.*

There was a long pause with no response. It stretched on for more than a minute. I mentally kicked myself. I was being too pushy, too demanding. It's not the first time I'd done that.

The phone rang. It was Lex. Dammit, she was going to break up with me via the phone.

I thumbed the call answer icon and wordlessly lifted the phone to my ear.

"Okay. I'll explain in person," Lex said. "Can you meet me at 10:00 AM at the Westway Diner on 9th Avenue?"

Chapter Seventeen: Hell Hath No Fury Like a Man Scorned

"Yes, I was angry," Lex said to me from across the table in one of the smaller two-person booths at Westway Diner. "And I needed some time alone. To think and to process things.

"I upended my life in Los Angeles to come here, Kal. To move across the country so we could be together. Yes, I know the desire to get as far away from the PFA as possible also motivated me. But that point is pretty much moot right now, isn't it?"

I opened my mouth, preparing to respond.

"No. Don't say anything. I'm not nearly close to done. Please just let me get through this. Let me finish."

It took everything in me to keep my mouth shut as I sat across from her, confused and scared that this was part of "the talk" that one gives when ending a relationship.

When I had first arrived the smell of the delicious food and coffee greeted me when I was approaching on the street, along with the scent trail of Lex who had arrived some time earlier than I had.

And when I first entered and made it to the booth where she was sitting, her emotive odor was filled with a deep love for me that was far more powerful than the scrumptious food in the place.

That meant little, of course, because for years I'd been able to pick up Gail's underlying love and passion for me—but that had never led to anything. Would I be taking that same path with this incredible woman?

Lex was also, of course, giving off the emotions of anger, confusion, and, more than anything else, fear. Was she afraid of me?

"Please," was the first thing she'd said to me when I sat down. "Let's just sit here and not say anything. At least not until I know your abilities have, you know, faded."

I had nodded wordlessly, and we'd looked at one another in silence, both of our eyes brimming with tears as we stared across the table at each other. We spoke only to our server, requesting coffee and food from their breakfast menu.

After an excruciating five minutes, shortly after our server had arrived with our food, I had nodded again, indicating to her I could no longer hear her heartbeat, scent her emotions.

That's when she'd begun. First with an apology for leaving without a note. And explaining that when she'd decided, she realized Gail and I would be back soon and didn't have time for it.

I silently nodded again, letting her know I wouldn't interrupt and would let her finish.

"Thank you," she said.

"I came to New York so we could be together. So we could build a new life together. Together, Michael. Not apart. When we were together in Los Angeles, it was just the two of us. And it worked. Things clicked. From the afternoon we'd first met sitting beside one another at that bar, everything fell into place so beautifully.

"And beyond that we had this compatibility related to our...underlying natures...or super-natures, if you will. As we were getting to know one another, opening up, sharing things we'd never shared with anyone else, I realized you had a way of completing me in ways I never imagined would be possible. And I know you feel the same way about me.

"But when we got here, I realized I hadn't considered the life you already had in New York. The relationships. And not just what you and Gail have had as confusingly intimate friends, but all of your relations. With Mack, with Anne, heck with the front door personnel at The Algonquin. Even with this traveling salesman mentor you regularly talk about—Buddy—who I haven't yet had the pleasure of meeting.

"You have an entire life that I haven't yet experienced here in the city. That alone was a bit of an adjustment for me. Because in LA it was just us. There was no other 'life of Michael Andrews' getting in the way.

"So partially, that has been difficult for me. But at least we had something between us, something special, something unique. A bond, a trust, a two-way clear, open, and consistent communication. Again, like nothing I'd ever experienced before."

Lex paused and picked up the napkin to dab at the single tear that ran down the left side of her face.

"When I found out you went to see Gail and didn't even mention it to me, that hurt as much as if you had physically assaulted me. And I'm still not over that.

"And, no, I get it. I'm not threatened by her. I actually like her, Kal. She's a good woman. A decent woman. It's easy to see how you fell in love with her and why you have kept her in your life as a friend. So, it's not jealousy or worry about any potential sexual transgressions between you and Gail.

"It's the emotional infidelity. That's what pains me the deepest. Do you get that?"

I nodded again, closing my eyes in an attempt to prevent the tears from flowing. But it was no use. My nose clogged up again, like it had earlier that morning when I had snotted all over Gail's blouse. I lifted my napkin to wipe my nose.

"I do, Lex. I get it. And I'm so sorry."

"I know you are. I'm still hurt, and not sure if I'll get over that. But I'm not angry about that. Not any longer."

"Lex, my love, I'm—"

"Don't. Stop telling me you're sorry. What hurts is that I know you will do it again. I know you, Michael. Oh, it pains me so much that I know this about you.

"It hurts, but the time I spent with Gail was helpful; it helped me to appreciate and understand how important a part of your life she is. How much you need one another. And I will not stand in the way of the special bond and friendship you have.

"So that's not why I left.

"I still love you, Kal. With all of my heart. With all of my soul. And I'm not going anywhere.

"But I can't be with you right now. And it has nothing—absolutely nothing to do with the pain I'm feeling. It has everything to do with what's going down, with the PFA, and what we need to sacrifice in order to fight them."

I felt an immense wave of relief that she wasn't dumping me. This was something we just needed to work out. Together.

"I was wrong," I said, "in thinking I could whisk you off to New York and we could leave the PFA behind. They're a virus that isn't going to just stay in one self-contained region."

"No," she agreed. "They're spreading. Or, more likely they started to spread a while ago. You read the *New York Times* cover story, right?"

"I did."

"They're here. They had to be here even before we returned. Perhaps they were always here. Marco never spoke about there being a faction of the group in New York. But I had overheard him a few times mention the PFA pocket in the east. I'd always assumed he meant the members in East Los Angeles or perhaps even the ones I'd heard about that were in Pomona."

"But Marco could be here now," I said. "Remember that guy in the jump suit and goalie mask I called Jason?

I saw and smelled him driving past in a car in Central Park.

"I do not know if Marco was with him or not, because when I encountered him, I didn't have my enhanced senses."

"He's here," Lex said. "Jason—his real name is Carl—must have become a member of Marco's inner circle after I left the group. He had to, for Marco to have put himself out to rescue him those two times back in LA. Marco would only do that for someone he is extremely tight with. If Carl is here, then Marco likely is, too."

"Do you think he's coming after you?"

"No," she said. "I mean, yes, he knows we're here. You're enough of a celebrity figure and where you live isn't a secret. So, I'm sure he knows. He likely suspected this is where we came. But nobody has attacked us. Not yet, at least.

"But with the way attacks, in general, have been increasing lately, I think it's Marco's way of relaying a message—a powerful and important message. That there's nowhere to run. No place to hide.

"I had some time to do some thinking about this, and I think I've figured it out. He can't attack me. Not directly. Not with magic. Remember all the times Carl wasn't able to hit me with that energy ball of his? They must have figured out that I do have some sort of power after all. My magic-nullifying ability.

"I still don't understand it, but the *luck* I have that prevents mishaps is intermittent. Yes, it has allowed me to skirt a few minor mishaps, and a few larger ones. But my power seems to have a consistent nullifying effect on supernatural powers. At least, that's the best I can figure it out."

"I know, right?" I said, with a wry grin on my face. "It's not like these things come with instruction manuals." I'd been about to share my frustration that I'd long wished there'd been some sort of *Werewolfs for Dummies* instruction manual for people like me, but the look on her face told me this was not the time, nor place, for my automatic humor coping mechanism to start up.

"Sorry," I said, lowering my head.

"Marco won't be able to attack me directly. But if he can incite violence throughout the entire city—an infestation of fear and hate, that we have seen can lead to mass riots and looting—there is a chance some of the cross-fire will end up harming me."

"You're saying that Marco is here to bring mass fear and violence to New York just to get back at you?"

"Oh," she said. "You have no idea how petty this man can be. I wouldn't doubt that. But with him, there's always something bigger. He never does something without having a larger plan or ulterior motive.

"Remember, when you fought with Carl that one night, he likely figured out that you have extraordinary strength. They wouldn't know about your wolf senses, but your super strength is likely enough for them to be cautious about attacking you. At least directly.

"But if they can inflame mass riots and looting, it's not just a violent mob they can blend into and hide within, but it'll also cause significant damage on its own.

"On more than one occasion Marco spoke about his desire to fuel and flame the kind of hatred that led to the 1992 Rodney King riots in LA. He used to cackle at the idea of kick-starting something like that. Only, he claimed, the riots he would inspire would be led by the superior race, not the inferior non-Aryans, as he put it.

"Look at the incidence of looting, of arson, of property damage, particularly against the black, Hispanic, Jewish, and Muslim communities. I think it's meant to draw all those groups out, to protest, but also, to inspire white people to react in kind. Look at the way white-supremacist groups have come out of the woodwork since last year's election. They used to cower and hide and pretend they believed in equality.

"But as a candidate running for the office of president of the US who was rising in popularity, his very rhetoric was empowering and enabling them. And when he got elected, that further emboldened them to show their true colors; it fueled their fear and hatred of *the other*.

"Marco is here to turn this city into a war zone. If LA burns, it's a spectacle for sure. But it's really just Tinseltown, a land of make-believe. But New York is the financial capital not just of the US, but of the world. It houses the United Nations. Remember what happened during 9/11 or the 2003 blackout when commerce seemed to just shut down?

216

"Imagine the 1992 LA riots magnified but happening in New York. Imagine the impact that could have. The perfect opportunity for a group like the PFA to gain even more power and strength."

She paused, taking a deep breath.

"As I said, I've been doing a *lot* of thinking about this." She looked down at her untouched plate of food.

"Wow, I haven't even started to eat."

I looked at my own untouched plate in front of me.

"I had the same reaction after reading the paper earlier," I said. "And it takes a lot to impede my appetite. Particularly after a night of howling at the moon."

"And that's just it. We stayed apart last night so you could do that. So that you could be the you that you need. The you that this city needs. Do you see why we need to be apart, Kal?"

"We make such a great team, Lex."

"We do. But we have to leverage our gifts, or curses, or whatever you want to call them, by staying away from one another. When I'm with you, you lose your abilities. And we can't afford that. Not right now."

I nodded. And, unlike the previous times, it wasn't a deferential action. It was filled with conviction. She was right. One hundred percent right. The only way we stood a chance of fighting what Marco and the PFA were up to would be if we maintained our distance.

"We need to separate, find out more about what they have planned, and reach back out to Hank in Los Angeles, anyone who understands the threat of the PFA, and see what they can do. You need to track down as many of these thugs as you can. Figure out where they're operating from locally. Relay that information to the authorities. And do whatever you can to physically stop them wherever and whenever possible."

My phone rang. It was lying face up on the table. I glanced over. It was Gail.

Lex nodded. "Pick it up. We'll need to discuss this with Gail, too."

I thumbed the button to answer and lifted the phone to the side of my head.

"Hello?"

"Don't say anything. Just listen. And get here *now*," Gail's voice was a whisper and coming through extremely faint, as if her mouth was far away from the phone's speaker. Her words also sounded as if she were speaking through clenched teeth—like was masking the fact she was speaking to someone that could see her.

"They're here. In my shop."

The line then disconnected.

Chapter Eighteen: You'll Need Your Seatbelt for This

I stared at my phone and then signalled our server for the check.

"What?" Lex asked. "What is it?"

"Gail said they're in her shop. She must mean members of the PFA. We need to get there now."

Lex shook her head.

"No," she said. "*You* need to get there now. I can't be with you, Kal. You need to be away from me for at least a few minutes so your senses and your strength can return."

Good point.

"Yeah, of course." I slid out of the booth and stood up. It would likely take about twenty minutes to get there from here, assuming I could get a cab or Uber immediately. "I need to get there now."

I pulled my wallet out to grab a few bills to cover the breakfast tab.

"Just go. I've got this," Lex said.

"She called me from her cell," I said. "Not sure if I should call back. It could alert them."

"I'll call her shop line. Go. I'll message you updates. And I'll follow, but from a distance."

I rushed out of the diner and onto the street, flagging down a passing cab immediately.

By the time I jumped into the back seat of the cab, I received my first message from Lex.

On the line with her now.

I gave the driver the address for Gail's store in the East Village without looking up from my phone, telling him there'd be an extra twenty-dollar tip if he could get me there in fifteen minutes.

"Hang on," he said, hitting the gas to swerve around a parked car and blow a freshly red light on W 43rd Street. "You'd best put that seatbelt on." he needlessly offered as I was already scrambling to pull the belt across my lap and lock it in place.

Lex's next text came in.

She's not able to speak openly. She's pretending I'm a customer.

Keep her on the line, I texted back, *so we know she's okay.*

The cab blew through two more red lights as we raced down 9th Avenue. This guy was already making good time.

Did she say how many of them are in her store?

No.

It was another minute, which seemed like an hour, before Lex's next text came in.

She had to hang up. They wanted her help. I think she's in the store alone.

That's right. It was Thursday. One of her part-time associates wouldn't be scheduled to come in until mid-afternoon. Gail would have been working alone for the morning.

Leaving the diner. On my way. Will stay at least one block back.

As the combination of the cab driver's overpowering aftershave, underlying body odor and the garlic he'd had for last night's dinner slowly came to me in ever increasing waves, I knew my enhanced powers were returning.

I glanced at the time on my phone. It had been less than five minutes since I'd left Lex behind.

It made me wonder if we should make a point of properly measuring the time it takes for Lex's nullifying powers to wear off. As in how long it actually took. It seems to be somewhere in the realm of about five minutes; but if we planned on putting up a solid fight with the PFA, the actual timing would be important to know.

Similarly, measuring the proximity for her abilities to have their effect on me would be important. And not just for understanding her effect on me, of course, but as a way of leveraging her powers against the members of the PFA that had their own supernatural abilities.

After having no choice but to stop at four red lights in a row on the southward journey down 9th Avenue, the cabbie turned left on West 23rd.

Another text came in from Lex.

I called the shop back. No answer.

Damn. We were still at least ten more minutes away, assuming we didn't run into traffic delays.

I called Enchanting Magic. It rang five times before going to voice mail.

Same, I messaged back to Lex.

She'll be fine. Gail is a strong woman. She can handle herself.

I was in awe of just how much had changed from a couple of hours ago; at least within my perspective of what was happening.

I thought Lex had been ready to dump me. And not only was she still sticking it out with me, but she seemed to be a member of the Gail fan club. I reflected on how both Gail and Lex, who would be expected to hate one another and be at one another's throats, showed their admiration and respect for one another.

I marvelled at how I could be so lucky as to have two such amazing women in my life.

The cabbie blew a yellow light crossing 7th Avenue and then another fresh red light on 6th. The traffic crawled to a snail's pace through the intersections of 5th and then Broadway but picked up again after we passed Madison Square Park.

"C'mon, c'mon," I muttered.

An odor of indignation came from the driver.

"I'm doing the best I can," he grunted.

"I know. Thanks."

As the traffic opened a bit, he again stomped on the accelerator and the cab shot down E 23rd and turned south again on 2nd Avenue.

Another text from Lex appeared on my phone.

How close are you?

Maybe five minutes.

I was hopeful that we were making good time, but then I heard the urgent blare of horns, the harsh squeal of brakes and the unmistakable sound of metal crunching against metal.

It was an accident of at least two or more vehicles.

It was difficult to tell from what direction the sound had come, particularly with the way sounds echo down the canalled streets of the city. I was just hoping it wasn't on the road ahead of us.

Sure enough, after we crossed East 11th Street, we could see it up ahead at 3rd and East 10th. A cube van, a black airport limo, and a red hatchback were blocking off the entire intersection, looking almost like a small group of people huddling together to share a secret. The hatchback was resting on its side.

The traffic in front of us was stopped. We stopped behind them. The cars behind us blocked us in.

Dammit.

Ripping a pair of twenty-dollar bills from my wallet, I passed them to the driver. We were only a couple of blocks away now. I could quickly get there by running. "Well done," I said. "I'm going to go the rest of the way by foot."

I leapt out of the back of the cab and raced down the sidewalk.

Chapter Nineteen: Urine for Another Delay

As I was racing toward the accident on East 10th Street, I picked up the medley of powerful emotive scents of the people who had been involved in the accident and a few of the sidewalk bystanders.

Amidst the shock, bitter annoyance, and anger—likely from the delay this accident had caused—there was an overwhelmingly intense sense of panic accompanied by a frail female voice.

"Help me. Please."

It was coming from the red hatchback. One bystander, a man in a dark suit, was standing on the road in front of the windshield in front of the vehicle. "I've called 911," he was calling to her, "they'll be here soon to let you out."

As I was moving past, I heard the woman respond from inside the car. "I'm stuck. I can't breathe. Please."

That, combined with the smell of the gasoline leaking from the car gave me pause.

I likely knew less about the way vehicles worked than the average person. But if Hollywood films and television programs have taught me anything, it's that the combination of a hot engine, any sort of spark, and leaking gasoline is likely to lead to a fire.

Not the types of exaggerated explosions you see in those shows, of course, but at least a minor explosion and fire—and why would you want to even take the chance?

The woman's heartbeat was racing—naturally. But I could tell it was an elderly heart; matching the timbre of her voice, and it was getting progressively worse as the panic and shock in her was growing. Her breathing was also stifled. She wasn't choking but was short of breath.

"Please," she repeated.

I stopped.

Gail wasn't in any immediate danger that I was aware of. PFA guys were shopping at her store. As far as I knew, they weren't trashing the place or doing anything to threaten her. But this woman could likely use my help. Now.

Rushing over to the car, I placed my left hand on the shoulder of the guy in the suit who was still standing there just looking at the vehicle.

"Get everyone to stand back," I said to him. "There's gas leaking from this car. A spark could set this off. I'm going to get her out of there in case her car catches fire."

The suit nodded, instantly deferring to the perceived authority and that common fear of the exploding car likely instilled in any of us who have watched more than a handful of television dramas.

I turned back toward the car, put one hand on the edge of it where the roof met the passenger door. In a combination of pulling myself up and jumping, I got onto the top of the car. It was resting on the driver's side. The woman was still strapped into her seat at the bottom.

I tried to pull the passenger door open, but it was locked.

Damn.

The window was rolled all the way up. I considered smashing it so I could reach in and manually unlock it. But I was worried about the glass falling onto the woman.

The wail of a firetruck echoed from at least a few blocks away. Proper help was coming, but they were still a minute or two out.

"Don't worry," I called to her. "I'll get you out of there."

After a second, I moved over to the back door on the passenger side. The falling glass from there wouldn't land directly on her.

I quickly peeled my t-shirt off and wrapped it around my right hand and forearm. Then I slammed my arm against the window, smashing through it.

Using my t-shirt covered forearm, I cleared the shattered glass remains from the rest of the window. Then I eased myself inside the backseat area.

The woman's heartbeat was still racing. I couldn't smell fresh blood, but I could smell urine. But it wasn't human; it wasn't hers. It was far more concentrated. And it smelled like dog urine. There was a dog in the car somewhere. I could smell it as well, hear a second, even faster heartbeat and a low whine I hadn't noticed before.

"Are you hurt?" I asked.

"No."

"Can you wiggle your fingers and your toes?"

"Yes."

"You have a dog in the car with you, right?"

"Yes. Rufus. He's in his cage in the back. Is he okay?"

"He's fine," I said. "I'm going to get you both out. You first."

"Okay."

Her heartbeat was still racing but started to slow a little. My reassuring words were helping her realize she wasn't alone and this would work out.

"First," I said, "I'm going to undo your seat belt. Can you brace yourself, hold onto the steering wheel, so you don't fall?"

"Yes."

"Okay, here goes." I reached around the seat and depressed the button the release her belt, then slipped it off her. I then put out my right arm, bracing it against the dashboard. "Can you grab onto my arm and pull your feet out so you can twist around and stand?"

She wrapped her right arm around my outstretched one and pulled herself from lying on her side to a crouch.

"Good. We're almost there."

I stood up and offered her my hand.

"Okay, let's get you around this seat."

Fortunately, she was thin and limber and had no issues maneuvering. And though her heart was still racing, and she was giving off an air of shock and fear, the progress was helping to calm her, at least moderately.

"Okay. Good. We're almost there." My constant short and simple reassurances and explaining every single step were helping ease her anxiety. "I'm going to climb out and then pull you up."

I grabbed onto the edge of the window and the front passenger seat and pulled myself back up out of the car. I then twisted and looked back down into the car at her.

"Okay. Now your turn. I'm going to pull you up now."

She nodded.

"Step onto the side of the driver's seat with one foot."

She did so with her left foot.

"Now grab onto the passenger seat with one hand."

"Okay," she said, reaching her left hand around the back of the seat's headrest.

"Now reach up with your other hand and take mine."

She took my right hand. I reached down lower and grabbed her upper arm with my other hand.

"On the count of three I'll pull you up while you climb. Are you ready?"

"Yes."

"One, two, three." She lifted herself up, and I easily pulled her through the window. Once she was out and crouched on the outside of the car, I wriggled off the car and onto the pavement.

"Okay, let's get you down now. Sit on the car with your legs dangling over."

She did that.

I was right below her with both arms raised up.

"Put your hands on my arms and slide off."

She did so, and I easily caught her from her upper torso under her arms, and gentle lowered her to the pavement.

"There you go," I said. "Safe and sound."

She nodded, and then her legs gave out from beneath her. Fortunately, I still had my hands on her sides and caught her.

I shuffled with her away from the car, which was still leaking gas, and over to the sidewalk. Two women— what looked like a teenager and her mother, rushed over to meet us, took a hold of the older woman and helped me lower her to the sidewalk. She was in good and caring hands.

"I'm going to get Rufus now," I said, and then moved back to the car where I launched myself back up onto it.

As I was lowering myself back inside, I could hear the approaching firetruck. It sounded like it was less than a block away. They could probably get the dog, but I was already here.

In for a penny, in for a pound.

The dog, a small white Maltese, was in its cage in the storage area behind the back seat. Its whines turned to chippy angry barks as it realized I was approaching. It likely picked up part of my own canine scent.

The cage door was on the far side, so I simply grabbed the thin metal bars and bent them open enough to reach inside.

"Okay, Rufus, let's get you out of here."

The dog growled and then snapped at me as I reached for it.

I uttered a short sharp growl from the depths of my throat, establishing my dominance in no uncertain terms, and the dog immediately squirted a shot of urine as it cowered to the furthest corner of the cage,

Reaching in, I grabbed it and lifted it out of the cage, then stood. I then climbed out of the car with the dog in one hand and slid back to the pavement.

As I was walking over to the where the old woman was sitting on the sidewalk with the mother and daughter who were comforting her, the firetruck arrived, and I felt my phone vibrate in my pocket.

"Here he is," I said, handing the tiny dog to the old woman. "A little shaken, but safe and sound."

The second before the hand-off, Rufus appeared to have had a temporary relapse from our neutering session a few minutes earlier. He twisted in my hands, growling, and snapping at me. Apparently being close to his mommy either brought back a little courage, or he felt he at least needed to put on a bit of an act.

I issued a curt low growl that put a stop to that BS. Except the little Maltese also squeezed out a fresh stream of urine all over my hands and forearms, including the arm still wrapped in my t-shirt.

"Dammit, Rufus," I said, quickly handing the dog over to her.

"Oh, my Rufus," she said, exuding gratitude and un-adulterated love for the little animal. The animal's pure and utter compassion for the woman was perfectly mutual.

I backed away, wiping as much of the dog's urine from my left hand and forearm with my shirt, tossed the smelly damp shirt to the ground, then slipped through the crowd standing behind where the old woman sat on the sidewalk and lifted the phone up to see that Gail had texted me.

They just left.

I slipped the phone back into my pocket and started running east down East 10th Street toward Gail's store.

Chapter Twenty: Smell Ya Later

I raced down East 10th Street and then turned right at the next block, cutting diagonally across a space in the traffic on 1st Avenue.

I did my best to ignore the emotive reactions I could sense in several of the pedestrians and motorists witnessing a crazy shirtless man with an intense panic in his eyes, tearing down the street, dodging around cars.

Unfortunately, it hadn't been the first time I'd run through the streets less than fully clothed. At least this time I had a decent pair of jeans on and sneakers on my feet.

Turning left onto East 9th Street, I picked up my pace. Gail's shop was about halfway down the block. I was almost there.

As I got closer, I picked up Gail's scent from earlier on what had likely been her morning approach to the store. And even before I was right outside and stepping down to the front door, I could tell she was the only one inside *Enchanting Magic.* There were too many lingering odors of strangers on the street, none of them, except for Gail's familiar to me.

If I were to be able to track them, I needed to get inside and try to isolate their unique scents.

Gail met me at the door, a confused look on her face and in the emotion she gave off.

"What happened to you?" she asked.

"Accident. Where'd they go?"

"They left the shop and picked up a cab. It went straight through the lights across 1st Avenue."

I must have just missed them—not that I would have even noticed. Yellow cabs in this city were just as common as red traffic lights when you were in a hurry.

She grabbed me by the arm and pulled me into the shop. "C'mon, maybe you can isolate their scent. The one guy paid cash."

We went over to the cash register where she keyed in the password to open it. She pulled a handful of twenty-dollar bills and handed them to me.

I held the bills under my nose. They had, of course, picked up Gail's scent from her handling them. The stack of bills contained numerous faint scents from the dozens of people who had each handled one or more of them in the past few days. But there was one specific scent, one I can describe only as a heavy male odor, common to all of them. I fixated on it.

"What else did he touch or handle in here?"

She came around the cash desk and brought me to the wall across from it. She pointed at a ceramic black skull.

"The guy who handed me the money picked this up."

I lifted the skull closer to my nose and, among the scents of the people who had handled it, that same heavy male odor was on it.

I had enough of a bead on him.

I lifted a hand with my index finger raised up to Gail to show *one minute* and headed back to the front door, fixated on the scent trail this man had left behind. I followed it out through the front door and to the spot on the street where he had gotten into the cab.

The scent faded from there.

I turned to Gail who was standing in the entranceway to her shop. I walked back over to her.

"I could head down East 9th Street, see if I could pick up the scent, he might give off through the open cab window. But I'm likely too far behind to catch up."

She nodded.

"I do have his scent, though. It could be worth trying. Maybe I could track them back to where they're staying. But," I gestured to my bare chest, "do you have a shirt I could borrow?"

"Yeah," she said, moving back into the store. "You gonna tell me what happened? You smell like pee. Did you get into some sort of pissing match on the way over here?"

"Something like that."

I quickly briefed her on the details of the accident and the older lady and her dog and my Hollywood-inspired worry about the leaking gas catching fire while Gail handed me a pack of wet wipes from a drawer behind the cash desk that I used to wipe the urine from my arms and hands.

"You never could resist stopping to help someone in need," Gail said. "Something I have always admired about you."

I thought back to how, several years after we had broken up, Gail returned to my life out of the blue because she needed my help tracking down her fiancé who had been kidnapped. She'd known about my enhanced werewolf powers; and she'd also known about my Spider-Man inspired belief that *with great power comes great responsibility*.

"And I know that you and Lex have this thing where, when you're together, you don't have those special abilities and you can live a normal life.

"But I don't think that's something you're actually *able* to do, Andrews. At least not for long. If it wasn't this PFA business, it would have been something else that came up. I think you *need* to be a hero. You *need* to help people. You *need* to make a difference."

She walked over to a rack of t-shirts she had for sale in at the back of the shop and searched through them.

"Like I said, it's one of the things I most admire about you. But it's also something I hate about you too."

She made a tsk-tsk sound as she pulled a shirt off the rack.

"There isn't anything left in your size except for this lady's style." She handed it to me.

It was a bright yellow xx-large ladies v neck t-shirt with the words *Witches do it with incense* printed across it in bold red letters.

"Really?" I said. "You bought this to sell in your store. It's not even funny."

"We all have our off days."

"Well," I said, laughing as I slipped the t-shirt on over my head. "I have worn worse."

On more than one occasion over the years, I've had to hastily acquire discarded clothing when my hidden stash of clothes for post-wolf romps had gone missing. It wasn't like I'd had anyone around to meet me with perfectly fitting clothes like Gail had earlier that morning.

She didn't have to say anything as she looked at me. I could easily sense her mirth about how silly I looked.

"Go ahead, say it," I said, laughing.

That set her off. She couldn't contain her amusement any longer. "I don't need to." She laughed so hard she actually snorted.

We laughed like that for a moment before she said. "The scary thing is you *have* worn worse, haven't you?"

I nodded and that set us both off laughing again.

"Okay," I said, finally. "Let me see if I can track them."

"Be careful, Michael," Gail said, "I lo—" she stopped herself immediately, realizing what she'd been about to automatically say. But she didn't even have to do that. The warmth and love she felt for me washed over me in an overwhelming wave.

I had to stifle back the automatic three-word response that was on the tip of my tongue. Of course I still loved Gail. I don't think I ever wouldn't love her; and I would be lying to myself to pretend anything other than that.

I didn't say anything in response. I simply nodded and slipped out of the store and turned to walk west down East 9th Street, feeling like a jerk.

A shift in the wind from the east brought me Lex's scent. I turned and saw her standing across the street in front of a vintage 80s and 90s clothing store half a block away. I waved to her. She waved back.

I reached to my back pocket to lift out my phone and text her, only to see she had texted me a couple of minutes ago.

I'm here.

I hadn't heard the beep nor felt the vibration of her text coming in. I hadn't even attended to it or noticed, not even with my enhanced powers. That was odd.

Hi. I texted back. *They left already, but I picked up their scent. Going to try tracking them.*

Okay.

There was a pause before she texted again.

What are you wearing?

Gail will fill you in.

Be careful, Kal. I love you.

Love you too.

I waved at her again, wishing I could cross the street and walk over to her and hold her in my arms. But to preserve my tracking ability and the rest of my enhanced powers, I needed to keep my distance.

It felt so surreal that, within the space of less than a minute, the only two women I've ever truly loved both told me they loved me. And I couldn't respond with what came natural with either of them.

My love life never had been all that easy. Heck, it had been pretty much non-existent for most of my life.

But this recent complication? This was just ridiculous.

I turned, pocketing my phone again, and then started walking down East 9th Street. Half a block away, I caught a pocket of that heavy male scent that must have drifted from the open cab window. Good.

I kept moving west and after I crossed 1st Avenue, I picked up another shifting pocket of his scent still lingering in the air.

This might just work.

I hastened my pace and moved at more of a jog as I followed the pockets of the man's scent along the same street for several more blocks.

There was a lingering scent of the man that led left on 4th Avenue, so I turned there.

I followed the scent up 4th Avenue as the road snaked off to the left, away from the previous square grid pattern the way some streets in Manhattan meander off. Fortunately, there were enough remnants of his smell to pick up as I moved.

The trail took me up 4th to where, at Union Square Park it became Park Avenue South, and continued to head north.

I kept moving north for several more blocks before, at the intersection of Park Avenue South and East 20th Street I picked up a different quite familiar scent that was fresh.

This scent turned my blood cold, because I knew it well. I had, in fact, tracked this very scent in this neighborhood just yesterday.

Knell.

And the odor I picked up wasn't from yesterday. It was fresh. Powerful.

He had just been here.

I stood on the corner, looking straight ahead up Park Avenue South where the PFA guy's scent led, and to my right down East 20th where Knell's fresh scent told me he'd been walking down on foot.

Should I keep heading north, or go after Knell?

As if I didn't have enough emotional strings pulling me in different directions.

Chapter Twenty-One: Alas, We Meet Again for The First Time

I decided to follow Knell's scent for several reasons.

First, the trail for Knell was a lot fresher, so it would be easier to track him down.

Second, based on what I knew about him, the people of this city were at far more immediate risk of being harmed or killed by him.

Third, he was only one guy. Stopping him would be easier than putting a stop to an entire gang. That would, I suspected, likely be a longer-term thing. If I could catch up with Knell, somehow capture him, I could at least make a quick positive difference.

And, okay, admittedly, fourth, I was intensely curious to figure out how the heck he had come back from the dead.

Because, like yesterday, this smelled like Knell, but it was mingled with a different body odor. One I could only presume, based on Gail's explanation, was a side-effect of the means of his resurrection.

I walked along East 20th Street following Knell's powerful and fresh scent, trying to anticipate what I might do when I reached him.

Yesterday he'd been in a cab heading to this area. Today he was walking here. I wondered if he perhaps lived in the neighborhood. That made sense.

As I walked, I had a vague and odd sensation that I had recently smelled him up close. Sure, I had picked up his scent yesterday when he'd been passing in that cab, and then I'd chased him on foot not all that far from here.

But a tingling memory, almost like déjà vu, suggested I had experienced this scent from even more recently—between yesterday afternoon and now.

And *that* scent had smelled more like the Knell I remembered from a few years back; not as tinged with this less familiar odor I was picking up off the fresh scent I was currently tracking.

I shook my head. I couldn't be bothered with that now. I had to keep moving forward.

Knell's scent led me right on Irving Place. I followed it down one block where it led into a building on the corner of East 19th Street.

Maybe he lived here.

There was a doorman standing at the front. He was looking over at me, grinning, and an emotion I knew well came off him. It was recognition; he knew exactly who I was.

"Hey there," I said, walking up to him with a big smile on my face.

"Mr. Andrews," the doorman said, sticking out his hand. He looked at the shirt I was wearing, and an air of confusion briefly came over him. But his excitement at meeting me was a more powerful emotion. "It's a real honor. I've read all your books."

"Thank you," I said.

"Even the short story collection."

"Thanks, my friend. Uh, I didn't catch your name."

"Gary."

"Thank you, Gary. I'm delighted to hear you've enjoyed my books. Even my, er, story collection. Not many people liked that one."

I laughed, knowing full well how the collection of short stories, *Silent Screams*, was the least-best-selling of all my books, by far. It had been panned by critics and book reviewers, and since its launch, I had repeatedly been told that the only redeeming part of the book was the one Maxwell Bronte story that appeared in it.

Gary laughed as well.

"Well, I enjoyed it, Mr. Andrews."

"Oh, please, Gary, call me Michael."

"Okay. Darn, I wish I had my copy with me so I could get you to sign it." His heart was racing. He was both star struck and intensely pleased that I was speaking with him.

"Tell you what, my friend," I said. "I'm happy to swing by again so I can sign it for you."

"Sure," he said. "That would be great."

We stood smiling at one another a moment, Gary's heart racing even faster.

"So," he said. "What brings you to 81 Irving Place, Mr. Andrews? Are you visiting someone?"

"Seriously, call me Michael."

"Okay," he grinned, "what brings you here today, Michael?"

"Funny you should mention it. That man who just recently went in a few minutes ago. He's also a big fan of mine. He just left an event I was at. Er, that's why I'm wearing this silly thing. Long story.

"Anyway, I just met him. I don't even know his name, but a mutual friend told me he left because he was too shy to approach me. I wanted to surprise him."

"Oh yes, that's Mr. Herschell. You're right, he is rather shy."

That didn't sound like the Knell I knew, but, then again, if he was living under an assumed identity in hiding, maybe it was part of his persona.

"Is there any way I might be able to pop up to his apartment and surprise him?"

I could immediately tell, from the scent I was reading from him, that Gary was going to let me do just that. There wasn't even the slightest suspicion coming off him.

I wasn't fond of manipulating people, but had, over the years, become used to being able to read people, understand what I might get away with, and leveraging that to my advantage.

"That sounds delightful," Gary said. "I'm sure he'd love that. C'mon."

He led me inside. Knell's scent was stronger inside with no wind movement to dispel it. Gary introduced me to Brian, the elevator operator.

"Brian," he said. "This is Michael Andrews. The Michael Andrews, the author of the Maxwell Bronte novels."

"Hi Brian," I said.

Brian wordlessly nodded, avoiding making eye contact with me. He had no idea who I was when Gary had first said my name, but he was familiar with the Maxwell Bronte movies.

"He's heading up to visit Mr. Herschell in unit 11D."

Brian nodded again, gesturing for me to enter the elevator.

I stepped inside. Knell's scent was strong inside the elevator, having just taken this ride a few minutes earlier.

"Good luck, Mr. Andrews." Gary said. "I'm sure he'll be delighted to see you."

"Thanks, Gary. And please, it's Michael. We're practically old friends."

"Good luck, Michael," he beamed a huge grin and then head back to the front door.

"So, Brian, how long have you worked here?" I asked.

"Long time," he said. It's not that he was uncomfortable. He just didn't enjoy small talk. My awkwardness made me want to double down on being friendly.

"Beautiful day today, isn't it?" I asked.

He nodded.

"Cooler than yesterday."

Another nod.

"I think they're calling for rain overnight," I said.

He nodded again, remaining consistent in his conversational acumen all the way up to the 11th floor despite me trying, awkwardly, to make small talk.

His emotions were subdued and suggested to me he did not engage in idle chatter. I forced myself to keep my yap shut for the remainder of the ride.

Brian let me off on the 11th floor and I didn't even say goodbye verbally. I merely nodded politely back at him as the elevator doors closed.

I then moved down the hallway to unit D following Knell's scent.

I considered how I was going to do this. Grinning and saying something like "Hey there, buddy! Remember me?" was the best I could come up with.

But before I could knock a shrill voice came from inside the door.

"Why are you stalking me?"

Chapter Twenty-Two: Where Wolf? There. There, Wolf! Aware Wolf.

I t wasn't Knell's voice on the other side of the door. It wasn't even close, despite the odor I was pulling off of him. This voice had a strong Yiddish sounding twinge to it. And though the voice was high pitched, the man had been speaking in a normal tone, as if he knew I could hear him perfectly.

"What?"

"You're stalking me. Why?"

There was more silence. I could hear his heart racing. He was filled with fear.

"I thought we had come to an understanding last night."

"What?" I repeated.

The door opened. On the other side stood a tall skinny middle-aged man I placed in his late forties, maybe early fifties tops with an upside down triangular shaped head, gray hair, big round spectacles, and large loopy ears that stuck far out from his head. He could have played George Burns in a biography of that famous comedian's later life.

But he still gave off that familiar scent of Knell. Or at least, the altered version of Knell I had smelled and then tracked yesterday.

So, while this was definitely the guy I'd thought was Knell based on his scent, he was not the shock rock star I had encountered on the set of the David Letterman show a few years ago.

"Come inside," he said, then paused, giving off an air of submission that, like earlier seemed strangely familiar, then continued. "I'm sorry. I didn't mean to be so confrontational. Please, if you prefer, would you like to come inside?"

I stepped inside, noticing how the man avoided making eye contact with me, keeping his head pointed toward the floor.

"No," I said. "I'm sorry. I thought you were someone else. I...you smelled like someone I knew. Or thought I did. Who *are* you?"

"I'm Irwin Herschell," he said.

I reached out my hand. Irwin was confused.

"I'm Michael," I said. "Michael Andrews."

He took my hand and shook it. I could tell that, like me, he was strong with superhuman strength and could likely crush my hand if he wanted. But he kept his grip loose and soft. Wow, here I had thought, all this time, that I was a major push-over and beta human. It looked like I was wrong.

"You have me at a bit of a loss, Mr. Herschell," I said, doing my best to reduce my dominant position in our awkward encounter to help put him at ease. "I'm a little confused. You smell almost exactly like someone I knew. I'm not sure how that is. And, except for that chase yesterday afternoon, I don't think you and I have ever met."

Irwin stepped around me to close the door, then gestured for me to step into the living room.

"Please," he said, pointing at the sofa. "Have a seat."

I stepped into the living room and took a spot on the edge of the sofa.

"You're like me," he said, remaining standing. "I can smell the wolf in you."

"Yes," I replied.

"But you don't remember last night?"

"No." I was confused and worried. Yesterday I had seen him change from human to wolf in broad daylight. He had full control over his change, just like Knell. This suggested that, also like Knell, he retained his human consciousness when in wolf form. And I could tell he smelled my unease. "I can't control my change. I never could. It comes over me when the sun goes down on the night of a full moon. I also have no awareness of my time as a wolf. Except perhaps for the occasionally flash of memory.

"Did we meet as wolves last night?"

"Yes," he said. "I realized, then, that you couldn't control the change. Or at least, that's what I suspected was the case. But I did not know that you also weren't aware.

"You see, I've already shared my story with you when you were in wolf form. But you obviously don't remember."

Irwin paused and turned to the bar set into the wall behind him. "I'm sorry, this is confusing. Frightening for me too. I don't understand what's happening. I'm going to need a drink. Can I pour you one?"

"Sure," I said, and watched him pour an inch of bourbon into a pair of crystal tumblers.

He walked over to the chair across from the sofa, handed me a glass and then sat down.

"L'Chaim," he said, raising his glass up.

"Cheers," I replied.

We both took a drink.

It burned my throat, but the shock and harshness of it felt good. It matched, perhaps, the shock of just how different this encounter had turned out compared to what I had been expecting.

"So, what happened last night?" I asked. "I can't remember."

He took another drink and then set it down before filling me in on the details of how we had encountered one another the previous night in Central Park in the field between Bethesda Terrace and Cherry Hill. How I had chased and cornered him and then he'd expressed complete submission. That he'd then morphed back to human form, fully expecting me to do the same, but I hadn't.

As he was sharing his story, I had a few brief flashes of memory from the night before. *Tearing across an open field while following the scent of the other wolf, enraged and ready to fight for territorial dominance.* The only other sensation that came to me was the *scent of fear and supplication from a human that smelled like an enemy wolf.* As much as I concentrated that was all I had.

"Since you weren't speaking, but were sitting there listening, I told you about me and asked for your help."

"My help?"

"As a wolf you are dominant, alpha. Pack leader. And though your actions and speech attempt to portray otherwise, you give off that same odor when in human form.

"You don't see that, do you?"

I shook my head.

"When I scented that dominance, I figured you knew more about this affliction we have. That you knew things. That you could help me. But after I told you my story, you raced off to go hunt. I didn't follow you. I thought you had abandoned me; rejected me as part of your pack.

"At least, I had told myself, you showed me mercy. At least you wouldn't attack me. Which was why I was surprised you tracked me down and showed up here, today."

I lifted the glass of bourbon to my lips and took a tiny sip.

"I tracked you down because your scent is so strikingly similar to someone else; someone I encountered who was like us. Only this guy was a raging psychopath. A killer. I thought you were him and had somehow come back from the dead.

"Are you, by chance, a close blood relative of Harold Neilson, the shock rock star known as Knell?"

Irwin gave off an air of confusion. "The musician who died here a few summers back after jumping off that building during the taping of the Letterman Show?" He shook his head. "No." He was being completely honest.

"But that was the same summer this had first happened to me. September 2014. I remember it like it was only yesterday.

"Oh yes, I remember it so clearly. Sunday September 14th. It was a clear night. I normally don't go out after ten at night, but it was such a beautiful night, and I'd been feeling stir crazy ever since the sun went down.

"That restless energy had been building all week. I could feel it, and it was particularly strong after dark.

"I hadn't realized, at the time, how it was connected to being bit by a wolf the month before. I should go back to that first."

He paused and took another sip of his bourbon.

"About a month earlier I had been bitten by what I thought was a wild dog. I didn't know much about dogs, so thought it had been a German Shepherd or a Husky or something. I only realized later, after reading in the newspaper that there had been a wolf attack where a pack of wolves had killed a man that I put it all together.

"But this wolf I had thought was a dog had lunged at me as if out of thin air when I was taking an early morning walk doing my daily laps around the path at Sara D. Roosevelt Park. It sunk its teeth into my left arm, but then a car on the adjacent street had backfired and it had bolted.

"Like I said, I thought it had been a wild dog. It shot off down the street and there didn't seem to be an owner anywhere nearby. So I went to the closest emergency room to have the wound dressed and to get a rabies shot.

"The bite healed and perhaps a week after I developed a fever. I thought I'd picked up a flu bug. It took me out for a couple of days. But as I recovered from the high fever, the chills, the sweats, I felt stronger and more youthful than I had in years.

"But that energy, youthfulness, strength, it came with a restless feeling. Instead of just going on walks in the morning, like I'd been doing for nearly two decades, I started going for runs. It felt like I'd needed to burn off that energy somehow.

"And, though I hadn't run like that since my high school years, I was surprised to find I wasn't at all out of breath. But the runs weren't enough, and every night the sensation of wanting to run, just tear free and run full out, hit me.

"And the night of September 14th, on a bright and clear night where the nearly full moon seemed to call me out, I left here and started walking north on 5th Avenue to get to Central Park. I sensed, somehow, that I needed to find some green space, large rolling hills, trees, a natural area. I walked more and more quickly feeling the moon almost calling to me, the desire to get to the park quickly, and then, after a few blocks I burst into a full-out run.

"I just kept heading north, ignoring traffic lights, but able to dodge and jump over cars in what became a relentless compulsion to get to the park so that I could properly ease the burning restlessness I was feeling in my very bones.

"When I finally made it to the park, I took the path around the pond near West 59th Street and then pushed into the wooded area of the sanctuary near that larger body of water.

"And that's when I took my clothes off, because I knew I needed to be free of them, crouched down on the bare earth, and looked up, through a break in the trees, at the moon and sobbed, asking what was happening to me.

"Then it came. It was like the release you feel after holding a bowel movement in. That's the best way I can describe it. But, looking up at the moon, I let the change come over me.

"One moment I was a man, crouched in the woods, staring up at the moon and whimpering, and the next, I was a wolf, baying at that same moon. Except, of course, it wasn't just a moon when I looked at it in wolf form. It was a powerful beacon that I felt connected with.

"It felt natural, normal. Like no other type of release I had ever experienced. I tore and raced through the park, delighted with the new sensations, the heightened senses I had experienced.

"Then I came up your markings. I knew, instantly, this was your park; that you had marked it as yours. I wasn't sure if you'd been the wolf that had at-tacked me, but I was instantly fearful of you. My instinct told me to back off, that I couldn't roam here.

"I rushed back to where I had taken off my clothes and then concentrated on returning to human form. I then got dressed and hastily left the park. I went to the subway and took the connections to get to the area I had grown up in. Brooklyn. I went to Prospect Park, switched back to wolf form and checked to see if there were any territorial markings.

"It was clear. No other wolf had claimed it. So I spent the rest of the night marking the boundaries of the park as mine and that's where I returned, regularly, to allevi-ate myself of the restlessness to be in wolf form."

"Wow," I said. "Where to begin?
"I think, for starters, I understand why you smell like Knell; or at least, so similar to Knell. He must have been the wolf that attacked you in August 2014. You're actu-ally his wolf kin. That's why I thought you were him. The wolf part of your scent reeks of him."

Irwin was incredulous. "Knell was a wolf?"

"Yes. And very much like you. He could control the change between human and wolf. And he also kept his human consciousness and memory when in wolf form."

I then explained how I had encountered Knell as a wolf, then our later encounter on the set of Letterman. How he had grabbed Gail and threatened her from off stage, the ensuing fight and struggle that led to him plummeting to his death.

"But that's the only way I can explain why your scent is so similar to his," I said. "He infected you and it's his wolf blood coursing through your veins that I was smelling.

"What I don't understand is why you're normal."

"What do you mean?"

"Knell was a sociopathic killer. I had always assumed that what made him lose his mind was being consciously aware of the change."

I explained to Irwin how, not only did I have no control over the change—that I was powerless to prevent the changes that happened when the moon was at least three quarters full—but that the changes I underwent were excruciatingly painful. That the trusted friends who had seen me transform had described it as a painful, childbirth like type of traumatic experience. And that I had always assumed it had been the conscious memory and awareness of that transmogrification that had snapped Knell's mind.

"But you," I said. "You're normal. Compassionate. Empathetic."

"The only thing I can suspect is at play is that, though we might both have werewolf blood running through our veins, we each have different strains.

"I work in the pharmaceutical industry, and I know that sometimes one person's biochemistry has a different reaction to a drug than someone else's. It's why, for example, a vaccine that is effective in most people may incite adverse reactions in a small percentage of the population.

"But it's not like there are clinical trials happening with our kind."

"I know, right?" I grinned, and paused for one beat, about to share the quip about my frustration over there being no sort of *Werewolves for Dummies* book for us—it hadn't gone over well with Lex earlier—but he replied immediately, annoying me that I didn't get the chance to try that joke out again. There were, after all, so few people I could use it with.

"I'm sure that, like me, you're afraid of being found out. Terrified of what they might do to people like us if they ever had the chance to lock us in a lab and study us."

"My people have been through enough, and I don't fancy my life being turned into a scientific experiment.

"My parents," Irwin said, turning his head to look over at a picture of an elderly couple on the wall shelves to his left, "were Holocaust survivors. Not a day goes by that I'm not thankful for the time and place where I grew up. So, I'm fine with never having to deal with that, thank you very much."

I nodded. "I'm with you," I said. My chagrin at missing the chance to share what I thought was a pretty good one-liner instantly fled. "I'm happy to keep our little secret as secret as possible."

Irwin stood up, reaching for my glass. "At that thought. I'm going to get myself a refill. Can I top up your drink?"

"No, I'm good." I said, watching him walk back over to the bar. "Listen, there's one thing I'm not sure I understand."

"What's that?"

"You said, after detecting that I'd marked Central Park as my territory you immediately left and never came back. That you christened Prospect Park as your place. And that's where, for all these years, you allowed your wolf self to roam and run free."

"That's right."

"So why did you return to Central Park last night?"

"Because," Irwin said, and the fear coming off him instantly filled the room, "of our common enemy. The one that is turning New York into Fear City."

Chapter Twenty-Three: And Then There Were Three

"That now makes three. We have a third supernatural being on our side," Gail said.

I was back at her shop, this time with Irwin, and we had just explained leaving the trail of the PFA members in order to follow the Knell scent, and how that led me to meeting Irwin Herschell.

We discussed how Irwin's ability to turn into a wolf at will, even during the daylight hours, brought a unique new possibility to our team.

Not that I was really sure, at this point, what we could even do. We first had to find them. But now there were four of us, not three of us. That was, at least, a start.

Gail led Irwin to the ceramic skull and brought out the bills for him to smell so he could identify the same man I had been tracking earlier. With two of us able to leverage that ability, we had doubled the possibility of finding them.

But, again, we are talking about two of us in a city of millions of people. Heck, Irwin and I had co-existed in this city for years without crossing paths.

"We'll have to keep Irwin and Lex separated as well," Gail said. I'd filled Irwin in on Gail and Lex before I had brought him to Gail's shop. Lex had left when I texted to say I was returning. Gail had given her the key to her place, where she would be staying. Gail also closed her store to the public so that Irwin and I could catch her up without the risk of being overheard. "But we need to figure out a way to leverage Lex's ability to diffuse the powers of Marco and any others that have enhanced magic abilities while allowing you and Irwin to overpower them."

I loved watching Gail ruminate on an issue; she was one of the best creative problem solvers I'd known. She could be intensely passionate in the moment but had an ability to chew on and ponder things in the back of her mind while going about other business or even engaging in other conversations.

I knew she was still doing that when she then shared what she had determined the PFA guys had been up to when making a purchase at her shop.

"I get the feeling they're planning on engaging in some sort of specific ritual," Gail said.

"They bought up every single black candle I owned as well as every piece of aggregate heliotrope, amazonite, black tourmaline, and labradorite. They also bought several rune stone sets, but only the ones made of actual bone. Speaking of bone, they also purchased every last item made of bone—including animal and human."

"You sell human bones in here?" Irwin asked. "Isn't that illegal?"

Gail shook her head. "No. New York does have particular import and export laws. And there is a federal law preventing the sale or trade of Native American remains. But several of my suppliers have a variety of bone products. Most of the bones are animal bones, skulls. But I have had requests for human bones from some customers over the years, so usually carry a few items."

"I had no idea."

"Bones, fangs, teeth, claws, feathers, and even shells are used for adornment and in different rituals. They can use skulls as a holding vessel, like a bowl, for mixing and blending.

"But I haven't been able to figure out what they would use those items for. The heliotrope, for example, also commonly referred to as bloodstone, is linked to courage, creative energy. It's meant to bring vitality, endurance, physical strength, to protect, even to prevent bleeding and protect the wearer from the effects of poisonous bites."

I remembered some of the research I had done which was led me to meeting Gail all those years ago. Christian traditions state the red spots on the dark green stone came from the blood of Christ, when, during his crucifixion, he was stabbed by a Roman solider. Ancient Romans would wear the stone to prevent bleeding.

"All I remember about bloodstones is that they're used to protect and to heal," I said.

Gail nodded. "That's right. But when used in a particular way, under the proper conditions, almost any artefact can be turned to be used for the opposite."

"Do you mean," Irwin asked, "instead of being used to stop bleeding, it's used to cause bleeding?"

"Yes. Or, instead of being used to inspire courage, it can instill fear."

"It's what they seem to be all about, isn't it?" I said. "Fear, hate, anger."

"Hatred, fear, and lies," Irwin said. "That PFA symbol has generated the same feelings in my people as the Nazi symbol has.

"*The Jewish Press* shared that they defaced more than four hundred synagogues in a single night with the PFA swastika along with the words 'die Jews' or similar wording, to make it perfectly clear what the intent of the graffiti should be.

"Over four hundred buildings across the city defaced overnight. There's no way the PFA itself has that many members. They are inciting and inspiring, manufacturing this behavior of hate."

"They are definitely good at doing that," I said. "And it's spreading like an unstoppable virus."

"That's exactly what it is," Irwin said. "Hate is the most insidious virus."

We were all quiet for a moment, reflecting, when Irwin spoke up again, addressing Gail.

"You mentioned how it's possible to take a gem or stone whose meaning is positivity and modify it in a way where the effect is the opposite."

"Yes, much of black magic applies such alterations to white magic. They derive spells of destruction from an alteration on spells of prosperity, healing, and protection."

"Altering their meaning and use," Irwin responded. "The swastika, which was originally used to denote goodness, prosperity, luck, and divinity by numerous cultures, got appropriated for Nazi symbolism by being rotated forty-five degrees, and it took on another meaning.

"But prior to that, in Hinduism, the right-facing swastika represented the sun, prosperity, goodness, and well-being. And, when altered so that it was left facing, called a *sauwastika*, it represented night, darkness, and Kali, the Hindu goddess of death, time, destruction, and power.

"Symbolism is important. Critical to a movement. History is rife with symbolism. Is that not what the runes are all about?"

"Exactly," Gail said. "People cling to symbols, find strength, commonality, a sense of belonging, or purpose and power. It seems like we need them. They can be used to motivate people."

"For goodness or for evil," Irwin said.

"Yes." Gail was quiet as she descended into the canals of deep thought. I was familiar with the odor coming off her and knew not to interrupt the thought process she had launched into.

I looked over at Irwin and could tell, both from the look on his face, and his own scent, that he was also picking up on the same thing I'd determined.

We stood quietly looking at one another for at least a full minute before Gail spoke up again.

"Okay," she said, and there was a long pause while she took a deep breath. "I have some research to do, some people to call. I need to be alone for this."

I nodded. "Understood."

Gail had work and research to do; I was filled with a restless energy and anxiety that I knew would only be satisfied by taking action, even if it was a futile one.

"I'm going to go wander," I said. "Explore, scout. See if I can pick up on any of the familiar scents I know. I can't think of what else I can do. I'm going to return to that spot on Park Avenue where I'd tracked them to. The trail scent will have long faded by now. But who knows? Maybe I'll pick something up."

Irwin nodded. "I'll do the same. If we split up, take different areas, we can cover more ground."

We quickly exchanged cell phone numbers and agreed upon an east/west division, using Broadway as the dividing line, then left the shop.

On our way out, I paused as I was stepping out the door and looked back at Gail. She had pulled down a small pile of half a dozen of the many books on the occult and black magic from the reference materials she kept behind the cash desk and had her laptop open as she was scanning something on the screen in front of her.

"Gail," I said. She was so focused on her research that she didn't hear me. The scent coming off her was infused with determination and concentration.

"Gail," I said in a louder voice.

She looked up, a sliver of annoyance crossing her face as the accompanying smell came to me. *"What?"* Might as well have been written in bold letters across her face.

"Do you want to lock the door behind me?"

She nodded, turning her head back to the computer screen. "No. I'll get it. Just go." She then fell right back into whatever it was she was looking up.

I closed the door and watched her for a moment through the glass.

It wasn't lost on me that this woman, who had absolutely no paranormal powers or abilities had found herself in the middle of what should have been an impossible to believe scenario.

She had teamed up with two werewolves—one that had full control over the changes and could transition at any time; the other who was prey to shifts between sunrise and moonrise—and a very powerful being whose supernatural powers were the nullification of magic itself in her presence.

With no powers herself, other than her deep knowledge of this realm, she'd found herself partnered to take on a malicious evil that combined the dark arts, black magic, plus an odd combination of fringe and border science linked back to Occultism from the Third Reich. All being shepherded by a modern neo-Nazi cult that sought not only to purify and white-wash America, but to create a new race of super-soldier paranormally enhanced humans.

Sure, she had studied, and then later curated supplies and materials associated with magic, the occult, and the paranormal. But it was one thing to study and read and learn about this realm; and quite another to be thrust into the middle of it.

And yet, at no point in the discussions she'd been involved in had I detected any sign of her experiencing fear for her personal safety.

Sure, there were threads of anxiety and concern emanating from her. But not a single scent or heart-beat indication that she was afraid of what she was getting herself into.

The only consistent essence radiating from her was that same determination and commitment I'd just seen on display as she was doing her research.

I reflected on how impressed I'd been when I'd first met her; how struck I'd been at the power and strength radiating off her. And fascinated with her innate sense of intuition in almost any setting.

No wonder I'd been some immediately taken and smitten with her. And not at all a surprising at how much I adored, respected, and admired her. Her strength, her passion, her integrity, it all inspired me beyond words.

"Oh Gail," I sighed quietly under my breath.

She looked up, as if sensing she was being watched, and the intense conviction I was feeling, and made eye contact.

Like so many times before, as her eyes met mine, they locked me in place, and I fell right into them. She knew, somehow, exactly what I was thinking.

"I know you don't see it in yourself," she said, and I could easily hear her quiet words, "but I see those same things in you."

She then turned her attention back to the computer screen, freeing the lock she'd held over me.

I turned and then began what I knew would be a very slow and methodical search for the proverbial needle in a haystack.

Hours later, exhausted from a long afternoon of scouting through the Rose Hill and East Midtown area of the city where I'd slowly made my way in a crisscross pattern of the city, I made my way back to the Algonquin.

I hadn't picked up a single trace of the scent I'd been tracking. I had, though, encountered many displays of the previous night's vandalism, graffiti, and the destruction of property.

And I had also picked up countless snippets of conversation in passing from people talking about the atrocities they had either witnessed or been told second-hand by a friend or family member.

Bad stuff was going down after dark in the city. It made me think about the *Fear City* pamphlets re-printed in the newspaper.

And here I was, completely useless to do anything about it, because, after dark, I was a wolf; with no conscious awareness of the evil plaguing the city. I was useless, at least during the nights, until July 14th, a full week from today.

Irwin would be able to, during this week, go out prowling and helping to put a stop to some of the attacks. Perhaps Lex's presence could reduce the impact of any paranormal assaults. But I was useless in assisting. And most of the attacks took place after dark.

As I approached the front entrance of the Algonquin, I was startled to detect two very familiar scents that I hadn't expected.

Bruce, the evening doorman, greeted me.

"Mr. Andrews," he said. "Welcome back. You have had two callers today. One of them is still here."

Chapter Twenty-Four: Being Pissed Off Never Felt Like This Before

I didn't need to ask Bruce who the two callers were. I could smell them.

My old traveling minstrel of a friend, Buddy J. Samuels had been here some time within the past several hours. "Your salesman friend, Mr. Samuels, stopped in to let you know he was staying at the Roosevelt."

I hadn't seen Buddy since nearly a month ago—that time in Los Angeles. His seemingly random appearances in my life had, more and more, come at the most fortuitous times. I would be curious to see him; because I had plenty of questions I needed to ask.

But the other familiar scent, far more recent, was immediately compelling and threw me for a bit of an emotional loop.

Lex was here. Recently. Her scent was extremely fresh.

"Lex," I said.

Bruce nodded. "Yes, Ms. Jones got here about ten minutes ago. She went straight up to your room."

It had only been perhaps six hours since I'd seen her down the street near Gail's shop, and not too much earlier than that, sat across from her at the diner; but I felt like it had been days since I'd seen her.

I didn't care that she would nullify my enhanced powers. I was exhausted, emotionally drained, and confused as hell for the strong feelings towards Gail that had been plaguing the back of my mind, making me feel guilty. I'd felt like I was being unfaithful to Lex, and I needed to make amends for that immediately.

I rushed through the lobby and to the elevator, huffing in her scent the entire way, anticipating the wondrous moment of pulling her into my arms and holding her tight.

All the rest of the side-effects be damned.

I needed to hold Lex, tell her I loved her, show her how much I loved her.

When I got to the apartment, I could hear her in the washroom, peeing. I was normally not one to intrude upon a person's privacy, even vocally, but I didn't care.

"Lex!" I called out in a loud voice. "Thank God you're here!"

"Kal!" she called out, her heartbeat racing, the anticipation and love strong in the air. "I'll be right out." I could hear her washing her hands and then she threw open the door.

I rushed over and pulled her into my arms.

"I can't do this!" I said. "I can't stay apart from you. I need you, Lex. I need to love you."

"We never go out of style," she whispered, then pressed her lips against mine and we melted into one another.

The intensity of the love and passion she felt for me enwrapped us as I led her to the bedroom. It took less than a minute for us to shed our clothes as we climbed up onto the bed.

By the time we finished, my enhanced senses and strength were gone. I basked in that feeling as we both lay entangled together, sweaty, and out of breath.

"You know I can't stay," she finally said. "I'd only come here to retrieve some of my clothing."

I nodded. "I know. I just needed this."

Lex reached over to the nightstand to pick up her phone. "It's 7:20. It's a little more than an hour before sunset. Gail said she was bringing some of the research material home with her so we could keep going through it tonight."

I looked over at her, impressed with how quickly she had adapted to both collaborating with my ex-lover and knowing the details of my moon-cycle schedule. She was strong, adaptable, committed, and passionate. I didn't deserve to be loved in such a way. Especially not after the emotions I'd been feeling towards Gail earlier that day.

She twisted out of my arms and slid off the side of the bed to her feet. "I should get going." She leaned in and kissed me gently on the lips before turning and retrieving her clothes from the floor.

I lay back on the bed, admiring just watching her; appreciating having her near and watching her go through the motions of something as mundane as dressing. But there was nothing mundane about this incredible woman. It seemed like her every movement, turn, and bend was part of some beautiful ballet. Yes, I know I have a tendency to idealize those I love, but I couldn't help the sheer pleasure of looking at her and the un-abashed joy it brought to me. It was still hard for me to believe that a mere few weeks ago I had not known her; she hadn't even been a part of my life. But now she was such an integral and critical component in it.

My emotions took a saddening dip to know that she was about to leave; that, in order for her and Gail and Irwin and I to fight the infestation of the Proud Fighters for America, Lex and I needed to keep our distance.

She got dressed, grabbed the bag she had filled with a few other personal items prior to me returning, and stood in the doorway to the bedroom.

"Maybe I can meet you at sunrise with a fresh change of clothes," she offered. "I'm sure it won't hurt for us to be together for a short time in the morning."

My heart lifted at that thought.

"I'd like that," I said. "That same spot, on the far side of the Bow Bridge."

"It's a date."

She blew me a kiss, and I listened to her leave.

I laid there, basking in the lovemaking's memory, of the feeling of holding her in my arms, and felt, almost in the way that you can feel the Novocaine wear off an hour or two after having dental work performed, the numbing of my senses returning to their full glory.

I picked up my phone. It was 7:32. It had taken less than five minutes for my powers to return. I wondered if we needed to fully and properly test a few things. The time required for her nullifying powers to take hold;

how long after she moved on that the lingering nullification would last. The distance or radius of her effect on supernatural abilities.

We'd need to know all this, wouldn't we, in order to properly leverage the extent of her power?

I rolled off the bed and pulled out a few of the cheaper throwaway clothes I kept for the nights of my change. Then I went into the washroom, to shower and shave.

When I stepped into the washroom, the overwhelming scent of urine in the toilet bowl struck me. Lex must not have flushed when I had returned.

I reached for the lever on the side of the toilet but then paused.

Something was off.

The ammonia-like scent should have been stronger as I'd leaned over the bowl to depress the lever. But, instead, it was fading.

I leaned back, away from the bowl, and stepped backwards out of the bathroom.

The powerful odor was stronger the further away I got from it.

I moved back inside, where the intensity of the urine odor was as strong as it had first been. But as I stepped closer to the toilet bowl to get my head back over it, the scent faded.

My hearing was fading too. As was my strength.

It was subtle, but it was there.

"Holy shit," I said. Of course, to be more accurate, I should have uttered *"Holy urine."* But that's not a thing. At least it wasn't a thing until now.

Lex's urine had the same nullifying effect as her physical presence. But unlike her physical presence, which took several minutes to impact me, the urine had an almost immediate effect.

I called Gail to tell her about this.

There should be a way we could use this.

Interlude—Wolf Night—Three

*S*omething was not right.
 It was a feeling; an overwhelming feeling that seemed to hang in the air.

At first the wolf thought it might be related to the other wolf it had recently encountered. And, as the feeling continued to grow, it stalked the fields, the forested areas, the rocky outcrops, but could not pick up any fresh scent of the other.

When the wolf reached a spot next to where the humans lived and moved about among their realm of artificial rock-like canyons a shift in the wind brought two things: A sudden and powerful odor of fear accompanied by a shrill scream of terror.

As the flash of emotion and the echo of the scream faded in the wind, the wolf recognized what that feeling it couldn't shake was; what had been ominously hanging in the air.

It had been difficult to determine because of the complexity, the layers, and the magnitude.

The air was charged with the sick-sweet odor of fear.

Not a burst of fear issued in the heights of trauma like it had just heard, but an intricately textured and interwoven quilt of fear that coated the air itself.

From some human-consciousness memory and knowledge that the wolf couldn't comprehend was buried inside its brain, it equated what it was picking up as likely being the subtle scent of an endless field of rotten apples, the remnants of soured milk, and the onion-like human body odor.

A unique and complex combination of those scents didn't float in waves on the shifts of the wind to the wolf the way most smells did. It hung in the air, like a sort of ominous and ever-present fog that infiltrated every square inch of the air around the green space.

A thickness that wasn't dispersed no matter how hard the winds blew.

Similarly, a heaviness that seemed to grow, continuing to be fed from some unspeakable, difficult to understand evil that remained hidden from sight, from scent, from sound, but was there just the same.

A voice—a male human voice—that the wolf seemed to recognize, came to the wolf's mind, speaking to it from somewhere inside. It was familiar, and yet didn't match any memory of the few humans the wolf had ever directly encountered.

"That's terror," the male human said. "The city is becoming consumed in a constant state of terror that is not only growing, it's replicating, like a virus."

The wolf, of course, didn't understand what those words floating through its head were saying.

All it could tell is that it wasn't good.

It whimpered and then raced into the center of the green space and as far away from the artificial human constructs as possible.

But there was no escaping the mass of terror and fear that had infiltrated every inch of the very air, like some giant cloud had descended and taken up permanent residence.

Friday, July 7, 2017

Chapter Twenty-Five: Batman, Bigfoot, & The Invisible Man Walk into a Chapter

I smelled the fear off Lex from the moment I woke.

As always when I first became aware—or at least human consciously aware—there was a disconcerting moment where I did not know where I was, and I had to quickly take in my surroundings to figure that out.

I was naked and lying on dirt, leaves, rocks, and twigs. Clicking and rustling movements of small critters scampering about the forest, birds flitting through the branches singing their morning songs, and the bustle of morning traffic slightly muffled by the foliage helped me realize roughly where I was in Central Park.

But along with the input from the surrounding green space came the scent of Lex from upwind. And she carried an underlying essence of worry and fear.

Something about the thick layer of fear coming off her reminded me of a similar scent. But it wasn't something I could pin-point smelling as a human. Was it the inaccessible memory of my time as a wolf reaching toward my conscious mind?

I sat up and then rose to my feet, recognizing I was in nearly the same spot I had awoken in the day before.

My wolf self seems to stick to a regular pattern of habits, much like I do.

As I stood, I realized—speaking of patterns—another part of me was also standing up.

My erection was painfully stiff; a not uncommon experience when waking. I remembered how, yesterday, when Gail had met me, it was an awkward situation.

Today, however, I briefly wondered, as Lex approached from the bridge just down the path, if the two of us could put this thing to good use.

The thought of that brought a throb of excitement.

But the next twist of the wind returned the scent of that underlying layer of anxiety from Lex.

Which had an almost instantaneous effect on reducing my little friend's rigidity. It gave up on the morning glory salute, retreating to its former normal self by the time Lex appeared around the corner of the path.

"Good morning handsome," she whispered under her breath.

"Good morning beautiful," I replied.

I stepped out from the bushes and onto the path to meet her. She dropped the plastic bag of clothing she'd brought and slipped into my arms. I held her for a moment, feeling her racing heartbeat and that persistent baseline of angst and fear, then kissed the top of her head and leaned back to look her in the eyes.

"What is it?" I asked.

As I was getting dressed—and yes, admittedly disappointed with the turn of events; making love in the morning with Lex in Central Park would have been a beautiful experience—she had filled me in on the cause of her emotions.

Things had gotten worse overnight.

Much worse.

There had been more attacks. Costumed members of the PFA had carried numerous attacks out; not all that different than the ones we'd read about and witnessed before in both New York, and previously in Los Angeles.

Most of the reported muggings where nothing was taken or stolen from the victims was an indicator that the motivation wasn't theft but more likely a hate crime. More than three dozen people had been admitted to hospitals following a surge of violent attacks across the city.

Two men—a gay couple—were beaten to death following a Midtown chase turned deadly, according to at least one eyewitness. The onlooker had reported seeing the couple fleeing from a pack of four men dressed in regular clothes with matching clown masks and had called 911 to report it. By the time the police arrived, the two men were found brutally beaten.

The incidence of arson, smashed windows, and blatant hate message graffiti to synagogues and mosques had also grown, making last night even worse than the previous ones combined.

But there were no longer stories of attacks by small mobs of people dressed in odd Halloween type costumes. The media was also filling with tales of monster-like sightings.

Several reports of the attacks included what witnesses described as monsters. In one an attacker with large black wings flew in like a giant bat, surprise attacking people from the air. The media was calling this creature The Bat Man.

Another report of an attacker known as The Invisible Force was responsible for no less than a half dozen surprise attacks. One victim described standing on the street corner with a couple of friends after having left an off-Broadway show, when from out of nowhere they felt a solid punch to the back of their head. When they turned to see nobody was there, a second punch struck them in the mouth, knocking out a tooth. There were similar reports of an attack from an assailant who could not be seen across the Midtown area.

Another bizarre story was of a Latino man who reported being pummeled and bitten by a large hairy man at least seven feet tall that he described as looking like a cross between Chewbacca and Bigfoot.

Several other reports had been of a wolf seen running down the city streets. One report was of a wolf leaping into the middle of a gang of costumed gang members who had been threatening a lone black teenager, scaring them off before their physical assault could begin. And another was of the wolf seen darting into an alley chasing a man in a clown mask.

We suspected those wolf reports were of Irwin out and about the night before doing his rounds of trying to protect the innocent from these growing attacks. It made me wonder if he'd been able to gain insights into fresh scents to help track back to the PFA.

The matter was so serious that the mayor and police commissioner were recommending people to not stay out after dark. When questioned about whether they were considering instituting a strict curfew the commissioner replied that if things continued the way they were heading, he wouldn't hesitate. If a move like that prevents further deaths, grave injuries or the reckless endangerment caused by arson, then it would be worth it, he said.

On our walk back to the Algonquin, Lex also filled me in on experimentation she and Irwin had done with both Lex's presence and a sample of Lex's urine.

While my own reaction to Lex's urine had been muted, because of the dilution of it with the toilet bowl water, they learned it was far more potent, and even faster acting when it was concentrated.

"Now I know what those beer taps at Gulp feel like," Lex joked when she was explaining to me how Gail and Irwin had her urinate in small sample bottles in an effort for them to store them up.

The three had spent much of the night testing Lex's effect on Irwin's paranormal ability, determining that a proximity of about a six-foot radius was the key for Lex to nullify the magic around her.

They also learned that, if Irwin was in wolf format—something he could do at will regardless of the time of day—once Lex stayed within five feet of him for several minutes, he morphed back. And because it wasn't under his conscious control, that shift between canine and sapiens forms was quite like the painful "childbirth-like" sensation I was more familiar with.

Irwin also took some samples of Lex's urine and a blood sample of hers that he planned on bringing back to the lab he worked in. His goal was seeing if there was a way he could isolate what it was in it that was causing the side effect. He hoped to manufacture either an injection or aerosol antidote to the paranormal members of the PFA.

"Like that classic shark-repellant Bat spray!" I joked, referring to that old 1960s campy Batman TV show episode. Lex had no idea what I was talking about, so like many of my quips, it resulted in the resounding symphony of crickets.

Oh well, at least I can amuse myself.

Gail had also made calls to the other occult supply stores in New York and had learned they too had sold out of the same list of supplies. Two of the other people she'd spoken with described the same pair that had visited Gail's shop; one of the other occult shop owners recognized the items on the list from something he had read but couldn't place it. He mentioned he would call Gail back if he figured it out. Gail told all of them to call her if those same men ever returned and cautioned them to be careful. She relayed her concern that these men had something to do with the night-time violence and attacks that had been growing in the city.

As Lex shared many of the stories from the previous night, both the experiments done with Gail and Irwin and the reports of the overnight attacks, I felt an ominous chill in my bones.

The PFA couldn't possibly have that many members of their inner circle group. The neo-Nazi terror they were injecting into the New York nighttime by attacking visible minorities was likely inspiring other racists to crawl out of the woodwork and perform copycat attacks.

That sinister chill in my bones remained, and I was convinced I could smell the fear that hung in the air even without my enhanced wolf senses.

When Lex and I got back to my apartment, we went to the bedroom where we made slow and quiet love to one another. It wasn't the sexually frenetic or heightened and energetic love making we had done in the past. Instead, it was measured, deeply passionate, and more about connecting and trying to be as physical close to one another as we could get.

After we finished, we lay quietly in one another's arms for about half an hour—not saying anything, just laying there entangled together. Then we both showered and headed over to Gail's shop.

Chapter Twenty-Six: A Tall Recipe for Disaster

"It's a recipe from a Third Reich era book believed to have been written here in America."

Gail was relaying the information she'd gathered from the colleague who had called her back, having recognized where they'd seen the ingredients from.

"Known as the *Constructive Chaos Cookbook* by Mobius R. Morningstar, it is extremely rare. It was long believed to be a fictional grimoire, much like the *Necronomicon* that H. P. Lovecraft imagined and mentioned throughout his writing.

"But apparently this one is a real thing.

"Mobius R. Morningstar is most likely the pseudonym of a collaboration of a group of disciples of Marvel Parsons, Aleister Crowley, and Madison Grant. The complete book itself may never have actually been published beyond a handful of manually produced copies. Though there are rumours that some printings do exist, nobody has ever confirmed owning one. But replicated copies of some pages from the text have appeared and been reprinted.

"My colleague from Catland Books in Brooklyn was the one who recognized the items as being from a recipe list from one of those manuscript pages. He faxed a copy to me.

"The recipe and incantations result in creating a fine powder referred to as *Berserker Powder* that can be ingested, burned as incense, or dissolved into liquid.

"It's made from Labradorite, Black Tourmaline, Amazonite, and Aggregate Heliotrope. These crystals are crushed and mixed in with the dust of the bones from humans using a chicken's foot."

Gail explained how the final blend is prepared inside a five-point star/pentagram with five bone runes:

- **Thurisaz** (Thor) - The Rune of Pain, Sharpness and Cutting. This is a destructive ruin of Chaos and Power.
- **Kenaz** (Torch) - Rune of light. The light of the soul. In black magick, it is used to incite stupidity and works so that the victim will remain unaware.
- **Uruz** (Aurochs) - Masculine in nature. Black Magic used to threaten and destroy.
- **Hagl** (Hail) Rune of Suffering and injustice, destruction, disaster and violence.
- **Wunjo** (Joy) - Rune of honors and rewards. In black Magick, used to instill overconfidence and trust in the wrong things.

That final mixture is prepared in bowls made from human skulls in front of the death throes of a group of humans.

"They add the blood of their victims to the mix?" I asked.

"No," Gail said. "Not at that point. The power comes from the death throes themselves, and not the blood. I read this in Levay's *The Satanic Bible* and a few other similar texts, but the impact of the victims isn't in the actual spilling of their blood, but in the discharge of bio-chemical energy they give off in their death throes. This is the same phenomenon that occurs during any height-ening of emotion.

"But the blood of those victims is preserved, and it's dried, then mixed into the main powder immediately before it is to be used.

"The ultimate effect of this powder is to infuse in-tense fear, anger, and hatred in anyone who absorbs it. It also has a side-effect of easy suggestibility.

"What we're dealing with," Gail concluded, "is a powerful toxin meant to produce mass anxiety and vio-lence. If we think things are bad now, just imagine what will happen once they can infect this poison to the masses."

"What are some ways they can do this?" I asked.

"It has to either be breathed in or ingested," Gail said.

"The water supply," Lex offered. "That feeds to eve-ry home, every office, every building in the city, doesn't it?"

Gail nodded. "That's one way."

I thought about the increased incidents of arson late-ly. "What about inhalation? When you set a fire, you send smoke into the air; particles are breathed in. Many people don't consume tap water in this city; but everybody has to breathe."

"During 9/11," Gail said, "the World Trade Center dust spread as far as three miles away. The towers collapsed in lower Manhattan, but remnants of the massive spreading cloud's debris were visible as far north as The Empire State Building."

"Do you think they could try to take down a skyscraper infused with the Berserker Powder?" I asked.

"That would bring chaos in two different ways," Gail said. "The immediate and outright terror of a major building coming down, which residents of this city are all too familiar with."

"Followed," Lex continued, "by the impact of tens of thousands of people inhaling the infection from the powder."

"Exactly," Gail said. "Combine that initial terror with an existing heightened state of hate and violence, and you've got one huge recipe for disaster."

I stared in awe at these two beautiful and brilliant women who seemed to be in complete sync with one another. They were not only finishing each other's sentences, but they were collaborating and working together like they were old friends rather than two women who should be in competition with one another for my affection.

That was, I recognize, a rather ego-centric thing to be thinking; particularly when there was a much more urgent matter at hand than who got to sleep with who.

"So, we should figure out what building or buildings they are most likely to target." Lex said. "But there's no shortage of tall buildings in this city. How would we figure out which ones?"

"Well," Gail said, swinging her laptop around so that the screen was visible to all three of us. She hit a few keys that brought up a Google Map of the city. "If the radius is anywhere between two to 3 miles, it would make sense for them to strike in a spot that would get maximum spread across the city.

"Some place in Midtown would be ideal for that. And it's far more impactful if the attack is on a recognized landmark; like the Empire State Building, the Chrysler Building, the New York Times, Rockefeller Plaza, Trump World Tower."

"Trump Tower would likely be under federal protection and not so easily accessible," I said. "Not as easy a target as some others."

Gail nodded. "It's also far east; too far from the center of the island. The same might be true for some of those other locations. The Chrysler Building, for example, is also further from center.

"Also, I'd think that places like the Flatiron Building, Radio City Music Hall, or the main branch of the New York Public Library wouldn't be tall enough to inflict the right reach or spread."

"Rockefeller Plaza is also pretty central," I said.

"What about that big white one with the funky slanted roof that we saw from the top of the Empire State Building?" Lex asked, turning to me. "It was pretty tall.

I remember looking up at it from that park behind the New York Public Library."

"Bryant Park," Gail said, then paused to think. "That's the Bank of America Tower. Yes, that's also quite central and one of the tallest buildings in the city."

"So that's something like four or five big landmark buildings in a fifteen-block radius of central Manhattan," I said. "If they strike a major landmark.

"But if they don't go with a landmark building, they have at least a dozen or more other really tall buildings that will do the trick. This is a veritable needle in a haystack situation."

Gail bit her lip as she reflected on the situation.

"If you and Irwin focus your tracking of the scent you have to that specific radial block area, you might pick up something," she said. "That could narrow it down."

"We should also alert the authorities," Lex said. "Let the Hate Crimes Task Force know about this. Call Hank back in LA."

"What are we going to tell them?" Gail asked. "About this magic powder from a cookbook that is only rumored to exist? That the PFA has a number of supernatural soldiers? People look down their noses at the occult. They think anyone who practices or believes is a little cuckoo. Heck, I was always a little skeptical myself, until I realized, then later saw the evidence that Andrews possessed special supernatural abilities."

I thought about Hank, the detective from the domestic terrorist task force I'd met back in LA. He trusted me;

and not just because I was friends with his brother-in-law. That came through clearly both times I'd spoken with him.

"Hank, back in LA. He trusts me. Even if we're vague about how we know, he'll likely listen."

"And that detective the other morning," Lex added. "Remember that strange thing he mentioned at the very end?"

"Wagner," I said. "Yes, he said that if we saw something that gave us the heebie-jeebies, or that looked like it was from The Twilight Zone, to call him. He is likely on to the fact the PFA is operating in a shadowy realm. He might just believe more than the average cop."

"Okay," Gail said. "We should call them both. Let them know about the supplies that were all bought up, the recipe we found, and our belief on how they might put it to use."

I nodded. I had Hank's number in my phone, but detective Wagner's card was back at my place. Just as I was lifting my phone to look up Hank's number from the recent calls list, my phone rang. It was Mack's office.

I answered. "Hello?"

"Hi Michael," it was Anne. "I'm just calling to remind you that the article about your experience with the PFA is due at end of day today. You're sending it soon, right?"

I had, of course, not thought much about that article in the past day.

"Of course, Anne," I lied.

She let out a knowing laugh, obviously seeing right through me. Anne knew me too well; she understood that I hadn't finished it but would get it in just on deadline.

"Since you still have work to do on it," she said, "Mack wanted to see if you could incorporate some of what's been happening in New York City into the article."

"Will do."

"Thanks, Michael."

She hung up.

I explained to Gail and Lex that I would head back to my place so I could call detective Wagner and get this article cranked out and back to Mack. I said I'd call Hank in LA as well to update him on what we knew so far. And that I'd then head to Midtown to resume my daily tracking for PFA members.

Gail said she would reach out to Irwin to see where he was with recreating whatever special effect Lex's urine had on magic. She also speculated about wanting to recreate the Berserker Powder and seeing if the urine had a neutralizing effect on it. The only challenge with that was that the materials needed for creating the powder were sold out from her shop as well as every other one she had contacted. She planned on checking for any other information in the books she had access to for a spell or ritual that could have a nullifying effect on the Berserker Powder or other dark arts magic.

Lex said she was going to put on another pot of coffee so she could use its natural diuretic side-effect to produce more pee. After saying that, she smiled, and asked if we could start referring to her liquid body waste as something else. The term *urine* felt too clinical, using *pee* made her feel like a little girl, and saying *piss* was far too crass and sailor-like.

"I vote we give it a unique and new name; something like Golden Charm," Lex smiled, and we all laughed.

It was nervous laughter, of course; because even though I wasn't able to pick up on any extrasensory scented emotions, the anxiety and fear in the air was still palpable.

I left the shop with the echoes of both that laughter and a deep and rich admiration and love for both women swirling through my mind and heart.

Chapter Twenty-Seven: No More Pussyfooting Around on These Wolf Paws

I decided to wait before calling Hank in Los Angeles. It was only 9:20 AM in New York, which meant it wasn't yet 7 AM Pacific time. I figured I'd wait until closer to noon Eastern to give him a call

But I called detective Wagner the minute I got back. My call went straight to voicemail, so I left him a brief message telling him who I was and that I had a potential lead on PFA activity.

Then I sat down at my desk and wrote the article I'd been pussyfooting around for the past couple of days.

The words flowed out of me like I had taken some sort of magic writer laxative elixir. Once I got into it, I was a writing machine and cranked out three thousand words in a little over two hours. I hadn't been on a roll like that in a long time; and it felt good.

While writing a non-fiction piece didn't have the same satisfaction as crafting fictional prose, it still came with a deep fulfillment that made me feel like I had returned to a state I hadn't felt in a while.

After giving the article a once-over, satisfied with the replay of what had happened to me in Los Angeles, and how the situation in New York was taking this terror to a whole new level, I emailed the article to Mack.

It was still ten minutes to noon.

I was expecting his surprised response to me turning it in early—something I rarely ever did—and remembered his comment about my arrival at his office the other morning a few minutes early. He'd said my trip to California and meeting Lex had been good for me.

He'd been so right.

I then called Irwin, confirmed he had already spoken to Gail about the specific fifteen block radius we suspected the PFA would plan their attack in. I let him know I'd take the area east of 7th Avenue. He mentioned he would do lab work most of the afternoon, but would resume his tracking after dark, and suggested that, instead of splitting by geographic region, we split our shifts into day and night.

This made sense, particularly because, at night, I wasn't all that useful while padding around Central Park howling at the moon.

Refreshed and recharged, both from the morning's accomplishments, and a solid plan of attack, I set off to do my sure-footed tracking.

Detective Wagner called me back after I had been out tracking for less than half an hour.

I explained what I'd learned about the purchase of occult supplies and the Berserker Powder recipe from those manuscript pages Gail had found. I also expressed our theory about how they might use a controlled demolition of one of the taller Midtown buildings to disperse powder.

"First thing," Wagner said, "leave the theories of how and where an attack might happen to the professionals.

"Second, how do you know this Gail Sommers? And can she be trusted?"

"We are friends." I paused, considering explaining we'd been more, but the reality was we had been friends for much longer than we'd ever been lovers. That detail wasn't necessary to share in this situation. Which made me wonder why I was even thinking about it. "Good friends. For a long time. She's not a member of the PFA. She would never be involved in anything like that."

Wagner started to say something and then stopped, paused, and started again. "Third, and perhaps most importantly: what makes you put any stock into some allegedly ancient chaos cookbook manuscript pages you found? It sounds like a bunch of *X-Files* kind of malarky."

"Back in LA," I said. "I've seen them do strange things. That one night when they attacked Lex and an East Indian woman, this guy dressed like Jason from *Friday the 13th* shot lighting bolts from his hands."

There was an extended silence on the other end. The sound of his breathing told me he was still there, but it was steady; he had no plans of speaking. I knew what he was doing, having studied this interrogation technique for research for the thrillers I wrote; not to mention having just experienced it the other day when officer Johnson had first interviewed me in that diner.

It's often inherent for a person to fill a nervous silence with words; to keep talking and perhaps say things they may even be reluctant to share—just to break the uncomfortable quiet. An investigator would often do that to allow a witness or suspected criminal reveal more than they had intended.

Despite knowing this, my nervousness of the fact I *was* hiding something—my own, and even Lex's paranormal abilities, not to mention her previous entanglement with the PFA—led me to keep talking, to fill that space.

"And then, more than a week later, when Lex and I saw that Jason guy again, after they'd attacked a mother and child, we saw a man step out of a giant ball of yellow light. A minute or so later, that same ball appeared in a different spot, and two of them stepped into it and disappeared into thin air. None of that stuff can be explained by any conventional means."

He remained silent; so again, I continued.

"That was strange. Something I'd never seen before. Now these most recent news reports of the attacks in the city have included sightings of strange things. Bigfoot in the city. A giant bat man. Some invisible force. And something you said to us the other day at that diner.

"You said if we saw anything that gave us the heebie-jeebies, or made us feel like we'd walked into The Twilight Zone to call you. And so that's what I'm doing."

After a long pause he replied. "So why did you tell *none* of this strange stuff to Detective Reynolds back in

Los Angeles? You obviously trusted him. You're friends with his brother-in-law Craig. You worked together on the set of *Tome of Terror*."

"We told Hank about the one guy seeming to appear out of nowhere and then how they disappeared into thin air."

"Neither of you told them about the giant light orb they stepped into." He paused. "Both you and your girl-friend, separately interviewed, said you couldn't explain how they were there one minute and then gone the next. You only mentioned the one guy had appeared out of nowhere and then the two of them disappeared.

"So, yes, you both mentioned them disappearing into thin air, but you neglected to mention the giant ball of yellow light—the light portal."

It was my turn to pause. This guy was good. He'd pulled info out of me that I hadn't been willing to share or admit to. But it wasn't just his technique; it was becoming more obvious that this guy had deeper insight into the paranormal background of the PFA.

"How do you think someone would react if we'd told them that? They would have thought we were crazy."

"You just told *me*."

"*You* don't think I'm crazy. You know what the PFA are capable of. And the paranormal crap they're into."

"I do."

"And you know that this powder isn't just some mystical theoretical incantation. This poses a genuine threat to the people of this city. And you have the resources to properly monitor and potentially stop such an attack from happening."

"Normally, yes. But do you have any idea how much manpower is already being leveraged in this city because of the rise of nighttime violence?"

"I can only imagine."

"You can imagine quite a bit from what I understand. So, tell me, can you also imagine the fact there are very few people working within the NYPD that believe any of the hocus-pocus stuff going down?"

"I can," I said. "I noticed how you lowered your voice before referencing the heebie-jeebies thing the other day."

"You get it, then. I can't be leveraging resources to prevent some attack from a magic spell concocted by some moonlight blood-spilling ritual. To get any play off this I'll need to compose a story about some other sort of airborne toxin, like an anthrax powder or something.

"Also, if they were to attempt a plot to take down a building, there'd be ways of tracking either purchases or thefts of the explosives or ingredients needed to make explosives powerful enough to do that."

That was a good point, and not something Gail, Lex, Irwin or I had thought of. You need a significant store of explosives in order to bring down a skyscraper.

"Unless..." Wagner said, leaving the thought hanging.

"Unless what?"

"Unless the PFA has someone in their ranks with the ability to pull something like that off."

We were both silent.

"We know they have at least one member that can fly, one that can transform into a giant Sasquatch, and potentially another one that changes into a wolf. There's a guy who can shoot lightning bolts out of his hands, and another that can open and close light portals to quickly transport in and out of places.

"These powers and abilities are pretty random. So what's to say they don't have other members with the ability to create an explosion without the necessary materials?"

I thought about that. We were already dealing with what felt like impossible abilities and powers. What Wagner was talking about was entirely possible. Heck, come to think of it, Marco's ability to pop in and out of a location, and to take others with him, could allow them to bypass any police or other guards protecting the perimeter of a building.

"So how the heck can we figure this out? How can we stop them?"

"What is this *we* you're talking about? I'm the cop. You're the citizen. Or are you some sort of vigilante?"

I was quiet. Could Wagner know about my ability?

"Listen, Andrews, speaking of vigilante antics, it's time for us to both cut the bullshit. I know you're not being straight with me. I know your little secret."

Chapter Twenty-Eight: I Know the Secrets That You Keep

After staring blankly at my phone, I realized I hadn't said anything for several beats. How the heck could Wagner know about me?

"What?" I asked. "What little secret are you talking about?"

"Stop bullshitting me."

"Seriously, I'm not sure what you're talking about."

"Fine. Let me lay it out for you.

"First, your girlfriend from LA. Hank and I both know her real background. We know she has ties to the PFA.

"Second, we know that the two of you have been meddling with the PFA. And it's not just because of the numerous times either you alone, or both of you have gotten into altercations with this group in the past month.

"I'm sure I don't have to tell you—because we both know how a group of them beat the crap out of you and left you for dead back in Hollywood—but these guys are hardcore and deadly. And not only that, but many of them also possess superhuman and paranormal abilities.

"Going after them with your fists and a bit of attitude fueled by your girlfriend's personal vendetta is only going to get both of you killed."

He paused, doing that silent thing again so that I would fill the silence.

What he didn't realize is how relieved I'd been to learn he hadn't been talking about my lycanthropic affliction, but about Lex's past.

So he knew. Which meant that Hank likely knew all along. Or, at least, he figured it out after the PFA had completely trashed Lex's apartment in LA.

They were holding what they knew close to their chest—as investigative authorities were wont to do. So why was he revealing this to me now?

"You must know, then, that they followed her here," I finally said. "As well as Lex's ties to Marcus."

"Yes."

"You've known all along. And so has Hank."

"Yes."

"So why are you tipping your hand now?"

"Because we need to fight this paranormal threat with the paranormal. The PFA has been engaged in a long-term plan to create a new race of super powered soldiers for their neo-Nazi cause. And we know your girlfriend has some sort of ability to nullify magic."

"Are you saying the NYPD and the LAPD are aware of the supernatural powers and rituals performed by the PFA?"

"No. Not everyone. I think you get an idea of the mass panic that would happen if this was widely known. This information has been entrusted to a small group lead by Special Agent Reynolds. Less than half a dozen of us within the New York and Los Angeles police forces working with the FBI know."

"Wait a minute. *Special Agent* Reynolds? You're saying Hank Reynolds is an FBI agent?" I had somehow believed he was an LAPD detective working with a group of CIA operatives. I didn't realize he was an FBI agent.

"It doesn't matter what he is. What matters is we are part of a special task force and I'm your local contact on these matters. What matters is figuring out a way to leverage your girlfriend's abilities."

I was quiet, trying to figure out, if they knew about Lex's powers and abilities, why they didn't just stealthily swoop in and apprehend her. Why was he speaking to me about it rather than just forging ahead?

Wagner seemed to read my mind.

"You and I both know," he said. "That her abilities occasionally seem to stop or prevent non-paranormal physical harm."

"You've already tried!" I blurted out, realizing that.

"Not here. But yes. Back in LA."

"You've been following her?"

"We have eyes on her now. We know she's with your ex at *Enchanting Magic* and that the two have been doing a lot of research, making a lot of calls; while you've been patrolling the city looking for these guys."

"And you need me to use her."

"Listen, son. The entire city—hell, this nation—needs her. She is likely going to be the key to helping us figure out a way to stop the PFA from the hell-bound spiral they're launching.

"And since we know that you and your little group of vigilante-wannabes are aware of the threat the PFA poses, it's time we figured this out together."

He was quiet again. I thought about Lex's urine, and what we had learned about it. I also thought about how Irwin was working to figure out a way to replicate whatever it was in the urine that negatively effected magic. I struggled with a way to tell him about this without sharing how we'd figured out her urine's effect. Because that would reveal both me and Irwin also possessed superhuman abilities.

"You don't have anyone else to trust," Wagner said. "So, you're going to have to put some of that trust in me that we will not harm Alexandria in any way."

I remained silent, my mind tumbling through the possible ways I could explain what we had found out.

"I can tell you're struggling with that. So let me make this easier for you. I've already shared a great deal with you; to show *you* trust.

"Let me share what we have planned.

"We captured one of them this morning. It's what I was in the middle of when you called. This one has special abilities. Superhuman strength. Even after we tased him, it still took six of our strongest officers to hold him down to inject him with a tranquilizer.

"We've already pumped enough tranquilizer in him to kill an elephant. And all it's doing is keeping him groggy. We need to bring your girlfriend close to him and measure her effectiveness on nullifying his powers. We have to perform experiments like that if we ever stand a chance to put a stop to this super-powered PFA threat."

I thought about this opportunity.

The four of us—Lex, Gail, Irwin, and I—knew Lex's proximity effect. But this was an opportunity for us to measure the impact of her urine more effectively. Not to mention, within a controlled environment.

"We have a theory," I said. "I know it sounds a bit whack—and let's be honest here Detective Wagner, everything that has been happening these past couple of months is most definitely not at all normal—but there's a different liquid to try injecting into this subject that we think might work to neutralize him better than any elephant tranquilizer."

Friday, July 7 through
Friday, July 14, 2017

Interlude: What's the Difference Between a Chapter and an Interlude Anyway?

Achapter is one of the main divisions in a piece of writing like a book. It may come with a number or a title; or, sometimes, both.

An interlude is a pause in a narrative. It typically is used to convey some sort of intervening time between two moments.

In the world of theatre, one might consider the intermission between two acts as an interlude.

In music, an interlude is often an instrumental passage that comes between sections of lyrics in a song.

In a podcast, it's often a short musical clip—often referred to as a "stinger" that adds character and effectively denotes a transition to a new topic or segment.

Within a television show or movie, an interlude might mark a transition in a character or story, often a montage of visual clips relayed with some fitting musical score. Training sequences, like the ones in *The Empire Strikes Back*, *Batman Begins* or the many *Rocky* movies, effectively denote what is understood to be an extended period of time, multiple try/fail episodes, and a main character or set of characters facing the reminder that 'this won't be easy.'

It's a trope that seems to be an essential element in sports movies as well as in thrillers and action films. They are meant to display the determination and persistence of the preparation to face the penultimate challenge. These scenes squeeze a significant amount of 'this happened' over the course of days, weeks, months, or even years into a shorter bit. To show all of it would simply take too long.

In a book, an interlude can be a break from the main story; an opportunity for the author to provide information that might supplement the main story. It may be a way to offer the reader background information and insights that would be difficult to relay because they might not come up organically. Let's say, for example, one wants to denote the perspective or experience of a different character, or the main character's furry alter ego. Or much like the movie montage sequences, it's a way to summarize an era or period that would otherwise simply take up far too much real estate in terms of pages, and could put the reader off or, even worse, bore them.

There's no one great way to express transitions in writing. Many writers pull it off effectively. For example, when denoting a passage of time, a writer might simply create an additional space between paragraphs. A distinct break in time might occur between chapters. Inserting date and time references or even relevant time indicators in the header of a scene or chapter can also work.

Writers do this because nobody wants to read about a character waking up, going to use the facilities, showering, making and eating their breakfast then locking and leaving their home and the boring commute into work. Especially when those normal routines are not infused with some sort of conflict, challenge, or pertinent character-defining or changing moment.

Transitions can be, like those short visual breaks in the text on a page, or the pause in the narration in the audiobook, seamless and executed perfectly. Other writers can often adeptly insert a single paragraph that relays the necessary information to the reader to fill them in quickly and effectively and allowing them to move along.

In my writing, particularly in my Maxwell Bronte novels, transitions are one element I've always been quite self conscious of. Perhaps that's because, in real life, I've felt awkward in those transitional moments.

When I first walk into a room, for example, especially in a large social gathering, unless there is a specific destination, goal, or focus, I feel like a blundering fool. If I were to walk into that same room where the expectation is for me to mount the stage and speak to the entire room, even were I not prepared for it, if it were sprung upon me out of the blue, I would heartily embrace the challenge. My graceless gawky nature would all but melt away as my attention centered on the task at hand.

While others may be fine lurking in the crowd instead and might faint with fear at the thought of speaking in front of a large crowd, I'm more comfortable with that defined purpose than in the awkward transitional mingling within a crowd.

It's been said that the typical person is more afraid of public speaking than they are of dying. Comedian Jerry Seinfeld said this suggests that at a funeral most people would rather be in the coffin than giving the eulogy. That's not me. I'm fine on stage—because with that task comes a specific focus that helps remove any of that clumsiness that comes with figuring out what to do in a social situation.

And that ungraceful floundering I do in those moments translates to the written word. When Maxwell Bronte is in the middle of confrontation or bold discovery, I'm all about zooming in and bringing the reader right into the depths of those moments.

But when it's one of those transitional pieces, where he is doing a lot of waiting, or engaging in repetitive tasks, conducting hours of research that are not likely to be all that compelling to a reader, well that's when those two left feet insert themselves. I suppose, with my writing, I should say that's when I start typing with all thumbs.

Or when I can take meandering asides before I even delve into the transitional passage.

I mean, there's nothing like demonstrating by offering a bold and blatant example, right?

A lot happened in the seven days between that ground-breaking conversation with Detective Wagner and the climactic confrontation with the PFA where too many lives were lost.

But I'm getting ahead of myself.

After I quickly relayed the suspected impact Lex's urine might have on supernatural humans, I told Detective Wagner to meet the four of us at Gail's occult shop.

I then called Gail to fill her and Lex in on the conversation I'd just had, and then called Irwin to get him to meet us there.

After all five of us synced up—leaving out the part about Irwin and I actually being supernatural humans ourselves—Irwin, Wagner, and I took one of the vials of Lex's urine to the secret location where they'd been holding the tranquilized PFA super-powered goon.

Neither Irwin nor I recognized the sight or scent of the guy who was bound in thick leather straps to a table inside a ten-foot square metal cage inside what appeared to be an old basement bank vault. The white man with thin black hair was maybe pushing forty and was small—perhaps five and a half feet high tops. He had a body shape and thin arms that made Olive Oil look like The Rock in comparison.

"Don't let his size fool you," Wagner said. "When he's not drugged, he could easily snap his leather straps and bend these steel bars with his bare hands."

He asked the officer guarding the vault room when he'd last been given an injection and learned it had been forty-five minutes since the last one. So far, they'd had to give him the tranquilizer every hour in order to keep him subdued and weak enough not to break free.

Wagner told the man to get two of the other officers guarding from outside the vault to come in and stand by as he performed an experiment. He also made Irwin and I stand outside the metal cage for our own protection.

All three of the officers stood with their tasers ready as Wagner opened the vial of the urine and held it near the man's face where he could breathe it in.

Wagner explained that, usually by the end of the hour, the man would normally wake from the effects of his last dose. And, shortly after waking, his strength would return.

As we watched, the man slowly opened his eyes. After a few moments of punchiness, clarity came to him. Irwin and I were both far enough back that the nullifying effect of the scent of Lex's urine only subtly impacted us. I could hear the man's heartbeat change as he rose from consciousness. In addition, I could smell the intense anger coming off him when he remembered where he was.

He strained against the leather straps holding him down and was surprised that he could not break free. That angered him further, and he struggled harder.

Wagner looked back at me, nodding. It was working.

The man then seemed to fall back under the effect of the tranquilizer in his system and lost consciousness again.

He didn't come out of the effects of the tranquilizer in his system so long as the vial of urine remained open and close to his head. Wagner placed the open vial on a small table less than a foot away from the left of the man's head. That seemed to do the trick.

Wagner then filled a syringe with half a milliliter of the urine, and once the man was again awake, he injected it into the muscle in the man's shoulder, like a flu shot.

It seemed to work. Without needing any other tranquilizer or even a second dose of the urine, the man's super-strength didn't return for the rest of the week.

We had apparently found a cure.

Irwin carried on with researching ways he might manufacture a replicant of the urine while Lex continued her regimen of drinking plenty of diuretics and producing and saving as much urine as she could.

We learned, during this time, that the average adult female bladder was about 500 millilitres and most people typically produced between 800 and 2,000 millilitres of urine per day. By remaining focused on urine production, over the course of about 6 days, Lex produced a little over 15,000 milliliters of what we were now calling Golden Charm. They would fill almost eight 2-liter soft drink bottles, but Irwin had 1-ounce vials for us to store them in. There were over five hundred of those little vials available.

Gail continued to work with her colleague from Catland Books—pretending she was helping me with research for a sequel to my novel *Tome of Terror* to find if there were any potential counter-spells to the Berserker Powder spell they'd discovered. They found at least one recipe that might undo the effects of it, but it required the fresh blood of a virgin spilled during sunrise mixed into the concoction. We debated about whether the "spilling" needed to be murder, or if we could figure out a way to solicit blood bank volunteers. Never-mind your blood type on these sign-up forms; we're more interested in whether you've ever had a sexual partner.

We opted, instead, to stick with Lex's Golden Charm.

During this research, Gail also uncovered, in collaboration with her fellow occult-specialist colleague, another powerful spell they could perform. She tried explaining to us how it worked, but the actual logistics of the recipe and ritual were confusing, involving more crystals, potions, incantations, and charms. The important thing was it didn't involve killing virgins, and that was enough for me. It took four days worth of timed and layered ritual procedure and additions to it, but by early on the Friday, Gail possessed a working magic-detecting orb.

It started off with a raw walnut still in its green husk and was made of repeated layers of a combination of wax, crystal dust, soaking in liquid, and continuing to add more layers until it got to the size of a small honeydew melon. It had a similar texture to a honeydew and was virtually indistinguishable from one.

Unless it was in the presence of magic or paranormal. As any supernatural spell or person got near—as close as half a New York city block away, the melon glowed. The closer and stronger the magic, the brighter the melon glowed. We tested it, with Gail sitting in her shop on

E 9th Street and neither Irwin nor I could get within a block of the store without it beginning to glow and then brightening as we got closer. It didn't seem to work on Lex, though. Gail suspected it somehow wasn't in tune with Lex's magic-nullifying abilities. The melon still worked for Gail even with Lex standing beside her.

The melon wasn't something we shared with the special task force. We didn't need them getting their hands on such a device and realizing that Irwin and I were also supernatural humans. In addition, it only worked for Gail—the person who created the object seemed tied to its effectiveness—it's not like they would have been able to carry it into a battle zone the way they could carry vials of Lex's Golden Charm.

Because it took so many days and rituals to create and then test the magic detecting melon, there wasn't time to create another one. We had the one. We called it, simply, the detection melon.

Over those same seven days the city continued its downward spiral into the throes of nighttime terror.

After three more nights of continuing escalated violence, racially motivated attacks and mob-like protests, looting and violence, the city had no choice but to enact a strict 7 PM curfew.

This made my need to get out and howl at the moon in Central Park a bit tricky. I had to navigate my way to the park well before sunset—at least an hour and a half early, so I could safely hide some clothes in a thick set of bushes in the park by the time the curfew was in effect.

Both the NYPD and the New York Army National Guard were involved in patrolling the streets of Manhattan, Brooklyn, Queens, Harlem, and the Bronx at night.

This almost military state approach reduced the incidents of violence and the destruction of property. But it wasn't enough to stop them completely. The PFA and emboldened citizens still struck out. Over two dozen deaths specifically attributed to targeted attacks on diverse citizens and businesses occurred.

Citizens who weren't driven to violence and protesting during the daylight hours were filled with unrest and anxiety. Many chanted that this lockdown was taking away their freedoms and liberties, which lead to further protests, particularly by enraged privileged whites from upscale neighborhoods. Half a dozen other deaths completely unrelated to hate-crimes or the PFA-incited violence resulted from infighting among neighbors in these boroughs.

The underlying smell of perpetual fear and anger and hatred across the city was stronger than ever. People were exhausted. Many, with the means, were leaving the city to cottages in the Catskills, other places, or even to stay with family outside New York.

Irwin and I continued to patrol the city as much as we could, both tracking for the scents we knew, as well as doing our best to stop violent crimes when they went down. But neither of us had picked up the scent of the one PFA member who'd been shopping at Gail's store. And the super-powered PFA members had been elusive in their night-time attacks. Irwin hadn't been able to do more than stop a handful of night-time muggings and arson attempts.

I was eager to get to the end of my monthly ten-day wolf transition cycle where I too could assist by patrolling the city streets after dark and looking to stop or capture PFA members.

But it seemed, to us at least, as if the leaders of this night-time chaos in action, the PFA, had set the wheels in motion and then all but disappeared back into the shadows.

Detective Wagner and his small team, joined by Special Agent Hank Reynolds and his additional insider resources, conducted a sweep of the city, the landmarks, and potential target buildings.

It was good for me to see Hank, but we only socialized once by meeting for lunch. Hank, Lex and I had enjoyed catching up with him and talking about my friend Craig, his brother-in-law, back in Los Angeles; but all of us were, of course, too distracted with what was going down in the city.

Hank relayed the fact that their intel confirmed the PFA leader Marco Bauer had left LA for New York, but apart from unsubstantiated whispers of him moving about the city, he hadn't been located.

Hank informed us that Lex was being followed and watched, in anticipation of Marco directly attacking her. That made her coming to meet me with a fresh change of clothes in the mornings in Central Park problematic— so I returned to my previous solo logistical tasks of stashing a bag of clothes in secret locations, and then meeting her at my apartment for a morning rendezvous between the sheets.

It was a different type of lonely than I'd had when I was completely single. Yes, I had time with Lex, and we made the best of our time alone together. But it had not been, at all, how I'd expected our time together in New York to be. It had been liked we'd skipped out on that fun *honeymoon* period together and had already started a family. The odd and yet wonderful collaborative family of me and Lex, Gail, and Irwin, and our cousins detective Wagner and Special Agent Reynolds.

Wagner and Reynolds made an effective team, and they kept us in the loop, at least at a high level on the progress their teams had been making. After all, there were only so many of us that understood we were dealing with an enemy with paranormal abilities. They had learned and tracked the purchase of material explosives that had led them to busting up a group with absolutely no ties to the PFA.

There had been no luck at all apprehending any further PFA members; but they had made progress in the ongoing interrogation of the short man they had captured, and whose super-enhanced strength never seemed to return. That single dose of Lex's urine injected into his body had, as I mentioned, done the trick.

By the end of a solid week of being questioned and re-questioned, and likely interrogated using techniques I'd prefer not to know about, he revealed several details. In combination with snippets of information gathered from various other intel sources, Wagner and Reynolds were able to piece a story together.

Three simultaneous attacks were being planned on July 15th. The Empire State Building, Rockefeller Center, and One Bryant Park, three of the tallest structures in Midtown Manhattan, were to be the targets of demolition. Two of the locations were decoys while they would fill one of them with the berserker powder that would disperse across the city.

The specific day was chosen because of its relevance to the 1099 battle of the Crusaders from Europe to capture the Holy City of Jerusalem, resulting in the mass slaughter of thousands of Muslims and Jews. On July 15, 1099, Jerusalem fell to the besieging Crusaders.

The PFA felt it was the most appropriate day to deliver the defining blow in their own relentless desire to take back the nation.

Lex was also interviewed—though she felt *she* was being interrogated—on everything she knew about the PFA. Sure, she had revealed plenty of details about them and Marco, to Hank Reynolds a few weeks earlier back in Los Angeles. She had mentioned that they engaged in odd occult-like rituals, but she'd left out any details about the extraordinary powers some of them possessed.

This time, though, she'd shared and outlined details about the various powers she knew different members of the group possessed. How there had been about twenty members she'd known with some sort of obvious paranormal abilities; but that maybe only a half dozen of them, including Marco, had abilities that were considered powerful.

When she'd known him, Marco's only ability had been super-strength in his left arm. Full on Lee Majors *The Six Million Dollar Man* type of strength through his entire arm, hand and shoulder area—giving him the ability to bench press hundreds of pounds with that single arm, punch hard enough to kill a person with a single blow, or crush bricks in his bare hands.

His ability to open portals and step through them were not something she was aware he could do and had only witnessed it that one night in LA; when during an encounter with PFA thugs, Marco had arrived in a portal, grabbed the one guy, who turned out to be his right-hand man, and then disappeared again.

Special Agent Reynolds shared with her that, since she'd known him, Marco Bauer had risen in the ranks from local group leader to overall PFA leader. He had continued to play Russian roulette with experimental rituals and injections, eventually gaining the ability to teleport, which he used to murder the previously leader and take over.

Wagner and Reynolds developed a plan to deploy resources to intercept and prevent the planned attacks on all three buildings on the day in question. They would be equipped with weapons, armor, and a significant supply of one-ounce vials of Lex's Golden Charm as well as a synthetic compound Irwin had developed that hadn't been tested—beyond the partial and somewhat weakened effects it had on us both.

Like I said, some writers are quite good at inserting important transitions and backstory details seamlessly into a piece of writing. Others, like me, are pretty obvious about it.

But one thing I've done in my Maxwell Bronte novels quite effectively—and it's something that readers and critics alike often agree on—is that I'm always entirely honest with my readers. That, and I have been able to insert the occasional effective hook that compels them to turn the page and get to that next chapter.

Like right now, for example, as I explain that, though these days were long, filled with stress and an underlying fear that we wouldn't be able to find and stop the PFA from the massive attack they had planned, they were also good. Because the four of us had bonded as a motley, yet well-functioning team. And they were the last moments I had working collaboratively and for so many hours with the only two women I had ever loved.

Because when that week ended, when everything finally went down, that team would meet with a fate shattering it beyond ever reuniting again, and I would be in for the biggest heartbreak I'd ever faced.

Friday, July 14, 2017

Chapter Twenty-Nine: Friday Night's Not Alright for Fighting

I felt and heard my heart skip a beat when I came upon them. A pack of four, all wearing different clown masks.

One of them, wearing a rubber Pennywise the Clown mask from Stephen King's It, was the only one also dressed in a white clown-style jumpsuit. The others were in street clothes and had on different style clown masks. One was a full head covering Jigsaw mask. Another was wearing a cheap plastic Heath Ledger style Joker mask. And the fourth one had on an evil leering clown with thin red hair.

They had surrounded a pair of teenage boys, had been taunting and shoving them around—I'd heard it from several blocks away—and as I arrived the shoves and verbal attacks were devolving into kicks and punches.

It was my first time being out at night in New York since I'd brutally injured that one attacker. And it was the first night I felt I could be doing something useful; trying to help.

In addition, it was the first time I had ever, since gaining these powers, actually purposefully gone out stalking or hunting for bad guys.

Sure, over the years, I'd used my special senses and abilities to perform all kinds of vigilante activities. I'd tracked missing people, taken down muggers caught in the act, chased and apprehended burglars and thieves, or used my super strength and agility to defend those who needed my help.

But I had never, before, purposely, gone out looking for trouble.

I know I was doing it for the right reasons—to help protect innocent people in this city from the infiltration of the hatred and prejudice of the PFA—but it still felt wrong.

Maybe I'd been conscious of the whole thing ever since Detective Reynolds had asked me if I was some kind of vigilante.

I thought about that a lot, and about how, back in Los Angeles, my getting involved as an untrained civilian, in a night-time attack, had led to the death of someone I considered a friend.

It was why I had been more than happy that Lex's proximity allowed me to be rid of my lycanthropic affliction, and my powers.

Back then it had all seemed so clear. Let the professionals handle the bad guys. Allow me to live a normal non-confrontational non-alpha male life. Spend my days and nights in the arms and companionship of Lex.

Heck, instead of prowling the streets looking for a fight, I could have been back at my place sharing a bed with Lex.

Yes, I know, Lex and I had made the best of it and been able to be physically intimate, slip between the sheets for repeated rounds of the vigorous sexcapades we mutually enjoyed. That was, of course, wonderful. But I wanted something a bit more mundane and normal. What I really wanted to experience was the simple pleasure of crawling into bed with a woman I loved and falling asleep for the entire night knowing she was beside me.

A basic creature comfort.

But of course, it couldn't be that simple.

So, there I was, stalking the New York night and looking for a fight.

Earlier, about half an hour before the city's curfew was enforced, I had dressed all in black, then snuck into and hidden in a set of bushes in Bryant Park, which was only a couple of blocks from the Algonquin. I waited until the streets had cleared and then made my way about, carefully staying in the shadows as much as possible while listening for sounds of trouble.

The streets were quieter than I had ever seen them before, especially that early in the evening. Occasionally, a police cruiser or military vehicle would drive by in a slow patrol, but it was easy enough for me to evade them by ducking into a nearby alley with plenty of time, particularly because I could hear them coming from a mile away.

At least a half dozen helicopters were patrolling overhead, in both north/south and east/west sweeps of the city, their spotlights beaming down and lighting up the shadows below. It was easy for me to avoid those as well.

I had been out patrolling the city for hours before, while moving through Hell's Kitchen, I heard a commotion coming from the south.

It was the catcalls and verbal insults from that group of clowns. I heard the pleas of the two males that had been cornered and repeated yells of the words "faggot" and "sick perverts" from the gang that had surrounded them.

I quickly made my way in the ruckus's direction and found them in the empty lot of an auto repair business south of where the Lincoln Tunnel connected to Union City under the Hudson River.

Before I crossed the street, I pulled the black fleece gaiter from around my neck up over my nose and mouth. It was Gail's. She used it when running in the winter to protect her face from the cold and wind chill. It, and the hood over my head, worked perfectly for covering half of my face and hiding my identity.

I suppose the mask was leading me to feel a bit more self-conscious about my vigilante activity. While I had always been fond of Spider-Man, growing up on a constant diet of the comic books, I had never gone out donning a mask to conceal my face.

And yet here I was.

Considering I was in Hell's Kitchen, dressed all in black, I felt a little like Daredevil in that Netflix series. Only, Matt Murdock wore a black cloth over the *top* of his head, covering his eyes (he was blind after all, so no need to see), and most of his nose. My mask was on the bottom of my face but obscured enough of it to my satisfaction.

By the time I made it onto the lot where they were, the kicking and punching started. My heart skipped a beat as I remembered the first night back in Los Angeles when I'd encountered a gang of masked men beating another man, and how that night hadn't turned out so well for me.

But that night I'd been weakened by a combination of far too much alcohol and perhaps the lingering effect of having spent most of the day, evening, and night with Lex—we believed that alcohol somehow helped extend the nullifying effects of her own powers.

Tonight, I was not only fully sober but the proximity to the full moon meant I was near the peak of my strength, agility, and enhanced senses and powers.

"Hey, you clowns!" I yelled, trying to distract them. It might have been easier for me to surprise them. But sneaking closer would have taken longer. They'd already injured their victims—I could smell fresh blood from one of the men they'd cornered.

Because I could run much faster than any normal human, it was still a surprise for most of the gang as I barreled into them with my arms crossed in front of me. The smell of surprise and shock shot out from them like a valiantly held fart released from a sudden physical impact.

I struck the one in the Jigsaw mask and he flew back hard against the Joker, his whip-lashing head smacking the Joker hard in the face and cracking the plastic mask right off as they both sprawled to the ground.

"What the—?" the one with the big bush of red hair said. He was stunned into inaction.

Pennywise struck out immediately, throwing a punch at my head.

I leaned to the left, dodging his punch easily, as if he'd been moving through jelly, and lifted my right leg up to knee him in the stomach. He doubled over.

Making a quick mental note that neither super-speed nor rock-solid abs seemed to be part of this guy's special ability, I turned to face Red.

Red wet his pants, then turned and ran, screaming for help. I let him run off, then pivoted to face the other three.

Pennywise was still doubled over, his breath still knocked out of him.

Jigsaw was still laying on the ground on top of Joker, now mask-less, who was actually crying, his nose all bloody from the head butt he'd received when I knocked his buddy into him. He was, like their victims, a teenager.

I attended to the heartbeats—yes, everyone's heart-beat was racing, but there was an underlying rhythm and cadence to them that suggested every single person in front of me, both the victims and the assailants, were younger. They were all teenagers.

Nobody got up or approached me.

The victims, holding one another, continued to whimper and shuffle away in an odd backwards crab-like shuffle. The scent coming off them was not one of relief, but of a deeper fear.

"Please," Jigsaw said, his terrified youthful voice muffled beneath the rubber mask. "Don't hurt us. We're on your side."

My side? What the heck were they talking about?

Pennywise, his breath coming back to him, joined in the pleas. "Please, mister. We're one of you. We want to join the PFA. Show these faggots they're not welcome. Rid this city of niggers and kikes and wetbacks."

They thought I was PFA?

Of course. I was wearing a mask, a hoody, and dressed all in black. I'd attacked out of the shadows.

These weren't even PFA members. They were a group of teens. A bunch of impressionable young kids. Copycats acting out on their white supremist and homophobic tendencies.

My heart dropped.

The PFA had truly started something far more evil than their own malicious attacks.

They were inspiring similar actions in others.

I turned to the two crab-crawling teens who had been their victims.

"I'm not going to hurt you. Get up. Get out of here." I could hear a vehicle approaching from south on 11th Avenue. "Head that way," I pointed. "There's a police cruiser coming up 11th Avenue. They'll get you home safe. And for god's sake, stay off the streets at night."

They scrambled to their feet. One of them yelled out a quick "thank you" and they rushed over to the street and south along 11th.

"As for you bozos," I said, turning to the three. "What the hell is the matter with you? Why are you so filled with hate?"

One helicopter patrolling over the Hudson River was heading in this direction overtop of the Javitz Center, its spotlight sweeping north.

They were heading west and would come over atop West 37th Street, a block away, but the spotlight would likely pick us up within a few seconds.

"Don't try to run," I said.

None of them moved. They were too terrified.

The spotlight reached the lot, picking up the three teenage clowns, but I ducked out of sight, hiding behind the cover of the side of a building. A booming voice commanding them to freeze came over an electrified amplification system as the helicopter descended in an approach to land on 11th Avenue.

Nearby, a police siren started up.

These teens would be apprehended. The other two were now safe. There was nothing more I could do here.

I raced down the street as fast as I could, away from it all, and chastising myself.

I'd come out here specifically looking for trouble, looking to fight a group of PFA goons.

And in the process, I'd given up a night of laying comfortably with Lex. For this? Beating on a bunch of weak and impressionable teenagers? A mis-informed group of youths who likely needed to perhaps open a book and open their minds more than anything.

We were no longer just fighting a bunch of neo-Nazi super-powered thugs. We were up against a far more pervasive illness in society.

Something that couldn't and wouldn't be solved with fisticuffs and masked vigilantes.

Saturday, July 15, 2017

Chapter Thirty: The Ides of July Are Come

D-Day was upon us.

Despite Detective Wagner and Special Agent Reynolds keeping us in the loop on how things were going, and what was being planned, this wasn't some odd episode of a television show like *Castle*, *Lucifer*, or *Medium*. Meaning, in reality, a civilian consultant for the police is not given unlimited special access to official agendas and crime scenes; nor are they brought into the front lines of a raid or a sting operation.

Gail, Irwin and I, though considered helpful to the work this special task force was doing, were regular civilians. Or, at least, that's what they thought. So, we were not to be on site with them at the three identified target locations.

Lex, however, possessed special abilities—her magic-nullifying effects, which could come in handy for any paranormal or magic-based assaults. And so, clad in a Kevlar body suit, she accompanied Reynolds at One Bryant Park. It being the middle location of the three, if there was activity at one of the other locations, the distance to move her the seven blocks north or south would be relatively equal.

Enough vials of Lex's Golden Charm had been available for each of the teams to distribute them, almost as if they were animals marking a territory, around the inside perimeter of each of the three buildings. If any magic enhanced PFA goons crossed inside, they'd be almost immediately affected, putting them on par with the awaiting officers.

Unbeknownst to the special task force, Irwin and I were outside the Empire State Building and Rockefeller Center, respectively. We'd be able to hopefully step in if the armed forces there needed any help.

Gail took up a station at Bryant Park at a table outside the bakery booth at the northwest corner of the park, where, via a group text, she remained in contact with all of us. We chose that location for her because it was adjacent to One Bryant Park and central to all three locations. She kept her detection melon with her and would be able to alert us if any paranormal presence came within range of that central area.

Maintaining a party-line text communication allowed us to stay in touch directly with the entire team. And, as strange as it might seem, I had grown accustomed to the time all four of us had spent together. Sure, we had been forced together to work under a tight deadline on potential defences to a domestic terrorist organization, but it wasn't all long faces and bitter tension. Throughout the previous week we had found moments of jocularity.

Irwin and I had the opportunity to bond. We had been, after all, quite nerdy in our individual ways—he a science geek, and me a lifelong comic and book nerd.

And neither one of us had previously had the chance to spend time or speak with someone else who suffered the same affliction.

While he could change between human and wolf at will and I had no control over the change, we shared so many mutual experiences nobody else would understand. The ability to intuit other people's emotions, for example, could also come in handy—which both of us had used to our advantage—but it could also be a bit of a downer. Sometimes, particularly when a person you are interacting with, had a big time hate on for you, it was overtly transparent. It could become all-consuming and there was no ignoring it.

And while I had experienced that over the years, Irwin had suffered in far deeper ways. I recognize, particularly with the incidents that the PFA were inciting, that racism was far from gone in America. If anything, it had merely been partially brushed away from the surface of society and sent to fester underground.

Most of us, particularly middle-aged straight white men, fooled ourselves into believing we lived in an enlightened time in history. We looked down our noses at the racial segregation of the past but fail to recognize the underlying economic and cultural segregation that continues. We aren't aware of the micro-aggressions or those things that pepper a person's emotions and feelings but remain unsaid or even visible to the average person.

Irwin, of course, had understood that.

He talked about growing up and having friends and classmates consistently use his ethnicity in a derogatory way in the small town in Ohio where he was raised. Hearing someone, when haggling, being told that they were trying to 'Jew' them in the deal was common.

There was also that one high school classmate, the beloved and charming class clown, who was also a trophy-winning track athlete, named Reggie Hart. Reggie had signed every single person in the senior class's yearbook the same: *What did Hitler get for Christmas when he was a boy? G.I. Jews and an Easy Bake Oven.*

Irwin had shown his yearbook to Mr. Hartley, his favorite English teacher. The bald man with the white flowing beard had always made Irwin think about Gandalf from Lord of the Rings, and Irwin respected and trusted him.

After seeing the joke scribbled in the yearbook, the old guy had squinted his eyes, stroked his long beard, and shook his head for a long time.

Irwin had expected him to say something supportive; to call out the injustice, the disturbing maliciousness of such an aggression. But instead, the trusted and long-admired teacher responded with words that had shocked him.

"It's just a little joke," he'd said. "Don't take everything so seriously."

That response cut deeper than Reggie's dark and disturbing joke.

Just a little joke?

A *little* joke about the systematic slaughter of over six million people; more than two-thirds of the Jewish population of Europe?

An eighteen-year-old had written an unspeakably cruel joke that mocked this atrocity in a 1988 yearbook. And nobody—not even an enlightened and educated man like Mr. Hartley, that Irwin had looked up to—saw anything wrong with it. That told Irwin more than enough of what he could expect to come up against repeatedly in his life.

Even though he had left that small town, he continued to face similar moments throughout his life. Perhaps none as dramatic and deflating as Mr. Hartley's inability to see the blatantly obvious wrong.

But they added up over the years.

And Irwin had been even more privy to those hidden and unspoken aggressions and feelings other people had about him ever since acquiring the wolf-enhanced senses.

I realized I had nothing to complain about. Absolutely nothing. Sure, a lot of kids had made fun of the way my ears had stuck out of my head when I was a kid. I remember being asked if, like Dumbo the ele-phant, I might fly home for lunch instead of walking. Yeah, they had mocked me for being a book worm. I'd even been beat up.

But I'd never faced anything like that.

Just like encountering those teenagers the night before I was reminded of just how far we as a society had to go with matters of equality, equity and justice.

Getting to know Irwin made me realize how few male friends I actually had in New York. When I'd been in Los Angeles, Craig, the carpenter I'd met on my first day on the set, had become a friend. But he was still on the west coast. Here in New York, I didn't really have any male friends. Mack, my agent, could hardly be called a friend. The only consistent male friend I had since moving here—Buddy J. Samuels—didn't even live in the city. He was a traveling salesman.

I looked forward to the opportunity to spend more time with Irwin well after this chaotic mess with the PFA was long past us.

It seemed, also, that Gail and Lex had been bonding in a similar way. The initial conflict and competition between them had taken a back-seat to the more urgent need for us to collaborate; and it warmed my heart to see them working together and getting to know one another.

While I'd come to terms with the fact Gail and I would only be friends, I hadn't wanted to not have her in my life. Knowing she was close to and respected the woman I had fallen madly in love with, was a truly heart-warming and spirit-lifting feeling.

Despite the fact we were in the middle of some of the darkest, most anxious and fear-filled days the city of New York had faced since September 2001, the four of us were becoming closer. Though a darkness was seeping up from below and threatening to destroy and divide the population, we found a light within each other.

So that simple digital connection, the group text we had, kept us bonded at a tense moment when we were all physically separated.

The operation started, as these things often do, at the crack of dawn.

Reynolds and Wagner's special forces teams were fully in place at their locations by 5:30 AM. They had been keeping a small and secret presence in place at all three buildings since they discovered the attacks were planned. But the full team wasn't engaged until the morning of the expected attacks.

Lex, who was with Reynolds—they'd picked her up at 4:00 AM—texted the rest of us to inform us they were in place. Gail had spent the night at Irwin's apartment, in his spare bedroom, as it was significantly closer to today's action than her place in the Lower East Side. So, all three of us were ready to move into our spots.

I took up my position on the south-western edge of the upper concourse area of what was, in the winter, the rink at Rockefeller Plaza. It was far enough away from the building that the territorial markings of Lex's Golden Charm, did not affect me. And that location offered me a decent view of the main entrance of the tall building across the pedestrian walkway, as well as visibility to the lower concourse area and the channel garden walkway that led to 5th Avenue. West 49th Street was also right behind me, so I could attend to people and traffic approaching from that area.

Several hours passed with not much happening. The usual Saturday summer tourist traffic was dramatically reduced—a racial inspired terror crime-wave and a city under partial martial law would have that effect—so it had been relatively easy for me to deduce any strange emotive scents among the small crowd. I had been focusing on the nervous energy that came from a planned attack.

But so far, the only scents of anxiousness I had been able to pick up had been from the agents and officers placed inside and nearby the building.

A little after 10 AM I noticed what appeared to be an old UPS van that had been converted into a florist delivery vehicle stopped on the far side of West 49th street. No driver had gotten out, and it sat there, idling, for several minutes. The wind hadn't yet shifted in a way that allowed me to pick up any nervous scent coming from it, and there was no distinguishable sound.

I quickly did a visual and auditory scan of the rest of the area, seeing if I could detect any other anomalies, and considered making my way closer.

Before moving, I sent a quick text to the group.

Florist van idling on W 49th. Going to check it out.

In that moment, I had been so focused on the van and the message to my team that I barely registered the familiar scent of someone sneaking up on me from behind until they were right behind me and within striking distance.

Chapter Thirty-One: I'm Not Sure if the J. is Short for either "Juxtaposition" or "Just When I Needed You Most"

My instincts kicked in, and I whirled, my left arm raised in a defensive block and my right arm poised to punch out before my mind had even placed the familiar scent.

Fortunately, I didn't strike.

The familiar scent and visual confirmation of who it was sneaking up behind me came simultaneously.

It was Buddy J. Samuels.

"Michael!" Buddy said in the jovial, upbeat, and energetic voice he often spoke with. He paused, then took a half step back and mocked bringing his left arm up to block an attack.

"Woah, you look like you were about to punch me, man. Is that any way to greet a dear old friend? Did that parking lot incident in Hollywood leave you with a bit of PTSD?"

Buddy was referring to the last time I had seen him, a few weeks ago, when he'd rescued me from getting my drunken ass handed to me by a bunch of PFA thugs. He had, as he often did, showed up in the nick of time to save my skin.

"Buddy?" It was all I could say.

"I went by your hotel," Buddy said. "Paul your doorman said he hadn't seen you either leave or come back this morning.

"He's an interesting fellow, that doorman of yours. Did you know he—like you—is a scribe?"

"I do."

"Have you read any of his short stories? I have. He sold a story to *The New Yorker* last year that I quite enjoyed. The man, I dare say, has genuine talent. Of course, I'm just a layperson when it comes to writing. I know what I like to read, and most of the things I read are non-fiction, but that young man has a great deal of untapped talent I dare say.

"I suspect that the richness of the characters in his fiction comes from his love of, and great experience with interacting with other people. I would venture to guess that he has encountered more than his fair share of characters in his role as doorman."

I tried waiting for a pause in Buddy's onslaught of verbal diarrhea to reply. But even when he asked a question, like whether I'd read Paul's stories, he just kept motor-mouthing along.

Buddy was an amiable fellow—perhaps the most gregarious person I had ever met in my life—but he also loved, more than anything, the sound of his own voice.

He did, however, love other people. Buddy was at home amid networking and living in the moment, eager to bring anyone within his vicinity into the experience of basking in the moment.

One couldn't help but immediately love Buddy, with his veritable cross between Buddy Hackett and Lou Costello in looks, and a personality like the good-hearted and amiable Del Griffith as portrayed by John Candy in *Planes, Trains and Automobile.*

He was like a favorite uncle, a reliable and loyal sidekick best friend. I automatically put up with the relentless one-sided conversations he so enjoyed because there was just something about Buddy that made you want to hug him.

I suppose the fact he saved my life when we'd met and then taken me under his wing when I'd first moved to New York could be two major factors in my adoration of him.

"But," Buddy said, reaching over and slapping me on the back, "I digress. I'm only in town for another few hours. I've got to catch a plane back to Chicago late this afternoon. But you've got me for the next few hours, and, lucky duck that you are, you can treat me to a late breakfast at Limani."

"Listen, Buddy, I—"

"I'm in town working a few deals with a Sandhog laborer conference," he interrupted. "Did you know the term Sandhog is one often given to urban miners and underground construction workers?"

"No, I didn—"

"The term was first used as early as 1872 for some of the workers performing work for the foundation of the Brooklyn Bridge. It was, of course, the first fixed crossing of the East River. And, at the time, it was the longest suspension bridge in the world."

"I—"

"Of course, it wasn't originally called the Brooklyn Bridge. That didn't happen until 1915. But in the early days it was called either the East River Bridge or the New York and Brooklyn Bridge.

"Sandhogs also, obviously, had a hand in the Brooklyn-Battery tunnel, the Lincoln Tunnel, the Holland Tunnel, the Queens-Midtown and a myriad of subway and water system tunnels throughout the city."

He paused for a moment, and instead of worrying about trying to tell him I was busy, I figured I'd let him ramble on while I focused on that cargo van still idling across the street. The driver still hadn't come out.

"The majority of the Sandhogs I met with this week have been working, for decades, on Water Tunnel Number 3, which is the largest capital construction project in this city's long and rich history.

"Stage One work on it started in 1970. Hell, you likely weren't even born then, were you? You likely weren't even a twinkle in your old man's sperm by then yet."

I messaged the group to let them know there was no change in the van, but I was monitoring it.

"Don't bother to double check on my facts with your phone, son. You know I'm never wrong on these things. Anyway, the entire Tunnel Number 3 is expected to be over 60 miles long—that's about 97 kilometers, my Canadian friend—to travel 500 feet below street level, and cost more than six billion dollars by the time it's completed some time in the early to mid 2020s."

I looked up from my phone to quickly eye Buddy before glancing back over at the van. I had never realized how much he also reminded me of the old Looney Tunes character Foghorn Leghorn. His bombastic personality, booming voice, and constant non-stop monologues definitely fit the bill. Not to mention the way he latched himself onto me as a mentor, the way the cartoon rooster regularly did.

"Did you realize," Buddy continued, "that there's an entire world beneath Manhattan that is a textured tapes-try of endless layers running as deep down as the Chrysler Building is high?"

The Chrysler Building? Why was Buddy bringing that up? I'd always wondered about how this good-time-loving and happy-go-lucky guy always seemed to show up at the most convenient times in my life, with just the right peppering of insights and trivia.

When we'd first met, for example, he not only saved me from the wolf attack that had led to my lycanthropic affliction, but he showered me with advice and insights about New York. I stayed with him for those first several nights on a chair, and later, a fold-out cot in his hotel room. While he benefited from talking my ear off, I gained a crash-course in the Big Apple.

Once, when I had been kidnapped by the same group of thugs that had taken Gail's fiancé hostage, Buddy showed up, his blathering distracting them enough for me to get the upper hand.

Then, last month, in Los Angeles, he'd appeared in the middle of the night, gun in hand, and saved me from the PFA guys beating the snot out of me. He took me to a hotel room instead of a hospital and nursed me back to health.

Sure, it had only been a handful of times in the past decade, but Buddy had a way of juxtapositioning himself into a key moment just when I need him most.

It was like he always knew more than he was letting on.

While I could scent and smell his emotions, there was never any specific tell in his mannerisms. Maybe it meant he was authentically falling ass-backwards into moments that saved my skin. Or perhaps he had that ability, like some people do, to successfully navigate my enhanced lie-detection sensory abilities.

Could this mean that his mention of the Chrysler Building was something I should attend to?

But he never brought up that building again as he continued.

"And within that underground world lies a myriad of both natural and man-made waterways. The most famously known one, of course, is Minetta Brook, one of the largest natural watercourses that was covered over by city planners in the 19th century. Then there are the sewer systems, and, of course, the fresh water that is fed to the city in tunnels running anywhere between 200 and 800 feet deep."

I watched a young woman who appeared to be in her mid-thirties who'd been walking through the plaza in front of Rockefeller Center head toward the van.

"Two main tunnels currently provide New York City with most of the 13 million gallons of water it requires each day. About ninety percent of it is pumped in from res-ervoirs in upstate New York fed mostly by the power of gravity."

The woman opened the passenger side door and got in. I briefly heard a male voice from inside the van quietly say: 'What took you so long?'

"The water descends through aqueducts as high as fourteen hundred feet above sea level, and gathers speed, rushing down to a thousand feet *below* sea level by the time it reaches the pipes beneath this city."

I tried to block out Buddy's rambling history of the freshwater system in the city and focus in on the conversation I could hear coming from that van. It wasn't easy, particularly with so many other conversations happening in and around the plaza, not to mention the booming voice of my distracting friend.

"I had to go to the restroom," the woman in the van said."

"You were meeting up with *him* weren't you?" the male voice said indignantly.

"No," she replied, as the van bolted back onto the road. "How many times do I have—"

They were then out of earshot. The van wasn't, of course, part of a PFA operated attack, and I'd just overheard a domestic quarrel.

"It was these gravity feeds and the upstate reservoirs' distance from the coast that saved this city's water supply from the wrath of Hurricane Sandy back in 2012. I was in town for that. I got stuck here on a grounded flight. Do you remember the loss of so much of the infrastructure? People were without lights, heat, phones, a subway line—even the internet.

"But imagine how quickly things would go downhill if something happened to the fresh water supply?

"I've heard rumors that there are only a few spots in the city where someone might access one of the main channels of Tunnel Number 1 feeding this city with its upstate fresh water."

I texted the group to let them know the van I'd been watching had just been a false alarm.

"One of them, the most easily accessible one is at the southwest tip of Central Park near Columbus Circle. You can get to it through an entrance off the 59 St. Columbus Circle subway station."

"Speaking of Subway, if you don't have time to eat a full meal at Limani—I mean, I imagine we might not be able to get in without a reservation—I'm down for a good old meatball sub at Subway down the street."

"Did you know that Subway—originally founded by a seventeen-year-old in Connecticut in 1965 as *Pete's Super Submarines*—was crowned the fasted growing franchise in the world a couple of years ago, is the largest single restaurant-chain and the largest restaurant operator in the world?

"So, whaddaya say, Wolfman? Feel like the two of us should *eat fresh* at Subway?"

At the mention of food my stomach grumbled. I'd always found it interesting how Buddy occasionally called me Wolfman, in honor, of course, of the way we had met on that highway in upstate New York. But I now wondered if he'd been trying to subtly let me know he knew about my powers and abilities?

Could that have been why he hadn't taken me to the hospital in Los Angeles when I'd been severely beaten? He said he hadn't wanted the police involved because of the illegal handgun he owned. But could it have been more than that?

My speculation about Buddy's peculiarities were shoved aside when my phone vibrated.

I looked down.

Gail messaged the group.

No false alarm here. A cube van just drove past, and the melon started to glow.

Chapter Thirty-Two: Hello Lamppost, What'cha Knowing? I've Come to Watch Your Anger Flowing.

I looked up at Buddy's chubby smiling face and my heart couldn't help but warm.

It didn't matter how much the guy liked to spew random trivia, nor the suspicions I might have about how he often showed up just when I could use his help, I admired and cared for him.

So, the idea of getting rid of him and shooing him off wasn't easy.

You can also, of course, blame that on my small-town Canadian upbringing. As my agent Mack once said about me, I wouldn't say 'shit' if I had a mouthful.

"Listen, Buddy. I'd love to have lunch with you. But I have plans to meet with Gail. That was her on the phone I was just messaging with. I'm already late."

It wasn't technically a lie. I was messaging Gail, among others, and I felt extremely late to be rushing over to One Bryant Park now.

"Are the two of you back together?" he asked. "I knew your time away from the city would be just the thing to remind you two kids you were meant for one another."

"No," I said. "We're just friends. But it's important that I get to her right away. I'm already late. Can I take a rain check on that lunch?"

He frowned and looked down at his shoes.

I felt the guilt seeping into me. But I could worry about Buddy's feelings later. I needed to get my butt over to that other building in case they could use my help.

"Yeah, he said. Sure thing, next time, my boy. Go make things right with Gail. You two have got this."

"Thanks Buddy. Great to see you. Have a safe flight."

I didn't wait for his response. I texted *I'm on my way* and then turned and started running down the Rockefeller Plaza walkway on the south side of West 49th Street.

Not caring that I was clipping at a superhuman speed, I ran at top speed, turning left onto the sidewalk on West 48th Street, crossing it diagonally, and then hanging a left onto 6th Avenue.

It was only 7 blocks to get to West 42nd Street, where One Bryant Park was.

After I crossed West 48th Street, I felt the phone in my hand vibrate. I slowed down enough to read the screen which showed another message from Gail.

It stopped glowing.

I slowed to a slow jog as another message from Gail came in.

The van is across the street. Half a dozen men just piled out of the back of it, carrying giant duffel bags. But the melon stopped glowing.

I picked up my pace and hoofed it another full block before the phone vibrated again. I slowed once more to read the screen. This message was from Lex.

It's the effect of the Golden Charm. It has already affected whomever among them has supernatural abilities.

I started running again and then slowed after feeling the vibration of another message. It was Lex again.

They're inside. I think those bags are filled with explosives.

I leaned into my run and gave it all that I had, racing at full speed. Less than a minute later, as I was rushing across West 44th Street I could hear Gail's voice calling to me.

"Michael! Stop!" She yelled. I looked down the street and saw her standing in the middle of 6th Avenue halfway down the block where the skyscraper of One Bryant Park stood, waving her arms madly over her head and repeating her pleas for me to stop.

"The Golden Charm!" she said, shaking her head.

I stopped running.

In a lower voice, one she knew I could hear, particularly now that I was tuned in to her from more than a block and a half away, she said: "Remember, they laced the perimeter of the building with Golden Charm. If you get too close, it'll mute your abilities too."

I texted the channel back in response to her. *But I need to get inside to help*.

"They've got this," Gail replied. "They are trained professionals."

Gail and I met about half a block from the Bank of America Tower.

"What do we do?" I asked, grabbing her by the shoulders. "I can't just stand back here and wait. What if something happens to Lex?"

My phone vibrated. Gail and I simultaneously looked down at our phones at the message from Lex.

We got them.

"What?" I said aloud.

As if in response, another message from Lex appeared.

The officers inside got them.

"They got them," Gail said, and the relief on her face and in her emotions was clear and powerful.

"They got them!" I replied and picked her up in my arms and swung her around.

Less than ten minutes later, Lex was outside and explaining to Gail and I how things had gone down. The PFA guys had stormed in from the street front and the subway entrance, apparently expecting to quickly lay a bunch of explosives at the base of the building around the perimeter.

The men carrying the bags must have had some sort of super strength ability, carrying bags heavy enough that it would take at least three or four regular men to carry them.

Because their powers were muted almost immediately, they simply collapsed to the floor under the weight of the bags they were carrying.

The special task force officers lurking on ground level jumped out and apprehended them.

They had filled the bags with enough explosives to blow an entire city block. But no detonation device had been detected. As had been speculated, one of them likely had the ability to detonate the explosives with some supernatural powers.

But the Golden Charm lacing the building had prevented that, as well.

One of the six bags hadn't contained explosives, but some sort of heavy and dark ash-like material. It was suspected to be the Berserker Powder. They dosed it with a vial of Lex's Golden Charm.

Reynolds had also injected all the captured PFA thugs with the same liquid, to remove permanently any special strength or abilities they had. If one of them could detonate the explosives with his mind or some simple gesture, he needed to render his abilities useless before they took away him from the proximity of the building laced with magic-nullifying properties.

I was just about to mention how easy this takedown had been, making me suspicious that something else was afoot, when our phones buzzed and a message from Irwin popped up. He was still at the Empire State Building.

Something's going down inside. I can hear the officers inside taking someone down.

Gail, Lex and I looked at one another.

Having been that close to Lex, and the outside of One Bryant Park, where the Golden Charm had been spread, I had no extra sensory ability. But the look of surprise on their faces was more than enough to relay what they were feeling.

I thought back to the building I had abandoned on my race here.

Reynolds popped around the corner just then, not at all surprised to see Gail and I standing with Lex. Of course he expected us to be nearby.

"We just took down another group at the Empire State Building. These ones came in from a series of wind tunnels that flow beneath the building. They were equipped with explosives and detonators. Not nearly the amount needed to take down the entire building, but certainly enough to do some massive damage."

"What about Rockefeller Center?" I asked.

"Nothing yet," Reynolds said.

"Was Marco at the Empire State Building?" Lex asked. "Because he wasn't among the ones taken down here."

Reynolds shook his head. "No. No sign of him yet."

Lex, Gail, and I exchanged glances. I knew what they were thinking. We should get over to the Rockefeller Center. Marco was likely going to be part of the attack there.

Perhaps One Bryant Park and the Empire State Building were the decoy attacks.

Reynolds lifted his head, distracted, then lifted a finger to the side of his left ear. He was listening to something.

He nodded, said, "Copy that," and then moved back into the building without acknowledging us.

The three of us decided it was time to head north to Rockefeller Center. Gail ran faster than Lex or I could. After a block, I told Lex to run on ahead of me, that I would hang back a bit, cross the street to create some distance so that my supernatural strength could come back to me, and then run up on the far side of the street so I could get there quickly.

I also messaged Irwin on the group text line to let him know where we were heading. He messaged back that he'd meet us there.

My strength and senses were just coming back to me when my phone rang.

It was Reynolds.

"We got them. We got the ones at Rockefeller. Same MO. Six guys carrying explosives and detonators. Taken down with no casualties on our side. It's over. We nabbed them all."

"What about Marco?" I asked.

"No," he said. "We suspect he set the wheels and motion and left town. But we'll interrogate the captured men. One of the eighteen of them is bound to give him up. We're taking them in now."

I sent a message to the rest of the group.

Reynolds just called. They took down the group at Rockefeller.

Lex replied.

Marco?

No, I messaged back.

Just then another message appeared on the group channel.

Slow down, you move too fast.

It wasn't from Gail, Lex, or Irwin.

Someone had hacked into our group chat. There was a pause before they sent another line.

Got to make the morning last.

Who could this be? Was it Marco?

Gail was the first to reply.

Who is this?

The response was another confusing line from the unidentified stranger.

Columbus kept going in circles until he thought it best to be looking for fun and feelin' groovy.

What the hell was this about? Could it be Marco toying with us?

Irwin was next to reply to the group line.

I recognize that. The first two lines at least. It's Simon and Garfunkel. The 59th Street Bridge Song.

I knew the song he was referring to. Only I'd always thought the song was called "Feelin' Groovy" and not, what he said: *The 59th Street Bridge Song.*

Irwin sent another message.

Except for the Columbus Circle thing. I have no idea what song that's from.

59th Street? Columbus Circle? Subway. Manhattan's water supply.

I suddenly made the connection to something Buddy had been babbling about. It wasn't a song. It was a message. Buddy had been going on and on about the primary water supply to Manhattan. And he'd specifically mentioned an access point at the 59th and Columbus Circle subway station on the southwest corner of Central Park.

That was it.

And why Marco wasn't at any of the three buildings. All three buildings had been decoys.

I didn't know who this stranger who'd hacked into our group chat was, but it directly linked to a flow of trivial information Buddy had shared. Perhaps the hacker was Buddy or was working in collaboration with him at least. Why the elusive tips? How was Buddy getting this info?

Now wasn't the time to figure that out.

Now was the time to act.

It's not a song. I messaged the group. *It's a tip about where the attack is going to happen.*

The actual attack wasn't going to be dust clouds from a fallen skyscraper. There were going to dissolve it into the water that fed the entire city.

We needed to get to the 59th Street Columbus Circle subway station, find the access entrance to Water Tunnel Number 1 and stop Marcus from poisoning the city's water supply.

Chapter Thirty-Three: We're Going Down, Down, Down, Down

It didn't take long to find the secret access that connected via one of the subway tunnels at the 59th Street Columbus Circle station.

Because the minute I arrived—ahead of Gail and Lex—I picked up the scent of one of Marco's right-hand henchmen.

The guy I had nicknamed Jason back in LA.

Lex told me his name was Carl.

Whatever his name was, I knew that scent well, and picked it up when I was descending the stairs from street level. It was fresh—he'd been here well within the last ten or fifteen minutes.

I traced it down to the track level and followed it— and the smell of four other males I didn't recognize, likely Marco and three other PFA members—along a set of tracks into the darkness of a tunnel leading away from the station. There was a door about one hundred feet down set in the wall's side there.

That door led to three maintenance passageways, but I followed the scent through another doorway leading to a circular staircase that dropped another thirty feet.

My cell phone signal was useless, so I quickly ascended to the track level platform where I messaged them to explain where I was.

Gail came down while Lex maintained her distance a good twenty feet back—she couldn't get too close to either me or Irwin, lest she nullify our abilities. And I needed to be able to use my heightened scent for tracking.

"Carl is here. With two others. I found where they went."

A subway train arrived, barrelling through the tunnel where I'd just tracked the three men. Among the people who disembarked from the cars was Irwin.

"As fast as I can run," he said, "nothing beats MTA for getting across the city quickly."

After a quick discussion we decided to message Reynolds and Wagner to tell them what we suspected was happening to Water Tunnel Number 1, and then head down ourselves.

We moved in a formation with me in the lead and Gail and Lex hanging back a solid twenty feet. Another twenty feet behind them, Irwin followed.

Gail wanted to take the lead so that the detection melon would light up. But it's radius reached too far, a full city block, meaning, for Irwin and I not to set it off we needed to be too far away for it to be useful in that manner.

Lex suggested that she go first, so that her nullifying power could work against Marco, Carl, and the third person with them. But she wouldn't know which way to go. Initially, we needed my scent ability for tracking.

I felt self conscious that we were being male chauvinists in insisting the two women in our party stay in the protected middle of our formation. But the reality was both Irwin and I possessed super strength and agility that the other two didn't.

We moved as quickly and as quietly as we could through the tunnels, stairways, and passages that kept leading deeper down below the city. Talking wasn't an option, out of fear our voices would echo through the cavernous spaces. And we couldn't text message one another either.

But as we continued, I occasionally heard the shuffling of footsteps far ahead, and the odd indecipherable male voice.

We kept moving. Deeper. Further down.

At one point we reached a metal circular staircase that descended around and around deeper through a large round shaft for what could have been a twenty-story building.

The bottom of that spiral staircase led off to another tunnel that zigged and zagged before another single-story flight of stairs and another tunnel. I was starting to wonder if the architects who designed these confusing and non-sensible passages might be the same ones responsible for the Winchester Mystery House.

During no point in the navigation of this underground labyrinth did I ever have to use my cell phone's
light app. Gail's magic detection melon, picking up me
and Irwin, was glowing bright enough to cast just
enough light, from about twenty feet behind, for me to
see where I was going, but without tipping off the men
we were tracking.

At one point I stopped, hearing the shuffling of feet
and voices around the next bend up ahead that lead to
what seemed to be a large open chamber because of the
increased echo effect. The voices were two men, neither
of which I recognized as Carl.

"Did you hear that?" a deep gravelly voice said in a
whisper.

"Yeah," the other male voice, much higher, replied.
"Sounded like footsteps. Someone is following us."

"Get ready to change. We'll ambush them."

"Okay."

A few seconds later, the most hideously awful smell
came wafting in from the room around the corner and
up ahead. It smelled like a huge stinking rotten garbage
heap—a cacophony of over-ripened fruit, sour milk, and
rotting vegetables.

Several years ago, I fought a profusely sweaty guy
with the obscenest body odor I had ever smelled. His
pungent stench was so intense it debilitated my ability
to think straight or fight effectively.

This smell was much worse. And it was from farther
away than the up-close encounter I'd had with Mr.
Hyperhidrosis. I worried about the effect this smell

might have on me when I got closer. Would it, similarly, weaken me?

And what the heck kind of power did this guy have? Maliciously odorous fart bombs?

The more the scent washed over me and seemed to thicken, the more I worried this was already an attack. A noxious airborne attack. And our cover had already been blown. They heard us, and were either preparing to ambush us, or had already launched their attack. I couldn't wait to see if this foul odor was going to reduce my powers or knock me out.

I had to attack. Draw them out. Do something.

Steeling myself up, I turned, trying to get my face as far away from the malodorous stink in the air, and took a deep breath.

I raised my left arm above my head and whipped it forward quickly, in what felt like that age old universal gesture of "charge."

Then I rushed forward.

I was a few feet away from the entrance to the larger chamber when a bright white blast of light exploded in the air in front of me.

My momentum continued to carry me forward, but the flash completely blinded me. I ran right into what felt like a carpeted brick wall and realized the smell was coming from it.

The intensity of the stench, that close to my nostrils, prevented me from smelling anything else.

Large meaty hands grabbed me by the shoulders and lifted me into the air, throwing me off to the side. My back and left shoulder struck what felt like a concrete wall, and I collapsed to the ground, still blinded from the burst of light.

The horrid odor filling the room also rendered my sense of smell completely useless.

But my hearing was fine. I heard the swift footfalls of Irwin racing forward from down the tunnel, then they ceased, and I heard the distinct growl of a wolf.

My vision was coming back to me, and I saw a large brown figure at least eight feet tall standing in the entrance to the room as a horizontal grey shape—Irwin in wolf form—launched itself at him.

Lifting myself to my feet, I looked to see where the second man was as a scream of pain echoed within the chamber.

My vision was almost back to normal as I spotted a guy dressed in black shuffling away from the melee. The fight taking place was a giant hairy creature that looked like a Sasquatch. It was stumbling back and pawing desperately at a large grey wolf latched onto its throat.

Irwin seemed to have Sasquatch on the defensive, so I raced around them as they struggled to the man who was crouched and cowering against the wall opposite me.

He held his hands in a flat locked praying position I recognized from one that Carl had used back in Los Angeles. It was a gesture he'd used when he was about to shoot an energy bolt out of his hands.

Suspecting he'd been the one who made the bright white blinding flash and was preparing to do it again, I rushed forward. He was wincing and squinting his eyes, as if concentrating hard. But nothing happened.

I swiped my right arm diagonally across his clenched hands, knocking them to the side, and punched him in the face with my left, knocking him immediately unconscious.

As he crumpled to the ground, I heard a yelp from behind me. I turned to see Sasquatch now had the wolf by its throat and was swinging its body against the concrete wall.

Irwin yelped again, as the monster slammed it a second time into the wall. I got up and rushed over, trying to tackle the immense creature and knock it off its feet. I hit it hard, but that seemed to do nothing. With my face buried in the putrid fragrance of the hairy beast, I felt my strength depleting.

I tried punching the creature repeatedly, but each blow seemed to be weaker, as if the foul stink was draining my abilities. Not that even the first hit seemed to have any effect on it.

It spun, swinging the wolf at me, and hitting me with it, launching me several feet into the air and tumbling onto my back.

As I scrambled to my feet, the Sasquatch let out an immense growl, stumbled to the left, and threw the wolf, hard, at me.

No, not at me.

Over my head.

The wolf struck the concrete wall behind me head-first, and landed, motionless, on the ground. Instantaneously it morphed back into Irwin's human form. He was unconscious, his face and head awash in thick fresh blood.

The Sasquatch creature stumbled to the left and took a step back, letting out a yelp of confusion and pain. I took a step toward it, feeling my strength, my sense of hearing, continuing to fade.

Then I saw noticed Lex standing in the doorway's entrance and moving her way closer to the large hairy creature.

Sasquatch yelped, trying to move away from her, and suddenly seemed smaller, shorter.

His hair receded, and the monster continued to shrink, until, within another couple of seconds, a skinny man who couldn't have been even five feet tall was standing naked in front of Lex.

The foul stench in the air was also gone.

The man let out a whimper and Lex moved in, punching him in the side of the head.

Her punch sent him stumbling backwards, and suddenly Gail was standing beside Lex, the glowing melon in her left hand, and her right hand swung in, striking the man.

Lex threw another left and Gail another right, and this time the guy fell back on his ass.

He crab-crawled backwards, trying to get as far away from them as possible, and then bumped up against the wall.

"Please," he begged. "No more. Please don't hurt me." I recognized his voice as the higher pitched one I'd heard earlier.

"No more is exactly what you're going to get," Lex said, pulling a vial of Golden Charm from a rucksack she wore around her waist, then using a syringe to draw the liquid in.

The skinny naked man passed out before she even injected him with it.

Gail took the needle from Lex and went over to inject it into the other passed out man.

I scrambled over to Irwin.

Lex's proximity still muted my strength and enhanced senses, but I could see and hear how ragged and rough his breathing was.

"Can you move?" I asked him. "Did you break your neck?"

"I don't know. I hurt everywhere."

I knelt beside him as his breath continued. "Hang in there, Irwin. We're here. We'll get you to a hospital."

"No," he said. "It's too late for me. Go. You still need to stop Marco. Leave me."

I looked up at Gail who was standing over us. Lex was in the furthest spot on the far side of the room.

Gail nodded.

"He actually stands a better chance of healing if we go," she said, pointing back at Lex, who scuttled back down the tunnel we'd entered the room from. "Remember how advanced your wolf constitution and healing can be. It's likely the same with Irwin."

I could feel the subtle and slow return of my strength and my enhanced senses the longer I stayed distant from Lex.

"Go," Irwin repeated. "Stop him."

I nodded and got back to my feet.

There was a large round metal hatch in the floor on the furthest end of the room with a circular crank on it. I moved over to it and turned the crank to open it. It let out a whoosh suggesting it was airtight.

I looked down the four-foot round hole at the ladder rungs that led down into the darkness. Gail approached with the glowing melon, and though the light reached down quite far, the rungs continued to disappear into shadow far below.

"They went this way?" she asked.

As my scent was returning to me, I picked up the faint scent of Marco, Carl, and the other of the five men whose scents I'd been tracking leading down the shaft.

I nodded. "Yeah. Let's keep going. Same formation."

I led the way, with Gail a good ten feet behind me, and Lex another dozen feet behind her.

The shaft seemed to go on forever, and I tried, above the slight scraping sound of my shoes, as well as my breathing, and the breathing of the women above me, to listen for any sounds coming from Marco and the others.

All I could hear, though, was the distant echo of water dripping in some unseen cavern below.

Each rung seemed to be about twelve inches apart from one another, and I was coming on one hundred rungs—about one hundred feet—when the echo of the dripping water seemed to change in sound a bit. The noise didn't seem to reverberate off the shaft as much. I peered down, and thought I could make out, via the light cast from Gail's melon above, the floor.

Finally.

I got to the floor and found myself in a square room that was perhaps ten by ten feet. The floor was wet with about an eighth of an inch of water that had been dripping from a crack in the ceiling. It seemed to drain into a fissure about the water's height along the wall across from where the rungs had been placed.

On the right wall was a rectangular watertight door with rounded corners—the kind you might see below deck on a ship—with a similar circular crank on it.

I opened the door as Gail reached the bottom of the shaft. The scent of Marco and his crew was stronger when the door opened.

Slipping through the entrance, I found myself in a narrow tunnel that led off a good fifty feet before it opened into what appeared to be a much larger room. There was light coming from that room ahead; what seemed to be the flickering light of a lantern.

With it came the sound of a male voice, one I recognized as Marco's—even though I'd only heard him utter a single syllable the one time I'd met him.

The voice was uttering something in a language I was completely unfamiliar with. It sounded like an incantation of sorts. Some ancient tongue.

All three male scents were coming from up ahead, and I could hear the other two breathing. They were in that large chamber with him.

I moved through the tunnel as quickly and quietly as I could, Gail coming up not that far behind me. Lex was, of course, still hanging back a good twenty feet.

Though it wasn't the best time, I wondered if we should have switched and had Lex try to sneak up on them, let her presence and nullifying effect seep into the room, taking away the powers I knew Marco and Carl possessed.

But it was too late. I couldn't speak this plan to Gail and Lex, or Marco and company might just hear us.

The chanting stopped. Whatever last step in the ritual it was, Marco had finished and was likely about infect the water supply.

I had to keep moving. Step into the room and do what I could before the other three attacked.

Remembering how I'd been ambushed during that last encounter wasn't a reassuring thing for me to think about as I stepped out of the tunnel and into the vast chamber.

"Marco!" I called out at the top of my voice.

Chapter Thirty-Four: Nothing Lasts Forever, But This Is Going to Take Us Down

The room was gigantic—at least twenty-five feet high—and my call of Marco's name echoed and bounced around, providing a rather eerie effect.

Marco, who had been pouring what looked like red flakes from a chalice into a large open duffle bag when I'd stepped in, let out the sound of a sharp intake of breath and sped up heartbeat at me having startled him.

He was off to the right, kneeling on the ground in front of a gigantic water pipeline about fifteen feet round that bisected the room.

The other two men, whose heartbeats and breaths let out matching patterns indicative of surprise, were standing on either side of him. Carl was on the right, sans the Jason coveralls and hockey mask he'd been wearing the other two times I'd seen him—I suppose he only wore that when out beating innocents. He wore different attire, a more formal black, for helping to poison the city's water supply. The other man, also dressed in black, stood to Marco's left. In front of them was a large open duffel bag that I presumed was filled with the Berserker Powder.

There was a lantern on the floor to the right of Carl, and to the left of the other guy dressed in black was a steel railing that ran around a huge well that was maybe twenty feet across.

"What the hell's wrong with you?" I said, wanting to keep them confused and bewildered. "When I yell out *Marco*, y'all are supposed to reply with *Polo*. Didn't they teach you any fun games at Nazi training school?"

Marco whirled, and the anger shooting off him was immediately clear.

"You!" he yelled, his steel cold blue eyes glaring at me.

"We meet again," I said. "But this time I'm the one dropping in unexpectedly."

To Marco's right, Carl took up the crouched position with his hands pressed tight together. It was the one I knew proceeded the energy bolt.

Just as I saw the glimmer of light that told me a yellow lightning bolt was about to shoot out from his clasped hands, I flung myself to the left.

Carl's energy blast missed me, but only by an inch or two, as I dove, tucked, and rolled back onto my feet. It exploded into the concrete wall behind me accompanied by a sickening crack.

I rushed toward the man standing on Marco's left, as he was closest to me, and he shot up into the air. I tracked his upward movement and saw that giant black bat-like wings had appeared from between the back of his shoulder blades. He had unfurled them to lift himself up.

"You!" Marco yelled again in the same outraged tone.

I looked down from the flying bat man to Marco, but he wasn't looking at me. He was facing the entrance I'd come from, where both Gail and Lex were now standing together.

The seething anger he had for Lex was beyond any anger I had ever smelled.

"Do you have any other words in your repertoire?" I said, mocking Marco as I stepped toward him, trying to get his attention back on me. "Seriously, dude, you really got to come up with some new material. How the heck did you inspire your troops to follow you without a solid moving speech? Single syllable words are—"

Marco spun, faster than I'd ever seen anyone move before, and his left arm shot out, striking me directly in the chest. The punch was enough to knock the wind completely out of me and send me flying backwards several feet.

As I was falling back, I saw Lex rushing across the room toward him.

Beside Marco, Carl was in that standing preying position to send another blast at Lex. He apparently needed about a minute to charge up between attacks. The blast emerged from his hands but fizzled in the air inches in front of Lex.

"Keep her away from me!" Marco yelled, taking a few steps back as Carl stepped in front to block her. He picked up the bag and moved further away, closer to the water pipe.

As I got to my feet and was rushing back over, Carl, who, as I remembered, was also super strong, grabbed Lex, preventing her from getting closer to Marco. While his energy bolt couldn't harm Lex, her magic nullifying power on his strength didn't seem to be an issue; at least not yet. He punched her in the head and Lex stumbled to one knee.

I reached Carl at that point and launched myself in the air, feet first, delivering a flying kick into the middle of his chest.

He went back, his head slamming hard against the thick steel pipe, and fell to the ground, unconscious.

As I landed and turned, I heard and saw the bat dude sweep in and grab Lex, just as she was getting back onto both feet. He pulled her up into the air, about twenty or so feet straight up.

Lex struggled within his grasp, but he held her tight with his right arm under her own right armpit and across her chest. With his left hand, he forced her head to the left, exposing her neck.

His eyes flashed red, and it was then I saw the elongated dual fangs of his front top teeth.

He wasn't a bat man; he was a vampire.

"No!" I yelled, as his teeth came down on Lex's neck.

Marco struck me then, coming at me fast and tackling me to the ground. Before I could get out from under him, he punched me three times with his left fist. I couldn't see from my right eye as the agony of his punches tore through my head.

Letting out a battle cry, Gail shot out from the side, catching Marco by surprise. He and Gail tumbled to the ground on my right.

I scrambled over and threw a left-right punch combo. My left caught Marco in the back of the head, and the right caught him in the side of the face, shattering his right cheek bone.

He might have had speed and strength in his left arm, but his face, and, presumably, the rest of his body, was normal.

I felt a shameless bolt of pleasure hearing him squealing out in pain.

He collapsed backwards, and I looked up to see the vampire, still hovering in the same spot and struggling to sink his teeth into Lex's neck.

The fangs weren't penetrating her skin. That was good.

Lex struggled, and he kept trying to bite her, looking like a dog trying hard to bite into and crack a bone, but her skin simply wasn't giving.

A yellow sliver of light opened in the air between Gail and me. Marco had crawled over to the duffel bag and was pulling it in the direction of the light portal.

It was obvious he was going to teleport the bag into the inside of the section of the water tunnel in front of us.

"Lex," Gail called out, her one hand pulling on the duffel bag. "Drop me a vial."

Lex fumbled with the rucksack, a task made more difficult because the vampire holding her was fluttering sporadically back and forth.

After a few seconds, Lex released a vial, but the vampire had taken a dramatic left spin that sent the vial tumbling down the shaft of the giant well in the floor.

Lex tossed out a second vial that dropped a few feet to Gail's right. She dove to catch it, having to let go of the duffel bag.

Marco pulled the bag closer and then shoved it into the portal. I reached in and we played an aggressive game of tug of war with the bag half in the portal as it was closing.

Because he was sprawled on the ground, and I was standing, I kicked at Marco's shoulder and wrenched the bag away from the portal a second before it sealed up.

Gail was beside me, the vial opened, and she dumped the Golden Charm into the black powder.

"No!" Marco screamed in what sounded like abject horror. Gail responded by kicking him in the face and catching him in the same cheekbone that I had shattered. He collapsed onto his back, unconscious.

Above us, the vampire fluttered against the ceiling of the twenty-five-foot cavernous room, letting go of Lex.

They both plummeted.

Gail and I both rushed to get under Lex and help break her fall. We managed to get under her, and she crashed into us, knocking Gail and I into the floor.

Beside us I heard a distinct cracking sound suggesting the vampire broke his neck or back as he struck the bare concrete.

I was in intense pain, and could only imagine how Gail, who didn't possess any super strength, was feeling. But I heard both Gail and Lex breathing. Gail's left arm was twisted underneath her and there was a fractured bone protruding from Lex's right leg.

They were both injured, and stunned, but still alive.

I carefully untangled myself from Gail and Lex and was getting to my feet when I heard a shuffling from across the room.

Lex's proximity to me was reducing the ability of my senses, so I hadn't heard Carl's breathing change to indicate he'd woken back up.

Carl had regained consciousness and was in his odd ready-to-bolt crouch position. He was about to fire an energy bolt in our direction. But the look of utter pain and intense concentration on his face was so overstated it was both ridiculous and disturbing. If I didn't know any better, I would say he looked like he was constipated while trying to pass a human-sized cactus out his anus.

As an intense sliver of yellow light brighter than I'd ever seen from him started to slowly glow from between his hands, I suspected this was going to be a lot more than the average energy bolt he shot.

It may have been easy for me to dodge the blast, but Lex and Gail were still stunned.

Stepping out to get between the women and Carl, I watched the small sliver of light building until his hands disappeared behind it.

As I braced for the impact, out of nowhere, a grey flash burst in from the right, followed by the low growl of a wolf.

Irwin, in wolf form, leapt at Carl, his fangs catching him in the throat and his front paws knocking his clasped hands in a downward direction.

The thick searing lightning bolt struck the ground a foot in front of me, more powerful than I had even imagined.

But it wasn't a single blast—it seemed to be a continuing firehose of power that lasted a few seconds.

As Carl's hands swung to his left, the powerful energy blast ripped through the concrete, lifting the entire section of the floor that all three of us were on. The force lifted the thick concrete, flipping it into the air the way a heavy wind might lift a piece of cardboard.

A hurricane-type force threw us, the concrete we were on, and several large pieces of rock, metal, segments of old rusted pipe, and smaller debris and dust, across the large chamber.

My back slammed hard into the wall, and as I fell to the ground, I heard the wall crack and crumble.

I landed on my stomach directly beside the huge opening in the floor with something heavy pinning me to the ground.

Carl was staggering to his right with Irwin, still in wolf form, attached to his throat and bounced backwards off a torn section of the steel railing that had been ripped from its mooring around the giant opening in the floor. They both plummeted down the hole, the echo of the man's screams and the wolf's growls spiraling back out of the depths of the deep shaft as they fell.

Struggling to get up, I realized I was wedged, from my shoulders down, under a massive chunk of the concrete.

To my immediate left, clinging to the other half of the steel railing that the blast had partially shredded and twisted sideways over the middle of the enormous shaft like some bizarro section of bridge frame, were Gail and Lex.

Gail, looking to be unconscious, was closest to where it was still partially attached to the floor, her broken arm and one leg tangled in the railing.

Lex was further down the same section of railing hanging from both hands to a piece of the rail that jutted at an angle slightly higher than the rest.

"Hang on," I yelled to her, realizing, as the words escaped my lips, how stupid they sounded. "I'm coming to get you."

I pressed my arms against the floor beneath me and pushed. The concrete pinning me down was too heavy. And my enhanced strength was weakening by the second, being so close to Lex.

Trying again, this time lifting with my arms, back, and shoulders, I strained.

I lifted the concrete slightly.

But not enough.

The slight leverage I'd gained gave as my strength gave out further, and the concrete pushed me tighter against the floor.

I looked helplessly at Lex, less than a couple of feet out of my reach in front of me.

She stared silently back at me, realizing it was her proximity that was preventing me from getting out from under the concrete slab.

The weight of the concrete on top of me felt like it was getting heavier by the second. It was becoming more difficult to breathe.

"Wha—?" Gail groaned, groggily coming back to consciousness.

As she lifted her head, the one section of the railing still attached to the concrete let out a protesting metallic squeal as one of the three remaining bolts holding it up pulled out and fell down the shaft.

The railing tipped downward a couple of inches.

"Don't move!" I gasped. "And hang on."

Apparently, in the heat of the moment, I was quite adept at stating the overtly obvious.

Gail's eyes opened, and I didn't need my wolfishly powerful sense of smell to read the outright terror in them. She realized where she was and what was happening.

"Kal," Lex called. "I have to let go. So you can get your strength back, get out from there, and save Gail."

"No!" I tried to yell, but with my chest being compressed, it barely came out as a wheeze. I pushed up against the concrete with every single ounce of all the draining strength I had in me.

I succeeded only in exhausting myself.

"If I don't let go, all three of us will die."

"Lex, please. I love you."

"I know. I know how much you love me. I've never felt more loved in my entire life. And I love you too. But so does Gail. Very much. And you her. I see it deep in your eyes when you look at each another."

The steel railing dipped another inch, shrieked the eerie song of metal stretching, the noise echoing down the shaft, as the two remaining bolts holding the twisted rail slowly pulled further from their mooring.

"Alexandria—"

"I know, Michael." Lex stared at me in a way that riveted my soul the same way the concrete slab on top of me pinned me to the spot. "Please just say you'll remember me."

She let go.

Chapter Thirty-Five: Two Hearts and a Fleeting Schrödinger Thought Experiment

"Nooooo!"

It was Gail who called out.

I couldn't even scream aloud.

There was barely any breath left in me, as I made a frustrating combination gasping and gurgling sound.

One second Lex was there, looking me in the eye, the next, she was gone.

She let go and dropped swiftly and silently out of sight. Because there was no other sound—no echo of her screaming, nor the sound of her body hitting the ground far below—I told myself she'd grabbed hold of something further below, out of my line of sight, and was hanging for dear life.

It could have, of course, been because the pulsing throbbing sound in my head that had drowned it out.

But I lay there, hoping against hope she was still there, clinging to something—anything—just a few meters below, and feeling the pressure of the concrete on me easing ever so slightly as my strength slowly returned.

I avoided looking at Gail the entire eternal two minutes of laying there; because I knew she had a clear view of whether Lex was where I hoped she'd be, or if she had indeed fallen down the shaft.

The metal railing had stopped squealing and pulling from its anchors, so I knew Gail was safe—at least for now. So long as she didn't move, the railing didn't seem to be going anywhere.

There was no rush, no urgency.

Knowing Gail was alive and safe—and imagining Lex too was also safe—was comforting. My breathing was getting easier, and I contemplated just staying there.

Like Schrödinger's cat, Lex could not be confirmed dead until that box was opened. But if I didn't look, never opened that box, she would still be here.

And I might have stayed there, unable to move, if not for a thought that suddenly came to me.

Marco.

I had forgotten about him.

Gail had knocked him out, but he could wake at any moment.

Straining my neck, I looked over to where he'd been laying, but I couldn't see.

I pushed my shoulders up against the concrete and felt it shift.

My strength was returning, but I couldn't lift it off of me yet.

I waited a few seconds, trying to attend to the sounds and smells. But my heightened abilities hadn't returned enough to listen for the sound of other people breathing.

Taking a deep breath, I tried again, pressing my hands against the concrete, and straining up like I was doing a push up.

It moved, shifting a little down off my back. I held myself in place and waited another few beats as the power and energy flowed through my veins.

Then I pushed up again, this time scrambling out from under the concrete as it collapsed to the ground.

Free, I turned to look where Marco had been knocked out.

He wasn't there.

I turned to survey the rest of the chamber. The prone body of the vampire guy was laying where he'd fallen. But Marco was nowhere to be seen.

I pulled myself to the edge of the hole and braced myself mentally and emotionally as I looked down.

Lex wasn't anywhere in sight.

I saw nothing but the huge shaft receding into the darkness.

For the second time in so many minutes I felt what I can only describe as a massive sucker punch to my gut, completely winding me.

"Lex!" I screamed down into the chasm below.

My voice echoed down through the darkness, and as my augmented sense of hearing increased, I listened for the sound of anything else—her voice, her heartbeat— coming from the shaft.

All I could hear was the sound of an enormous volume of rushing water from what must have been hundreds of feet below.

That and the sound of Gail's labored breathing and racing heartbeat.

Hers, and my own, were the only two heartbeats I was able to pick up.

I looked over at Gail. She was staring at me, silent tears streaming down her face. A flood of emotions—grief, horror, excruciating pain, compassion—poured out of her as powerfully as the running water deep down the shaft.

I got onto my hands and knees and shifted as close to her as I could.

"Give me your hand," I said softly.

She lifted her right arm out and I grabbed her with my right hand reaching around her underarm, my fingers locked around her triceps.

With my left hand pulling the fabric of her shirt on the back of her shoulder, I lifted her gently toward me.

A powerful pulse of pain shot through her as her broken left arm disentangled from the steel bar it had been caught on. As I pulled her, she unwrapped the one leg that had been twisted around the rail.

A moment later, she was back on solid ground in my arms.

"Oh Michael," she said, her right hand on the side of my face, her eyes bursting with tears and compassion. "I'm so sorry."

I pulled her tight against me with both arms, our devastated hearts beating in sync a mere inches apart, and let my own tears explode.

As Gail rubbed the back of my head with her one good hand, I buried my face in her neck and let out a deep and low mournful howl that seemed to go on for eternity.

Epilogue: Much More Work to Do

The grief, and the mourning over losing Lex still hadn't faded, even well after Gail's broken radius bone had healed.

I wasn't sure if I would ever be over that loss.

It had ended as suddenly, and unexpectedly, as it had begun.

And, though I was in pain, slowly unraveling the heartache and anguish, a solid part of me was grateful for the time Lex and I had together; of the connection we had made.

I listened to her favorite album, Taylor Swift's *1989* on repeat, while letting myself cry. "Wildest Dreams" that song she'd told me she listened to after the first night we'd met, and the song she referenced in her last words to me, hit me the hardest.

Of course I would remember her. And not just in my wildest dreams, but in countless waking moments, forever.

She was *a gift I never dared to ask for*.

That was a line from the Alicia Witt song I heard the night before I'd met Lex; but of an experience that opened my heart up to being able to accept what Lex and I found. At the time, I'd been thinking of the song differently.

But now, it made me think about Lex, and that gift she brought to my life.

Lex brought something not only to me but also to Gail.

Throughout my misery, I was grateful to have Gail, and to know that, in the short time they'd gotten to know one another she had loved Lex like a sister. Gail was there for me in a way I didn't realize I needed.

On the plus side of things, the PFA had been destroyed. A few of the members captured in New York during the sting operations had given up information on their secret operations both locally and out west. The PFA was no longer a threat. Most of their members had been captured, and their abilities neutralized thanks to the Golden Charm from Lex.

Marco had disappeared. We assumed that some time after Carl's blast had torn up half of the chamber, Marco had regained consciousness and escaped into one of his portals and crawled off somewhere to lick his wounds.

He never resurfaced either in New York or back in Los Angeles, and if he did, he would have no PFA gang to lead.

Reynolds and Wagner had recovered the body of the dead vampire and hidden it away to be studied in a secret lab. They, similarly, kept any mention of the involvement Gail and I had in stopping Marco, from any official reports.

Despite numerous searches they never recovered the bodies of Lex, Irwin, or Carl. The deep running water at the bottom of the chasm was assumed to lead into the

Hudson River. But no combing of the Hudson ever resulted in their bodies turning up.

There were moments, in my grief, that I speculated Lex might be alive out there somewhere and would miraculously return to me.

But that was a fantasy—and something I never shared with anyone. Not even Gail.

Lex's selfless love would live eternally in my heart.

Her sacrifice—and Irwin's sacrifice, saved our lives.

I was determined that Gail and I would not let their loss be in vain.

The PFA's ultimate blow had been prevented. Thanks to the quick thinking of Gail and Lex working in unison.

But the impact of the terror they had unleashed on the city was slow to unravel. With the Proud Fighters of America no longer instigating white supremist fear and hatred, the violent riots and unrest, and racially motivated attacks slowed down.

New York's martial law days were in the past.

But we knew, deep down, that racism, fascism, hatred and fear of the other was not gone. It had, like in the past, merely been buried just below the surface. But it would continue to fester and would rise, once more, given the right circumstances.

In August, a Unite the Right rally took place in Charlottesville, Virginia that led to a violent and internationally covered clash between neo-Nazis and anti-fascists. When the president expressed that there were "very fine people on both sides" many groups of white nationalists and neo-Nazis took that as a sign they were being praised for their hard work liberating America in their anti-Islamic and anti-Semitic hate. And that the threads of racism and prejudice weren't reserved for the deep south, but were prevalent across the United States, up the nation's highest office.

Sure, the PFA were no longer a threat.

But they were merely the tip of the proverbial iceberg. There was a seething base of putrid hatred and fear-mongering constantly writhing beneath the surface that needed to be dealt with.

And not just by a special task force secretly tracking and investigating paranormal occult members or superpowered vigilantes raising their fists and punching Nazis.

This was work that needed to be done by every single member of society, looking deep into their hearts about what it meant to hold genuine compassion for fellow humans.

I had thought I could give up my special powers, my enhanced abilities, and live a normal life.

But Irwin and Lex had given their lives.

And I had been given a special gift—still not sure of the source or origin of it—that I could continue to use to help wherever I could.

Despite not having any special abilities herself, Gail was the perfect companion to help me with whatever good I could do, at least on some small level.

She was brilliant, resourceful, brave of heart, mind, and spirit—and I trusted her to the core of my being.

And she was working on other charms, elements, and tools—like the detection melon that revealed the proximity of supernatural forces.

Teaming up, in honor and memory of Lex and Irwin, Gail and I could keep this city safe, should other paranormal enemies—which we both now knew existed—or other threats arise.

Because it was clear there was a significant amount of work to be done.

Hatred, crime, unrest, and ill-will would not rest.

And neither would those who stood against them.

Author's Notes and Acknowledgements

I'm not an outliner, nor do I plan that far ahead when writing. Sure, I do have some ideas of major milestones along the way. But mostly I'm what is sometimes referred to as a "discovery writer."

This may just be a fancy term for someone who makes it up as he goes along or is considered a "pantster" instead of a plotter. (For those unfamiliar with the term a "pantser" is someone who "writes by the seat of their pants" without an outline or even specific direction in mind.)

Do you see why the term "discovery writer" can be a much-preferred substitution? It comes with a sense of adventure, like some major epic quest.

For this series, much of what I've written had been discovered along the way.

I didn't know, when I sat down to write a short story about a guy who wakes up naked in Battery Park with a bullet hole in his leg, the taste of blood in his mouth, and no memory of the night before when he was running around as a wolf, that it would be anything more than that single short story.

Readers of the story suggested it could be a novel; that I could explore the entire day of the then-unnamed narrator.

It took me ten years to finish that book. I started it during NaNoWriMo (National Novel Writing Month) in 2006. I got about 30,000 words into it and then put it on the back-burner where so many of my unfinished novel projects still linger.

And, when I finally finished and released *A Canadian Werewolf in New York* in 2016, I had no idea it would be a series.

Again, readers told me they were interested in that.

To satisfy their desires—as well as my own curiosity about what other adventures Michael might have—I had the idea for *Fear and Longing in Los Angeles* and started work on it during NaNoWriMo 2017.

Like the previous novel, I never finished it. I "won" NaNoWriMo by writing 50,725 words that year (To "win" NaNoWriMo you need to write at least 50,000 words during the month of November), but I was only halfway through the story I wanted to tell.

As I faced a major career crossroads during November 2017, my work and personal life was undergoing a major overhaul that occupied most of my attention.

I hastily made room for the book on the crowded backburner. You really should see this incredible spacious burner at the back of my writing stove. The multitude of pots there may just be able to feed a small army of writers with projects to keep them busy for a decade.

It was, interestingly enough, a short story that brought me back into the series. An intriguing thing, considering it was a short story that led me to this in the first place.

Stowe Away was originally written as a short story for an anthology called *Monster Road Trip*. The idea of having Michael trapped on a train headed from Manhattan to Stowe, Vermont but with the train arriving after sundown on the night of a full moon was appealing.

Within that story—which anthology editors Jamie Ferguson and DeAnna Knippling told me they knew would be much more than 10,000 words long—I had to give Michael a reason for heading to Vermont.

His reason was Gail. She was there for a family emergency. And Michael was going to be there as a friend for the only woman he ever loved. He, of course, made a friend along the way: the precocious and observant young bookworm, Bridget Wells.

She was conceived as a temporary distraction on Michael's journey. A victim he senses needs his help; a distraction along the way to his actual destination.

But she became much larger.

In the same way Michael enjoyed the young teenager's company, seeing her as a combination of a daughter figure, protégé and a mentor, I did too. Once Bridget first spoke in the novel, I immediately wanted to hear her speak even more. The unique bond and friendship between the two of them works effectively in this story. And she is too important to not return to Michael's life some time in the future.

It was as I was finishing that story, which ended up running about 20,000 words, that I knew I needed to return to that series.

Stowe Away first appeared in print in the anthology *Monster Road Trip* in 2019. And once it was published as a stand-alone novella (technically Book 1.5) in the "Canadian Werewolf" series in the summer of 2020, I retrieved *Fear and Longing in Los Angeles* from the back-burner and finished the first draft of it during NaNoWriMo 2020.

It was during the re-writes of *Fear and Longing in Los Angeles* in early 2021 that I came up with the idea for *Fright Nights, Big City*. I was in the middle of re-drafting the book that had bloated to a little over 100,000 words (working on it in two pieces of separate rounds of a 50,000-word NaNoWriMo might just do that) when that idea struck.

I paused in my re-writing to contact Juan Padron, the excellent designer who'd come up with the concept for the series look and feel, and had him design *Fright Nights, Big City* which I hastily put up for pre-order later in 2021, that same year.

So, for the first time, I knew how a book in this series was going to end before I'd even begun writing it. Partially because I was exchanging what I'd drafted as the original ending of *Fear and Longing in Los Angeles* over to the ending of *Fright Nights, Big City*.

Like Bridget, Lex was meant to be a slightly larger walk-on role—a distraction. She was to be a love interest to help get his mind off Gail for a while. And her nullifying powers were to give him the temporary belief that he could live a normal human life again. Lex's ties to the PFA were to bring them back to New York for the climactic encounter.

But, also like Bridget Wells, Alexandria Jones would become far more important than I, or Michael, would initially realize when we both met them.

You see, we both feel deeply in love with her.

Yes, Lex was supposed to die, sacrificing herself to save Michael and Gail's lives while acknowledging her awareness of just how much Michael and Gail still love one another. That was the original ending for *Fear and Longing in Los Angeles*. But I didn't have enough space to develop her character in a satisfying way, or to demonstrate the life-changing impact she would have on Michael. I also needed her to become more intimately connected with Gail so that her sacrifice is one made by a heart-felt friend who truly loves both Michael and Gail.

There just wasn't enough space to do that effectively within a single novel. So, the entire Lex storyline needed to be re-conceived into a two-book story arc.

I did purposely allow Marco to get away in the end—he disappears into the shadows but might just come back some day. It's always important to have some long-term nemesis to be fearful of and whose presence is felt, like the Professor Moriarty to Michael's Sherlock Holmes. You might also notice that the dude with the power of invisibility still hasn't—please pardon the pun—been seen.

I may have done that on purpose.

But apart from the intriguing things I discovered in the process of writing, a lot of research went into this novel.

My reading of Eric Kurlander's *Hitler's Monsters* which I first picked up when researching Nazi Germany's involvement in the occult for *Fear and Longing in Los Angeles*, played a good part in details within this novel.

But I also bought and poured through so many other books on the occult and black magic so I could come up with the "big nasty" that the PFA were going to try to pull off in New York.

Among those texts were *The Black Arts* by Richard Cavendish, *The Complete Book of Black Magic and Witchcraft* by Arthur Edward Waite, *Spells of Destruction* (no identifiable author), the 2016 edition of *The Book of Forbidden Knowledge* edited by Tarl Warwick, *Raising Hell: A Concise History of the Black Arts - and Those Who Dared to Practice Them* by Robert Masello, and Anton Szandor LaVey's *The Satanic Bible*.

Articles such as "Fear-Based Anger Is the Primary Motive for Violence" by Scott A. Bonn (Psychology Today, July 2017), "How Fear Leads to Anger" by Paul Thagard (Psychology Today, November 2018), "Was Yoda's Advice Any Good Psychologically?" by Kyle Hill (Discover, May 2014) and "The fear that leads to racial anger, and hate" by Beth Lefever (Commercial Appeal, August 2017) were helpful for understanding the ways the PFA would impact society.

I combined research from the occult and those more scientific studies of fear and hatred to create the "Berserker Powder" which is completely fictitious. Though I spent countless hours combing the occult texts for potential actual spells, potions, or crystals that would do the trick, I came up only with pieces and elements.

So, I used my research to help invent something that could sound authentic. I also, of course, made up Mobius R. Morningstar and the *Constructive Chaos Cookbook*, hoping it would sound like a legitimate "forgotten" text.

I plummeted down at least a dozen different rabbit holes when looking for a way for the PFA to effectively infect the population of the city and speed up the growing hatred and violence.

If I'm not on some FBI or CIA watch-list by now, I would be surprised. The number of instances over months that I searched and read about how to bring down a tall skyscraper or ways to access New York's water system are likely entirely suspicious.

So many articles and City of New York websites helped me learn about the water systems of the city. But the October 2013 Vanity Fair article "What Lies Beneath" by William Langewiesche and Randall Sullivan's "7 Days: The City Below" from an April 2019 The Village Voice article were extremely instrumental.

After further hours of trying to figure out a real spot for the PFA to conduct their attack, I decided, much like the fictional powder recipe, to just invent something that sounded legitimate. To the best of my knowledge, there is no entrance to Water Tunnel No. 1 off the 59th Street Columbus Circle subway entrance.

So much of the growth and depth to the "Canadian Werewolf" novels are due to the support of numerous editors and story consultants I've continued to work with over the years.

Michael and the characters, situations, and challenges in his world, are a product of my imagination. But they are also strengthened from the support, encouragement, advice, counsel, and heartfelt discussions with numerous people.

I know I'm likely forgetting at least a half dozen others, but here's my vain attempt to capture as many as possible to offer my gratitude.

Joshua Essoe, Jamie Ferguson, DeAnna Knippling, Clark Chamberlain, and Julie Strauss are all masters of developmental and story structure edits. Their careful council and insightful questions continue to help my writing—not just with this series, but my other writing as well.

While I'm no proper student of the Story Grid method, J. Thorn and Zach Bohannon have helped me, via in person, virtual conversations and their podcasts and their book *Three Story Method*. My ongoing chats with Valerie Francis, where she has been under the impression I'm helping her with book marketing strategies, have further informed me of solid story techniques. (BTW, the Staadt Publishing in this book is a nod to the fictional publisher of the same name from her amazing steamy romance thriller *Masquerade*. If you like love stories with heat, you will enjoy that novel.)

Mentors Kristine Kathryn Rusch and Dean Wesley Smith have long inspired my writing, and in more recent years have reminded me of the important fundamentals of what good storytelling is. Their faith in me as an editor for their *Fiction River* series has helped strengthen my writing in ways I could never have previously imagined.

Though Ellie Clarke and I haven't done our virtual morning coffee chats since 2019, so much of the philosophical, metaphysical, and deep meaningful discussions we had continue to inform and inspire me as both a writer and a person, resulting in strings that appear in this, and other books. Her own writing, creativity, and passion is a powerful force that I respect and still learn from. While I miss those moments, threads, and elements from that connection echo throughout my words and worlds.

Steve Gaydos, my dearest friend, might never read a single word of my Michael Andrews novels—particularly because "werewolf" is something that truly terrifies him. But our life-long intimate and meaningful conversations continue to fuel me as a person and as a writer. And something he expressed to me years ago regarding his appreciation of my comedic chops, particularly in writing, is what inspired me to believe that I could write a novel that is a dark fantastical adventure while inserting a constant thread of humor. Simply, these novels wouldn't have humor in them if it weren't for Steve's influence.

I wouldn't be where I am today in my writing and business career without the ongoing support and encouragement of my incredible partner and Love, Liz Anderson. Liz inspired me with the strength and courage to take a career chance in late 2017 and focus on my writing more than I ever have—and I owe much of the success I've had in my writing in these past several years to her belief in me.

Liz is often the first person to hear about the many ideas that are bouncing around in my head—and she often puts up, with good humor and a wry smile, with my boasting about "how proud" I am with myself whenever I finish a particularly challenging moment in one of my creative projects. Her own creativity and innate sense of adventure inspire me as a person and as a writer, and I marvel in the way we collaborate not only in creative and artistic endeavors, but in our life journey.

While many readers have told me how much they appreciate the powerful relationship and love between Michael and Gail, I owe an enormous debt to Jan Ehrlich for being the first early reader who kept hounding me to write more, and to share more about Michael and Gail. I had asked for her advice to ensure I was getting location and setting elements for New York City correct, but she became a champion for the entire larger story, and, of course, the ongoing relationship between Michael and Gail.

And, speaking of readers, as always, where would I be without you, dear reader? Thank you for reading this, for being an integral part of this journey. I hope that the adventures of Michael and his friends and loves have allowed you a fun escape, the occasional laugh, some thrills, and maybe even a few contemplative reflections.

Earlier, I mentioned a story arc, Lex's, that lasted two books. But there's an obvious longer story arc taking place in the series itself. And that is the complex love/friendship relationship between Michael and Gail.

When the series started, Michael realizes, when Gail walks back into his life, that he never stopped loving her. And he wants more than the friendship she is willing to give him—despite him knowing she still loves him too.

I've kept that tension strong.

But I've shared none of the back story to that.

So, as Michael and Gail are left, at the end of this novel, to figure out what their future together as a crime-fighting duo—who very obviously deeply love one another—might hold, I'm going to take readers back to the story of how they first met.

A while back, editors Jamie Ferguson and DeAnna Knippling asked for a story for their *Monsters in Love* anthology. That inspired the idea of telling the backstory of how Michael and Gail met in a novella I planned on calling *Lover's Moon*.

That book has remained, like so many other projects, on that infinitely growing aforementioned backburner.

It has remained there partially because it's more of a romance than anything I've ever written. And I struggled with how to write it. Particularly since this would be the first time that a "Canadian Werewolf" story would be told from someone else's perspective.

Lover's Moon must be told in alternating points of view between both Michael and Gail.

And, with me being as head-over-heels in love with Gail as Michael is, worshipping her and placing her on a pedestal, I could not do it. I was unable to give her character the richness and justice and flaws her perspective deserves.

I wasn't, at least, until my good friend Julie Strauss stepped in.

I've long wanted to collaborate with Julie on a writing project. And she agreed to co-author *Lover's Moon* with me, helping me weave a plot and taking on the perspective of writing Gail from Gail's unique point of view.

It will be the stand-alone novella length story of Michael and Gail's original meet-cute love story. It won't get in to how or why they broke up, nor any of the other still-hidden details of their relationship.

However, there is some planning that Julie and I have done to properly and fully flesh out the story which leads to some questions—some of which you might even have intuited when finishing this novel—that suggest there's more to the reason why Gail dumped Michael than Michael ever suspected.

Lover's Moon will dig into more of Gail's past, explore the complexity of her feelings toward Michael, as well as, perhaps, some of the reasoning she doesn't even yet understand about why she felt she couldn't be with Michael.

Of course, we also need to learn more about Buddy and why he regularly seems to show up at just the right moment when Michael needs help.

So many questions and answers to come.

And perhaps you wouldn't be surprised to know that I only partially understand what those answers might be. Sure, I have plenty of ideas, but it'll be the moment of writing them when I fully discover what those things are.

In the meantime, thanks for joining me on this chapter in Michael's life and some of the behind-the-scenes details about the creation of this book.

I do hope you'll join me on the flashback in *Lover's Moon* and the "as yet" untitled next full-length book in the "Canadian Werewolf" series.

Mark Leslie
November 2021

Next Book: LOVER'S MOON

WHEN IT INVOLVES A WOLF, IS IT CALLED A MEET CUTE OR A MEAT CUTE?

The complex relationship between Michael and Gail introduced in *A Canadian Werewolf in New York* has long been layered with mutual attraction, deep love, and sexual tension. Though now friends, they started off as lovers.

But we've only ever had the opportunity to see Gail or learn about their past relationship through Michael's adoring and biased memories.

This novella, told through both Michael and Gail's perspectives, shares the romantic story of how they met. It also explores Gail's past, the complexity of her feelings toward Michael, and some deeper, more intriguing reasons behind why she feels the two can't be more than good friends.

A special "Canadian Werewolf" tale co-authored by Mark Leslie and best-selling contemporary romance author Julie Strauss.

A CANADIAN WEREWOLF NOVELLA

LOVER'S MOON

MARK LESLIE
JULIE STRAUSS

books2read.com/loversmoon

About the Author

Like Michael Andrews, Mark Leslie considers himself a beta human. However, unlike his fictional character, Leslie doesn't have an alpha-wolf persona, despite hair growing on his aging body in all the wrong places.

When he's not writing, he attaches "Lefebvre" back onto his name and works as a writing and publishing coach and consultant. A bookselling veteran since 1992 (the same year his first short story was published), Mark has worked at virtually every type of bookstore, has sat on the Board of Directors for BookNet Canada and also been President of the Canadian Booksellers Association.

He can most likely be found behind the keyboard or with his nose stuck in a book. Or, at times, he can be found tracking and enjoying craft beer, or collecting and sharing musical earworms and dad jokes.

You can learn more about Mark at **www.markleslie.ca**.

Selected Works by Mark Leslie

Fiction:

- *One Hand Screaming* (2004)
- *Evasion* (2014)
- *I, Death* (2016)
- *A Canadian Werewolf in New York* (2016)
- *Nocturnal Screams* (Short Fiction Series) (2017/2018)
- *Stowe Away* (2020)
- *Fear and Longing in Los Angeles* (2021)
- *Fright Nights, Big City* (2021)

Non-fiction paranormal:

- *Haunted Hamilton: The Ghosts of Dundurn Castle and Other Steeltown Shivers* (2012)
- *Spooky Sudbury: True Tales of the Eerie & Supernatural* (2013) – Co-written with Jenny Jelen
- *Tomes of Terror: Haunted Bookstores and Libraries* (2014)
- *Creepy Capital: Ghost Stories of Ottawa and the National Capital Region* (2016)
- *Haunted Hospitals: Eerie Tales about Hospitals, Sanatoriums and Other Institutions* (2017) – Co-written with Rhonda Parrish
- *Macabre Montreal: Ghostly Tales, Ghastly Events, and Gruesome True Stories* (2018) – Co-written with Shayna Krishnasamy

Editor:

- *North of Infinity II* (2006)
- *Campus Chills* (2009)
- *Tesseracts Sixteen: Parnassus Unbound* (2012)
- *Fiction River 23: Editors' Choice* (2017)
- *Fiction River 25: Feel the Fear* (2017)
- *Fiction River 31: Feel the Love* (2019)
- *Fiction River 32: Superstitious* (2019)
- *Obsessions* (2020)
- *Pulphouse 10* (2021)
- *Halloween Harvest* (2021)